DELL BOOKS by Valerie S. Malmont

Death, Guns, and Sticky Buns
Death, Lies, and Apple Pies
Death Pays the Rose Rent

A Tori Miracle Mystery

DEATH, GUNS,
AND
STICKY BUNS

VALERIE S. MALMONT

To Ruth Cook —
So nice meeting
another mystery
fan. Valerie S Malmont

A Dell Book

Published by
Dell Publishing
a division of
Random House, Inc.
1540 Broadway
New York, New York 10036

Cover art by Mark Burckhardt
Copyright © 2000 by Valerie S. Malmont

Dell ® is a registered trademark of Random House, Inc., and the colophon is a trademark of Random House, Inc.

ISBN 0-440-23598-7

Printed in the United States of America

Published simultaneously in Canada

March 2000

10   9   8   7   6   5   4   3   2

OPM

For my children, Paul, Andrea, and Jason,
who have taught me the meaning of
unconditional love.

ACKNOWLEDGMENTS

I was assisted by many people during the writing and publication of this book.

I wish to thank the following: Françoise Harrison, Helen Platt, Laura Schramm, Susan Backs, and Jackie Werth for their valuable critiquing.

Jody Barthle, who gave up her own precious writing time to chauffeur me around Gettysburg, pointing out places and sights I'd missed during many previous visits.

Shirley Katusin, Linda Lake, and Helen Moe, who shared with me their recipes for sticky buns.

Barbara Lee, who offered daily support and encouragement.

George Nicholson, my agent.

Maggie Crawford, my editor, whose suggestions made this a more readable book.

CHAPTER 1

RESERVED FOR EDITOR. AFTER ONLY A WEEK ON THE job, it still gave me a thrill to park in front of the sign. Granted, I'd only taken the job as editor of the Lickin Creek *Chronicle* on a temporary basis to help out P. J. Mullins while she recovered from major surgery; granted, I didn't have the foggiest idea of how to run a small-town weekly newspaper; and granted, the paper only had two full-time employees, including me, plus a few freelance writers, and a delivery staff all under the age of twelve. None of that mattered; for the present I was The Editor for whom the space was reserved, and that was a necessary ego boost for me, Tori Miracle, recovering journalist and mid-list author.

I couldn't find the key to the back door, even though I was sure I had dropped it in my purse last night when I left. But that was okay; I preferred using the front entrance. Maybe someone I knew would see me—the editor—going in.

With the hem of my sleeve, I wiped a smudge off the little brass plaque on the front door that said the building had been constructed in 1846. Last week, as my first official duty, I'd polished it with Brasso until it gleamed. Inside, the little waiting room stretched the entire width of the building, almost twelve feet. The furniture was red vinyl with chrome arms, dating from the forties, two chairs and a couch, and an imitation-maple coffee table that held an empty ashtray and a pink plastic vase full of dusty plastic daisies.

"Morning," I called out as I hung my blue linen blazer on a hook behind the door.

Cassie Kriner came out of the back office. "Good morning, Tori. Can you believe this weather?"

"Is it unusual?" I asked.

"Sorry, keep forgetting you aren't local. Yes, it's very unusual for this late in October. Almost like summer."

In the office we shared, she handed me a mug of coffee. I took one sip to be polite and put it down on the edge of my rolltop desk. As always, it was dreadful, but I hadn't quite worked up the courage to tell her so.

"You had a phone call this morning. From a Dr. Washabaugh. She wants you to call her back."

"Thanks, I will."

"Nothing wrong, I hope?"

"Of course not. She's probably just calling to tell me I'm fine." I smiled reassuringly, but inside I was feeling a little alarm. Would a doctor really bother to call if the tests were all okay?

"She said to call her back, Tori."

"There's no urgency."

I hoped I sounded less concerned than I felt. Last week, at the urging, no, nagging, of my friend Maggie Roy, the town librarian, I'd gone for my first checkup in about five years. Pap smear, mammogram, the whole nine yards. Dr. Washabaugh had said she'd call me with the test results. Or had she said she'd call me if the test results were positive? Or did she say negative? Is positive good or bad? I couldn't quite recall what she'd said.

Cassie perched on the edge of our worktable and drank her coffee as if she really enjoyed it. Today she wore a beige cashmere suit that probably cost more than I had earned in royalties from my ill-fated book, *The Mark Twain Horror House.* At the V of her rust-colored blouse was an amber necklace that looked antique and expensive, and her silver-gray hair was pulled back into an elegant Grace Kelly–style French twist. She always managed to look like a million bucks, I thought, which was a lot less, P. J. had told me, than what Cassie's husband had left her when he suffocated to death in a silo a few years ago.

In comparison, I knew I looked all wrong in my favorite navy blue slacks and red-and-white-striped Liz Claiborne T-shirt. When I dressed this morning, I thought it was a perfect outfit for the warm weather, but it was autumn, despite the temperature, and I now realized I had committed a seasonal faux pas. Even worse, the pleats on my pants were making me feel fatter by the minute, and the contrast between my light-colored T-shirt and my dark slacks cut me in half and made me look even shorter than five one. Why hadn't I seen that before I left the house?

The regular Friday morning routine, I'd learned last week, was to check the paper for obvious errors and to make sure all the regular features were in place. I took the front section, Cassie took the middle, and we began to read through the articles. It all seemed to be there, the things our readers expected each week: church schedules, real estate transfers, births, deaths, marriages, divorces, comics, high school sports, and a single column of national and world news. The extension service's column was extra long this week, full of helpful tips about fertilizers, apple storage, and the need to turn over one's mulch on a regular basis to prevent fires.

The police blotter was very short, for which I was grateful. The worst crimes Lickin Creek had experienced during the past week were the theft of some plastic flowers from a cemetery plot and some rolls of toilet paper tossed into the trees on the square during the high school's Homecoming Week. It looked like life had returned to normal after Percy Montrose's poisoning death during the Apple Butter Festival a few weeks ago. Despite my role in finding his killer, I knew many locals had added the closing of the medical clinic to the list of things they blamed me for, starting with the burning down of the Historical Society last summer.

After we'd finished our individual sections, we spread the classified section out on the table so we could check it together. The classified ads were of major importance—without them, the paper would fold. We'd found only a few errors before the bell over the front door tinkled, indicating somebody had entered.

"Come in," I called. "We're in the back room."

A young woman appeared, and my first thought on seeing her was she had to be about eleven months pregnant. The visitor's chair echoed her groan as she lowered herself into it.

"Only six weeks to go," she said with a weary sigh.

It flashed through my mind that she must be expecting quadruplets at the very least to be as big as this at seven and a half months.

"I'm Janet Margolies, vice president in charge of marketing and public relations for the college."

By college, I knew she meant the Lickin Creek College for Women, the only one in town.

"Nice to meet you, Janet. I'm Tori Miracle and this is

Cassie Kriner. How can we help you?" I asked as I pointed out a typo to Cassie.

"Have you heard about the Civil War Reenactment we have scheduled for Parents' Weekend?"

I shook my head.

"That's the problem. Nobody else has, either. We need some publicity, and we need it fast."

"If you want to buy an ad, we still have time to get it into tomorrow's paper," I suggested.

She grimaced. "That's the second problem. President Godlove thought it would be great to do something different this year, something that would pull in townspeople and maybe even some tourists. Trouble is, I don't have any money in the PR budget to promote it."

I sensed she was preparing to ask a big, big favor and waited to hear what came next.

"I was hoping you could give us some free publicity." She smiled hopefully. "Please don't say no," she said as I began to shake my head. "Maybe we can work something out, something that would be beneficial to both of us."

I ignored Cassie's groan. "Like what?"

"I've got an article all prepared. If you do a big feature about the reenactment this week and next and scatter some ads throughout the paper, we could . . . we can . . ." Her voice faded away as she tried desperately to come up with an idea.

"How about listing the *Chronicle* as the cosponsor of the event?" I asked. "I'd like to get involved in community work."

"Cosponsor? I'm not sure President Godlove would approve."

I stood up and extended my hand. "Well, good-bye then. Maybe you'll have better luck with the other paper in town." The only "other paper" was the weekly shopper, and she knew it.

"Deal," she said, quickly reaching up and shaking my hand. I suddenly realized she had cleverly manipulated me into doing exactly what she wanted.

She opened her briefcase and pulled out a folder. "Here's the article I mentioned and some camera-ready ads."

"You've certainly made it easy for us," I said. Cassie was standing behind Janet's chair, glaring daggers at me.

"Can you attend a planning meeting on Monday?" she asked. "I'll introduce you to the college president and some of the staff."

"I'll do my best."

After she left, Cassie smacked herself on the forehead and looked as if she wanted to smack me. "What on earth were you thinking?" she asked. "We don't have the resources to cosponsor anything."

"You heard her—it won't cost the paper anything, and we'll get a lot of good publicity for being so community-oriented."

"P. J. never did anything like this," Cassie said doubtfully. "I sure hope it doesn't backfire on us."

"Don't worry about it, Cassie. It's a win–win proposition. How could anything possibly go wrong?"

Friday was our short day. After we plunked the article about the reenactment on the front page, put the camera-ready ads on subsequent pages, and finished the proofing, the paper was ready for Cassie to take to the printer in the next town, twelve miles away. It would never win me a Pulitzer, but I found the work very satisfying.

We left the office together. "What're your plans for

the afternoon?" Cassie asked as she put on her sunglasses.

"It's moving day," I reminded her. This was the day
I was to leave the Gochenauer home, where I'd been
living for several weeks with Garnet and his sister,
Greta Carbaugh, to take up residence as a house-sitter
for a college professor who was going to England for a
year's sabbatical.

It's funny how things never seem to work out the
way I plan. When I accepted the temporary position at
the *Chronicle* to give P. J. time to recover from her lung
surgery, I'd done so thinking it would give me time to
get to know Garnet Gochenauer better, time to decide if
being the wife of a small-town police chief was really
the life for me. Ironically, he, not knowing my plans,
had accepted a job as a police advisor in Costa Rica and
was due to leave this weekend for his training in Washington, D.C. I tried over and over to convince myself
that this was okay, that I could use the time alone to
finish writing my second novel. Besides, I'd sublet my
little apartment in Hell's Kitchen for six months, and I
really had no place else to go.

"Good luck with it. See you Monday." Cassie
walked smoothly away on high heels that would have
crippled anybody else.

Garnet's blue monster truck was parked under the
porte cochere in front of his house, already loaded with
my two suitcases, a box of paperback mystery novels
I'd picked up for a song at a yard sale, three bags of
kitty litter, two 20-pound sacks of Tasty Tabby Treats,
various sizes of feeding dishes and water bowls, and
two litter boxes. I had a feeling Garnet wasn't sorry to
see those last two items go.

I stepped inside, into the dim foyer, where the walls
were red, the Oriental carpet on the floor was blue, and

the ceiling was paneled with dark brown mahogany. When I flipped the light switch, the hall came ablaze with light from the priceless Tiffany lamp that hung from the mahogany ceiling. In my opinion, the place would look a lot better covered with a coat of antique-white enamel. My two cat-carriers sat side by side next to the door. Noel sat in one, glaring at me with her round gold eyes wide open. The other carrier was open.

I walked into the front living room, where I discovered a body lying facedown on the floor.

The body's head was under the Victorian sofa. What was visible was a crinkled broomstick skirt, a silver concho belt, and a pair of very large feet, clad in Earth shoes. "Hi, Greta," I said. "What are you doing?"

From under the couch came a mumbled reply. "Trying to get this stupid fat cat out so I can put him in the carrier. Of all the stubborn . . ."

From my purse I pulled an old prescription medicine container in which I always carried some Tasty Tabby Treats for emergencies like this. "I'll get him, Greta."

Garnet's sister rolled over and sat up. Her long gray hair was full of dust bunnies. Greta was always too busy saving the whales, the rain forests, and the Chesapeake Bay to worry about something as mundane as housecleaning. She removed a fuzzball from her face and said, "Be my guest."

Fred always responded to the word *treat* even when he pretended not to recognize his own name. The poor baby's life was ruled by his stomach. I pulled him onto my lap and plucked lint off his orange and white fur.

Greta sat cross-legged facing me, looking exactly like the aging hippie she was. "You should put him on a diet. He must weigh twenty pounds. And it's all fat."

Diet. How Fred and I hated that word. "He's just pleasantly plump."

It took the two of us to get him into the carrier. "I'll get some iodine," Greta said. "You don't want to take a chance on those scratches getting infected."

"Maa-maa," came a plaintive wail from the carrier.

"Did you hear that? He called me mama." I dabbed at my bloody arm with a Kleenex.

"Mama, indeed! What you need is to settle down and have a real family."

I saved my snappy retort for later because Garnet chose that moment to come in from the kitchen.

"All ready to go?" In my opinion he sounded much too cheerful for a man whose ladylove was moving out. I thought he could show a little dejection.

"Will you two be here for dinner?" Greta called from the porch as Garnet boosted me into the cab of the truck. "I'm fixing scalloped weiners."

"No thanks," we said together, a little too quickly. Garnet and I had fought about any number of things during the past weeks, but we stood united in our dislike of Greta's Pennsylvania Dutch cooking.

I took one last look out the side window at the Gochenaur home, at the white gingerbread trim dripping from the eaves, the Corinthian columns on the front porch, the slate-shingled fish-scale roof, and the four round brick towers topped with onion-shaped domes. The southeast tower was still under repair, a reminder of something very scary that had happened to me a few weeks ago. Then I turned face forward and looked ahead, as I had countless times in the past during my many moves as a foreign-service brat.

This one's different, I told myself. This time, Tori, you're only moving a few miles across town, not half a world away. But the familiar sadness was still there.

"Are you crying?" Garnet asked.

"It's the iodine. It smarts."

Sometimes Garnet shows remarkable sensitivity. This afternoon was one of those times. He took my hand in his and squeezed it gently. I studied him as he drove over Lickin Creek's cobbled streets. His straight sandy-brown hair fell forward on his forehead. He was the kind of lucky person who always looked tan, sort of like Don Johnson on the reruns of *Miami Vice,* which was one of my TV addictions. Today he wore what I thought of as the Lickin Creek uniform, a plaid shirt, tight jeans, and hunting boots. On him, it looked good.

Within five minutes, Garnet had driven his truck through the rusty iron gates that marked the entrance to the old resort community of Moon Lake. The lake itself marks the southern border of the borough. Great mansions, built before the turn of the century to be the summer cottages for the very rich from Baltimore and D.C., had crumbled there for years beneath ancient trees.

When the so-called cottages were first built, in the days before jet travel made the rest of the world easily accessible, women and children from those cities used to come to Moon Lake to escape the summer heat, bringing with them their servants and huge steamer trunks full of clothes for every occasion. Husbands and fathers visited on weekends. But all good things come to an end, and the "cottages" eventually fell into disrepair as World War I and, later, the stock market crash, put an end to those leisurely, elegant times.

Fortunately, the development had sprung to life again in the past few years, rescued by young professionals, mostly from the D.C. area, who were entranced by the charm of the spacious old homes and wanted to restore them to their former glory. When I'd come for my interview with Ethelind Gallant, it had been night-time and I hadn't been able to see much. But this morning, with the trees changing from green to autumn gold, and the sun sparkling on the blue water of Moon Lake, I gasped with pleasure. I could hardly believe I was really going to live in a place like this!

While many of the grand old places had been subjected to costly renovation, not so the largest and once grandest of them all, the house owned by college professor Ethelind Gallant, who was soon leaving for merrie olde England to collect information about the use of contractions in medieval writings. I had gratefully agreed to house-sit while she was gone. After all, I'd be living there rent-free and I'd only be responsible for paying the utilities and making sure the house didn't collapse while she was gone. Did I think for a minute that heating a house with thirty or more rooms might strain my budget? Of course not. And now, looking at the gloomy structure in broad daylight, I realized there was a real possibility that indeed it might collapse—the front-porch roof had already been propped up with some two-by-fours. A fluttering piece of paper, tacked onto one of the two-by-fours, warned visitors to use the back door.

Garnet stopped in the circular driveway, and I jumped down. Clutching a cat carrier in each hand, I walked around to the back while Garnet followed me pulling my suitcases.

Ethelind greeted us on the enclosed back porch, which was obviously used as a laundry room and a dumping-off place for last winter's coats and boots. She was about Garnet's height, five ten, and shaped like a barrel. I guessed her measurements would be fifty-fifty-fifty. Her hair was dyed Lucille Ball red, and she'd applied her makeup with such a heavy hand that it would have looked artificial even on a stage. In one hand was a skinny brown cigarette. In the other, a half-empty sherry glass.

Her smile of greeting, which showed big yellow teeth smeared with lipstick, faded as she looked down at the cat carriers. "You didn't mention you had cats!"

"Didn't I?" I tried to look surprised, as if I couldn't believe I hadn't told her about Fred and Noel. "I'm sure I did."

She kept staring at the carriers. "Filthy creatures," she muttered.

I held my breath and waited. Finally, she shrugged. "Well, nothing we can do about it now. I'll be off for England in a few days, anyway. Come on in. We'll have a drink to celebrate your being here." She turned her back on us and marched into the house.

Garnet put his hand on my shoulder and held me back. "It's not too late, Tori. You can still come to Costa Rica with me."

The weekend went by so quickly I knew my memories of it would always be blurred. I picked one of a dozen or more bedrooms to be mine, unpacked the boxes sent to me by my next-door neighbor and best friend in New York, Murray Rosenbaum, and tried to adjust to Ethelind Gallant's constant cigarette smoke. While I had thought she was leaving for England right away, it now turned out there was a slight change of plans and she was waiting for a vacancy on the QE II. Then there was the farewell dinner for Garnet at the home of his Aunt Gladys and Uncle Zeke, where I dozed off during dinner and distantly heard someone say, "Probably into drugs. She's a New Yorker you know."

On Sunday morning, I stood in the Gochenauer driveway with Greta and waved good-bye to Garnet until his rental car turned the corner. To hide my tears, I bent down and hugged Bear, Garnet's German shepherd, whose dark eyes looked as sad as I imagined mine must look.

"Stay for dinner?" Greta asked kindly. "I thought I'd fix a little beef heart."

I shook my head. The thought of Greta's cooking made me cry even harder.

On the following Monday morning, I drove to Hagerstown, Maryland, where a young doctor replaced my plaster arm cast with a soft cast that weighed about a thousand pounds less. I'd broken my arm nearly a month ago when my car was forced off the road during the Apple Butter Festival. Feeling free and mobile without the restricting cast, I checked in at the *Chronicle* and was assured by Cassie that there was nothing I needed to do there. "Except for calling Doctor Washabaugh," she added.

"I will," I said as I left to drive to the Lickin Creek College for Women, where Janet Margolies had scheduled a meeting to introduce me to some of the people who were to be involved in Parents' Weekend. I was glad to be kept busy. It was a lot better than sitting at home feeling lonely and sorry for myself.

From a distance, the white Victorian buildings of the campus were graceful reminders of days gone by. But as I trudged up the hill from the visitors' parking lot, I began to notice the flaking paint, the woodwork in need of repair, and the cracked flagstones of the walkways. The Lickin Creek College for Women was in the process of redesigning itself for modern women, but it still suffered from a severely declining enrollment. Was there really a place in today's high-tech, fast-paced world, I wondered, for a small, nineteenth-century, women's liberal arts college? I hoped there was.

I was ushered into a large lounge in the administration building, filled with priceless antique furniture and a half dozen oil paintings of past college presidents. After pouring a cup of tea for me out of a silver teapot on a mahogany breakfront, Janet led me to where a handsome gray-haired gentleman was seated. He stood, smiled, and shook my hand firmly, and I knew he must be someone important even before Janet told me he was President Godlove. "Glad to have you aboard," he said.

"Former Navy man," Janet whispered as she guided me toward a large group of people engaged in a lively conversation. They were almost all professors, except for the campus security chief and two members of the senior class. The names whizzed over my head and out the window, but I shook hands with everybody and said "Glad to meet you," several times.

Janet took my arm and pointed discreetly to two people seated on a red velvet sofa. "You can sit with them," she said, and I noticed she was wheezing pretty badly.

"Are you all right?" I asked.

"Nothing that a few weeks won't cure," she said with a wry smile as she clutched her back. "I feel like the Hindenburg blimp right before it exploded. Maybe I'd better sit down."

"I can introduce myself to the others," I told her. "You go take care of that baby."

The man and the woman on the sofa acknowledged my presence and shifted ever so slightly to make room for me to sit beside them. "I'm Helga Van Brackle, Dean of Students," the woman said in a voice that sounded as if she were used to scolding people.

"And this is Professor Ken Nakamura, the Academic Dean."

His shock of thick white hair fell into his eyes as Professor Nakamura took my hand and bowed. "I understand you speak Japanese."

It took me a second to realize he was speaking that language to me. "Only a little," I automatically responded in Japanese, using the proper and self-deprecating answer that I knew was expected of me. "Are you from Japan?"

He shook his head. "*Nisei*. From southern California. Welcome to the college."

His eyes smiled warmly at me, and I could imagine him being the surrogate grandfather of hundreds of young women students.

The three of us chatted for a minute or two until we were interrupted by a student passing a tray of pastries. I took one, then wished I hadn't, since President Godlove tapped his cup with his spoon to get everyone's attention. With a glance at his watch, he announced he had no intention of waiting any longer. The grandfather clock in the corner told me the meeting was twenty minutes late in getting started.

"He's never on time," Helga mumbled.

"Who?" I asked.

"Shh," someone cautioned. Helga's infuriated look would have scared anyone, but not the student who had done the deed.

President Godlove introduced me to the stragglers who had just come in, then asked Janet Margolies to go over her plans for Parents' Weekend. I nibbled at my pastry and admired the furniture while she described at long length the Friday night activities, including a banquet, a tour of the dormitory, a poetry reading in the library, and a short production of *The Tempest* as adapted by a local playwright and alumna, Oretta Clopper.

From the groans that greeted this announcement, I guessed Mrs. Clopper was not everybody's favorite writer.

Janet shushed the crowd. "I know, I know, but it won't kill any of us to sit through it. This brings us to Saturday. After coffee and pastry in the dining hall, we will all move outside for the reenactment." She smiled at me and said, "Generously cosponsored by our friends at the *Chronicle*." A smattering of applause greeted this announcement.

"As some of you know," she continued, "The chairman of our board of trustees, Mack Macmillan, has agreed to play the part of the condemned man."

I jerked around to stare at her. What was she talking about?

She ignored me. "As you all know, Mack Macmillan is a well-known Civil War historian and will provide his own costume. Because of his years in the public sector as a United States congressman, he is highly visible and his participation will be a great asset. . . ."

"Excuse me," I said rather timidly. "What do you mean by 'condemned man'? I thought this was to be a Civil War battle reenactment."

"It is," Janet said, not looking at me. "Sort of." She looked relieved as the door opened and a tall, stately man with a vaguely familiar face entered the room. Although he was dressed in the Lickin Creek uniform of jeans, plaid shirt, and boots, he gave off an aura of aristocracy that set him apart from the citizens of the borough.

"Congressman Macmillan," Ken Nakamura said softly. "The great man himself."

Mack Macmillan worked his way around the room, shaking hands, slapping the men on the back, and kissing the women, until he reached me. "This is Tori Miracle," Helga said.

"I had an Aunt Dorie," he said, gazing into my eyes. "Lovely woman. Lovely name. So nice to meet you, Dorie."

He moved on before I had a chance to correct him.

"Anybody seen my wife? I thought she was going to meet me here?"

"Problem at the stable," the security chief said. "She's probably down there."

"Then I'll just pop into the dining room and see if I can't catch her." He paused in the doorway with one hand raised. "Carry on. I know Janet's got everything under control."

I must have looked confused, because Ken said softly. "Stable—table. Tori—Dorie. He had a viral infection five or six years ago that left him deaf. He can only read lips if someone talks slowly and directly at him. Most of the college people can deal with it. The rest of the time he depends on his wife to interpret for him. It's what ended his career in Congress."

Helga Van Brackle frowned at us, and Ken stopped talking to me and smiled innocently at her.

"Let's get back on task," she said in a rasping voice. "Where were we?"

I raised my hand as if I were back in school because that's the way she made me feel. "Janet was starting to talk about the plans for the Civil War reenactment." I turned to Janet, whose face was flushed. "Something you said about a victim confused me. Can you explain to me in detail what's going to happen?"

Janet took the floor as Helga sat down and told us of her plans for the reenactment, while I listened in shock.

I could already hear Cassie saying, "This is *not* the kind of event P. J. would want the *Chronicle* involved in."

When the meeting ended, I left fuming. The least Janet could have done was be up-front with me when she asked me to cosponsor the event. However, the wheels were in motion, the publicity was out, and there was nothing I could do about it now.

CHAPTER 2

A Saturday Afternoon

IT WAS NOT QUITE NOON WHEN CASSIE AND I arrived at the college and found a vacant spot on the lawn close to the college administration building. Cassie had apparently been to events like this before, because if there was something she hadn't brought, we wouldn't need it. She spread her pink blanket on the grass, urged me to sit next to her, then extracted two ice-cold Diet Cokes from her cooler. As usual, she was perfectly groomed and expensively dressed, today in a gray knit pantsuit that emphasized the silver in her hair. Casual, yet professional. She made me wish I'd worn something other than jeans and my NYU sweatshirt.

Cassie turned around to survey the crowd and waved to several people, who smiled back and nodded their greetings. She believed it was her duty to inform me who everyone was and what they did for a living. "That's J. B. Morgan—president of the Old Lickin Creek National Bank."

"With a name like that he'd have to be," I commented.

"Why?"

"Never mind. It was just a silly notion."

"There's Oretta Clopper—she thinks she's a play-wright. Oh good—Marvin Bumbaugh is here with the rest of the borough council." She continued naming names, which I promptly forgot.

"Lots of unfamiliar faces here," she mused.

"It *is* Parents' Weekend," I reminded her.

"Out-of-towners! Right here at our own Lickin Creek College for Women. This is so exciting. Tori, I'm finally beginning to think you did the right thing."

I didn't gloat. Instead, I noted what a beautiful fall day it was, with not a cloud in the sky, and still practically summer-warm. The mountains surrounding the valley looked so close in the clear air that I could nearly count the trees. A perfect day and, I hoped, a perfect way to make my mark as acting editor and publisher of the Lickin Creek *Chronicle*.

Several weeks ago, when I'd agreed to cosponsor the event, Cassie's first thought had been that P. J. Mullins would never have gotten involved with something like this. I admit I'd had a few doubts, especially after I'd attended my first planning meeting at the college, where I learned Janet Margolies had not been completely can-did with me. But now, seeing the eagerly waiting crowd, I was sure I'd done the right thing. I hoped Cassie would still think so, when she learned what kind of a reenactment we were about to witness.

We finished off Cassie's ham sandwiches, the potato chips, the chocolate cake, and the homemade pickles. "What time is it?" I asked.

"Nearly half past one."

"This thing was supposed to start at twelve-thirty. I wonder what's happening."

The sun beat mercilessly down upon the crowd of men, women, and children who were showing their dis-content. The picnic hampers were empty, the drinks were gone, and not even the small brass band playing "The Battle Hymn of the Republic" for the fourth time could drown out the complaints about the delay and the wails of bored children.

Janet Margolies appeared at my side and lowered herself to the blanket. Her face was bright red, whether from the heat or from her pregnancy, I couldn't tell. She fanned herself with a program and gratefully accepted Cassie's offer of a soda.

Although Janet and I had officially collaborated on the final plans for the reenactment, she'd done the lion's share of the work. Basically, all I'd done was show up at a few meetings, keep my mouth shut, and write articles for the paper.

"Has something gone wrong?" I asked her. "This thing was supposed to get going an hour ago. The crowd is turning ugly."

"Mack Macmillan showed up late. Guess when you're a VIP you don't have to think about other people."

"Are they nearly ready to begin? What time is it anyway?" Every now and then it crossed my mind that I should replace my broken Timex.

Janet glanced at her watch. "It's one thirty-five. I have to admit this isn't all Macmillan's fault. After he finally made his appearance, I couldn't get the door to the storeroom open." She touched me on the arm. "Hey, it looks like something's starting to happen."

A soloist stepped forward and, after a brief musical introduction, began to sing "Old Abe Lincoln came out of the wilderness," to the tune of "The Old Gray Mare." After some urging on his part, a few people in the waiting audience perked up and began to sing along. Their voices faded away as Federal troops marched out of the administration building and down the white marble steps onto the field, trailed by a small group of civilians. Murmurs of "Finally" and "It's about time" fluttered through the air until the crowd fell silent.

The men's dark suits were dusty, as if they'd survived a long tramp over miles of Pennsylvania's dirt roads, and most of them wore stovepipe hats in the style of President Lincoln. The women wore stiff, brightly colored silk gowns, except for one who was wearing a black bombazine mourning dress and was dabbing at her eyes with a tiny lace-edged handkerchief.

With faces growing red and sweaty from the relentless afternoon sun, the soldiers formed several haphazard lines, facing a shallow hole about six feet long and three feet wide, with fresh earth heaped beside it in a neat pile on the well-tended grass. It wasn't really deep enough to be a grave, but it was as deep as the campus groundskeepers would let us dig.

An officer stepped forward, turned to face the men, and unrolled an official-looking document. The soldiers snapped to attention as he began to read.

"Men, today, at the hour of three p.m., you will witness the execution of a Deserter, who will be shot to death by Musketry by order of a Court Martial, approved by General Hooker."

The soldiers remained impassive, but a wail from the woman in the black bombazine dress attracted the officer's attention.

"Madam," he said to her, "whilst you may think the killing of your husband is unjust and heartless, it behooves you to remember the many good men who died bravely here. Perhaps some of those lives would have been saved if we had executed more deserters in the past."

The woman slumped into the arms of one of the civilian men and sobbed quietly into her handkerchief.

From behind the college library came a horse-drawn wagon, and as it drew closer the spectators could see it carried a coffin. It was followed by another wagon carrying the condemned man himself, his hands tied behind him. And finally came the shooting party, fifteen soldiers in blue wool uniforms.

The coffin was lifted from the wagon and placed before the freshly dug grave. With his eyes upon his wife's face, the prisoner was helped out of his wagon. With his deeply lined face and silver hair that sparkled in the bright sunshine, he looked much older than the other uniformed soldiers.

The officer who had read the execution order a few minutes earlier asked the prisoner if he had any final words. The prisoner, still intently focused on his wife, ignored him.

As the officer placed a gentle hand on the man's shoulder, the prisoner turned to face him with a stunned look on his face. "Do you have any final words?"

The condemned man took a step forward, in the direction of the woman in black. "I beg of you, my dear wife, to forgive me. Please tell my beloved children that my last thoughts were of them." His voice boomed in the silent, sultry air.

The woman in black buried her face in her handkerchief.

Next, the prisoner addressed the soldiers. "It is only since I was sentenced that I have realized the error of my ways. Please remember the oath of allegiance you have taken. Look upon my execution as a warning. In all ways be true to your country and to your God."

He turned to the firing squad and spoke in a loud,

firm voice. "Gentlemen, I bear you no ill will. Please pray for God to have mercy on my soul."

A guard stepped forward, tied a handkerchief around the prisoner's eyes, and led him to the waiting coffin. Almost deferentially, he urged the prisoner to sit on the edge of the coffin's base.

The officer in charge read the sentence. "By Order of the Court Martial approved by General Hooker, you will be shot to death by Musketry. The number of bullets detailed is fourteen. As is our company's custom, one rifle is loaded with a blank cartridge, so that each member of the firing squad may console himself with the thought that he may not have fired a fatal bullet."

The prisoner hung his head.

"Pastor Kleinholtz, will you lead us in a prayer?"

A civilian gentleman in a somber black suit and stovepipe hat stepped forward and opened a large leather-bound Bible. "Psalm 23," he announced. "The Lord is my shepherd . . ." When he read, "Though I walk through the valley of the shadow of death . . ." the soon-to-be-widow fell to the ground in a faint. The preacher paused for a few moments until she was revived, finished reading the passage, and closed his Bible with a snap. "May God have mercy upon his soul."

The shooting party came to the ready, and in a moment a volley of shots rang out and the law was appeased. In a cloud of black smoke, the prisoner toppled backward into his coffin.

The woman in black broke away from the sidelines and ran toward the wooden box where her husband's body lay. She dropped to the ground beside the coffin, raised her arms to the sky, and cried out dramatically, "My life—my love. What shall I do without you? What shall I do?"

A young soldier tried to raise her to her feet, but she

clung to his knees and moaned, "Let me say my last good-bye. One last kiss before we part."

She leaned over the side of the coffin and reached in to embrace her husband. A bloodcurdling scream pierced the summer air. "Oh my God, he's dead!" she cried.

The spectators burst into applause and began to sing along with the band, "Oh we'll rally 'round the flag, boys, we'll rally once again . . ." I was thoroughly pleased with the way the reenactment had gone, especially after the annoying delay. I couldn't resist nudging Cassie and saying, "Didn't I tell you it was going to be great? Lickin Creek's going to be talking about this for a long time."

The woman in black rose to her feet and faced us angrily. "Shut up, you idiots," she yelled. She reached her arms out toward the crowd, and something dark dripped from her outstretched hands. "Didn't you hear me? The man is dead. He's *really* dead!"

CHAPTER 3

THE SUN WAS JUST APPEARING OVER THE TOPS OF THE trees lining the banks of the creek, and although it was not quite eight, it was obvious that today was going to be another scorcher. I met no one as I hiked up the hill toward the imposing building housing the administrative offices of the Lickin Creek College for Women. But this wasn't surprising since I knew the enrollment was fewer than two hundred students, most of whom I assumed were still in bed—where I wished I were.

On the footbridge over the Lickin Creek, I paused for a moment to catch my breath. Wishing I'd worn sneakers instead of my unsubstantial Italian sandals and something cooler than my dark blue dress, I rested my elbows on the rail and watched a pair of ducks floating on the sparkling water a few feet below me. I was to meet with the police, the president of the college, the president of the borough council, and who knew who else, to discuss yesterday's tragedy. The prospect made me more than a little nervous.

Although I had the urge to linger, I knew I was only delaying the inevitable. I had to make my appearance and face the music. My attempt to get some good PR for the *Chronicle* had turned into the worst disaster in Lickin Creek history. As the lone outsider involved, I was pretty sure I knew where the blame would be laid. After taking a deep breath, I continued my march up the hill.

The yellow police tape enclosing the grassy lawn didn't stop me for a minute. I ducked under it and kept going. A man in the gray uniform of the campus security force yelled at me, but I acted as if I didn't hear him. After the hike I'd just taken, I wasn't about to risk any more blisters by detouring around to the back of the building. I shuddered as I skirted the shallow grave, six feet long and three feet wide, for it brought back in vivid detail the ghastly events of yesterday afternoon. I paused once more to let my pulse rate subside, and while I waited for the pounding in my chest to stop, I feigned interest in the tall white building, complete with turrets, gingerbread trim, and a mansard roof and vowed, once again, to start a diet and maybe even an exercise program on Monday.

To get into the building, I had to push my way through a mob of television reporters. On the porch, a woman I recognized from one of the Harrisburg TV stations was speaking to a video camera. She looked hopefully at me as I climbed the steps, but I shook my head and pulled open the massive oak door.

Since no one was expected to enter through the front door today, I wasn't surprised to find no one at the reception desk.

"Yoo-hoo," I called. My voice echoed in the high-ceilinged hall. "Anybody home?"

An enormous black door on my right opened, and a woman's head popped out. "Shhh!" she warned with a frown that caused her half-moon reading glasses to slip off her nose and dangle from a chain around her neck. I recognized her immediately as Helga Van Brackle, the Dean of Student Affairs.

She slipped through the door, letting it close quietly behind her, and said, "Please hold your voice down. We're having a meeting. I assume you know about Saturday's unfortunate incident."

She obviously didn't remember meeting me. I stuck out my hand and said, "I'm Tori Miracle, the editor of the *Chronicle*." I loved the way the title rolled off my lips. "If by 'unfortunate incident' you mean Representative Macmillan's being shot to death by a firing squad in front of this building yesterday, I certainly am aware of it. But I think I'd use a stronger phrase than 'unfortunate incident.' "

"Did you say you were from the *Chronicle*? We have no comment."

"I'm not here for statements. I'm here to attend the meeting."

Her eyes widened as it finally dawned on her who I was. She tried to cover up. "Why, Toni, of course. We've been expecting you."

"It's Tori," I said.

"Come right in. We're just getting organized. Still waiting for that new police chief to show up."

Helga patted her short steel-gray hair, plucked an invisible piece of lint from her navy blue suit jacket, replaced her glasses on the bridge of her nose, and opened the door to the meeting room. "Come in," she said, holding the door open. I stepped inside to a room where some grim-faced individuals sat around an oval table.

"About time," someone muttered. I glared at him. The meeting was supposed to start at eight, and according to the antique grandfather clock in the corner I was seven minutes early.

"Anybody seen Janet this morning?" a woman asked.

"I did," a man said. "She was on her way to the basement for coffee."

"Someone go get her," Helga Van Brackle snapped.

"I'll go," I volunteered. I'd already noticed there was no coffeepot in the room, and I figured I could get a cup from wherever Janet was getting hers.

"Better take the elevator," the man said. "It's faster than the stairs."

"No it isn't," the woman contradicted. "Damn thing sticks half the time."

I left while they argued.

Rising up from the left side of the hallway, near the back, was a circular staircase with a bronze goddess serving as the newel post. Looking up through the hollow center of it, I saw metal rods at each landing, extending across the empty space. When I realized they were braces placed there to keep the staircase from collapsing inward, I decided to use the elevator.

The elevator was a marvel of turn-of-the-century engineering, with a brass grille I had to pull shut by hand. It creaked slowly to the basement, and I stepped into a dim area, nearly conking my head on the overhead tangle of pipes. I spotted a row of snack machines at the end of the long, dark hallway. In front of them was a small round table, and seated at the table was Janet Margolies, along with two other young women. All three looked startled when I appeared out of the shadows.

"Oh my, that dress! I thought you were a ghost!" Janet gasped. They all laughed nervously.

What an odd thing to say, I thought. Did ghosts wear navy blue dresses? Janet introduced me to one of the younger women, a pretty ponytailed brunette who was in her early twenties. "My assistant, Lizzie Borden," Janet said, and looked at me as if eagerly awaiting my reaction to the name.

"Okay," I said. "I'll play along. What were your parents thinking of?"

Lizzie giggled. "Not that their precious baby daughter Elizabeth would grow up to marry Timothy Borden."

I shook Lizzie Borden's hand and asked, "What was your maiden name?"

"Swineheart. I think Borden's an improvement, don't you? This is Jennifer, today's receptionist." She smiled at her younger companion, who grinned back. "You don't need to remember her name—she won't be here tomorrow—too competent—actually knows what she's doing—probably be fired by lunchtime."

I shook Jennifer's hand, which felt a little peculiar.

"Sorry," she murmured. "Just finished a sticky bun."

I knew about sticky buns, a favorite Pennsylvania Dutch treat: yeast dough, slathered with real butter, sprinkled with brown sugar, cinnamon, and nuts, then rolled, sliced, and baked in a mixture of melted butter, brown sugar, and pecans. A sticky bun served warm with the sugar-butter mixture dripping onto your fingers was food fit for the gods. Also, it was guaranteed to go straight from the lips to the hips in a matter of minutes. Yes, I knew all too well about sticky buns.

Janet glanced at her watch. "Guess it's time." She waited while I got a cup of coffee from the machine, and then we rode the creaky elevator to the ground floor.

"You're late," Helga said as we entered the room.

"I was in the middle of something important." Janet winked at me and sat down.

"Hmmph!"

While I'd been gone, some more people had arrived.
I took the only empty chair, across from Luscious Miller, who looked nervous. It was odd to see Luscious
wearing the chief's uniform. I knew the young man had
absolutely no confidence in his own abilities, and
smiled reassuringly at him.

Marvin Bumbaugh, the borough council president,
sat at the head of the table next to the college president.
He didn't look quite as important in these surroundings
as he did when presiding over council meetings.

It was a small and very serious-looking group who
sat around the grand table. Besides President Godlove,
Helga, Marvin, Luscious, Janet, and myself, there
were only three other people present: the vice-president
of the college, the head of campus security, and Professor Ken Nakamura, who was sitting to my immediate
right. He smiled at me and said, "Be wary of the drag-
ons, although they generally produce more smoke than
fire."

I guessed from the way he spoke that nobody else in
the room understood Japanese, and I bowed my head to
acknowledge the wise advice of my elder.

"If you're quite finished, Dr. Nakamura . . ." Helga
said briskly, "I'm sure President Godlove would like to
get on with our meeting."

The twinkle in Ken's eyes was more than light re-
flecting from his glasses as he bowed toward her. "I am,
as always, your humble servant, madam."

"Hmmmph!"

I'd been wrong about one thing—they weren't laying
all the blame on me. And oddly, I thought, campus security wasn't picked on at all. Poor Janet was the target
of most of their fury.

The questions rained down upon her. Though she

tried valiantly to answer them, nobody gave her time to finish a sentence.

"Why was Macmillan playing the condemned man?"

"He asked to—"

"Who loaded the guns?"

"Two of the reenactors—"

"What were their names?"

"Woody Woodruff. And his helper, Darious De-Shong."

"When were the guns loaded?"

"Friday night. Woody said he wanted to do it himself. For safety's sake."

"Why weren't they locked up?"

"They were. In the basement storeroom. I locked the door myself."

"How many keys were there? Who had them?"

"There are only two keys. I had them both with me all night."

"Could someone have picked the lock?"

"It was still locked on Saturday morning. It's an old-fashioned kind of lock—takes a key to both open and lock it." She opened her purse and produced a ring with a pair of keys dangling from it. *"They're still here. See."*

"Did you watch the man load the guns?"

"Of course I did. Lizzie was there, too."

"And you're positive the guns were loaded with blank bullets?"

"They didn't use bullets at all. Woody explained that they use black powder and Wonder Wads to keep it from falling out for reenactments."

"What the hell are Wonder Wads?"

"That's what the men called them. They looked like big foam-rubber ear plugs."

"Where were the reenactors when you arrived?"

"*In the hallway waiting for me. We all then waited together until Mack Macmillan arrived.*"

"Who . . . ? Why . . . Where . . . ? How . . . ?"

The questions flew furiously over the tabletop, but instead of answering any more, Janet gasped, grasped her abdomen, and moaned.

The Lickin Creek Volunteer Fire Department ambulance arrived in record time and left for the hospital in Gettysburg with Janet in the back.

After that flurry of activity, when everyone was settled, President Godlove looked directly at me and said, "So, young lady, since you insisted on cosponsoring this event, it looks like this is now all your responsibility. Let's hear what you're going to do about this disaster."

And the questions started again, only I had no answers. Luscious looked sympathetic, but offered no help. I knew there really was nothing he could do; I was in this one on my own.

I had no idea of what time it was when I staggered out of the meeting. President Godlove had entrusted me with the job of quietly looking into the disaster, probably because he figured if I was involved in the investigation, I wouldn't be writing nasty articles about the sorry event. I stopped at the desk and asked Jennifer, the receptionist, to direct me to Janet's office. I'd been given carte blanche to go through her files and get the names of everybody who had been involved in the reenactment.

The elevator carried me to the top floor of the building.

"Nice garret—for a starving artist," I remarked, looking around the public relations office. All the meetings I'd attended for planning the reenactment had been downstairs in a Victorian parlor. Now that I saw Janet's office, I understood why we hadn't met here. The ceiling came down nearly to the floor on the outside wall, and the only window was in a dormer that looked like an afterthought. The wall below it was water-stained and blistered.

Lizzie laughed. "Our department is regarded as a necessary evil, not an important part of the college hierarchy. We just does our job and keeps our mouths shut. How about a cup of coffee?"

She ducked through a low doorway into another room and reappeared a moment later with two mugs of coffee. "It's better than that stuff in the basement machines but kinda strong."

I sipped the coffee and nearly gagged. Didn't anybody in Lickin Creek know how to make decent coffee? Maybe I should give up journalism and open a Starbucks. "Do you have any milk?"

Lizzie brought me a jar of powdered whitener. I stirred a liberal amount into my coffee mug and tasted the brew again. It didn't help at all. "It's fine," I fibbed as Lizzie anxiously watched me. "Any word from the hospital about Janet?" I asked.

"Yes, mother and child are doing just fine, thanks to God and no thanks to Godlove." The way the phrase fell from her lips made me think it was used often in the college's PR department, and quite possibly in the whole college.

"She only had *one* baby?"

Lizzie giggled and nodded. "Poor Janet's got a lot of weight to lose."

"Why is the college blaming Macmillan's death on Janet?" I asked. "Surely, the reenactment wasn't all her idea."

Lizzie shook her head. "You'd think none of them have ever heard the word *accident*. I guess they're putting the blame on her because she was ordered to come up with something different for Parents' Weekend. And she did."

"I'll say it was different!"

"The college desperately needs some good publicity. Our enrollment is under two hundred and still shrinking. Janet thought staging a mock Civil War execution would get us a lot of press."

"It certainly did, but I don't think this kind of publicity is going to bring any students in," I said.

"I'm afraid you're right. Half a dozen girls left with their parents this morning. Including the senior who played the prisoner's wife. Her parents said she was so traumatized, she'll probably need years of therapy. Which, I'm sure, the college will have to pay for."

"I wonder what made Janet think of staging an execution? It's something that would never cross my mind."

"We saw one last summer over in Gettysburg. She hired the same people to do it here. Except for Mack Macmillan, of course. He has, I mean had, an office across the hall, and when he learned of our plans he burst in here saying he thought it would be great fun to play the victim. He reminded Janet he was very well known, which was true, and that we'd get a lot of notice with him participating. Janet didn't have any choice; she had to agree."

"Why?" I asked. "He was way too old for the role."

"Because Macmillan is, I mean was, the chairman of the college's board of trustees, a position he assumed at the beginning of this semester. And like the proverbial eight-hundred-pound gorilla—the chairman of the board of trustees can do exactly what he wants to do.

And what he wanted to do was participate in the reenactment since he's a big-time Civil War buff. You do know that he was also a retired U.S. congressman? That's what got him on the board of trustees in the first place."

"I can understand why he might want to participate. What I don't understand is how real bullets got into the guns. Lizzie, were you there Friday night when the guns were loaded?"

She nodded.

"Could you please tell me exactly what happened?"

Lizzie sat down on the ugliest sofa I've ever seen and patted the seat beside her, raising a little cloud of dust. "Sorry about that," she said. "I picked it up at the Goodwill. Cheap. Now I know why. Have a seat. I'll try to tell you everything."

I sat on the sofa and found it smelled nearly as bad as it looked. "Go on," I said.

"Like I told Chief Miller yesterday afternoon, Janet and I went out for hamburgers at about five. When we came back, the building was deserted or seemed to be. Nobody in their right mind sticks around here after dark. We wouldn't have been here either, except we were waiting for the reenactors to bring the guns.

"There were two of them. One guy was big and fat, with a bushy beard. The other was younger and pretty much of a hunk. They each carried a big box, full of guns, we found out later."

"Did Janet know who the men were?"

"Sure. At least she knew the big one. I forget his name, but it's in my file cabinet. We stood around the lobby for a while chatting, then the five of us took the elevator down to the basement."

"Five of you? You only mentioned four: you, Janet, and the two reenactors."

"Mack Macmillan came with us, saying he wanted to 'savor the entire reenactment experience.' As usual, he was late, but not as bad as yesterday, only a couple of minutes. He didn't have any reason to think so highly of himself—it's not like he was a senator, you know. Just a congressman. That's not nearly as important, is it? And he's been retired for more than a year. Anyway, Janet unlocked the door to the storeroom where we had already decided to keep the equipment and let us in."

"Why was the door locked *before* the guns were put in the storeroom?"

"Things used to disappear. You know how it is, a box of thumbtacks, a ream of paper, a case of ballpoint pens. After Janet put a lock on the door, the pilferage stopped."

"I noticed keys hanging on hooks next to the door as I came in. Is that where you keep the storeroom key?"

"No. Those are for the other doors on this floor. Offices, mostly empty, and the rest rooms. People kept misplacing their keys, so Janet said she'd keep a spare set here. But she always kept our keys in her purse."

"You didn't have a key to the storeroom?"

Lizzie shook her head. "I'm not saying she didn't trust me, but she made a point of keeping both keys. I had to ask her for them every time I needed to replace a pencil."

"I see. So what happened after the door was opened?"

"The reenactors opened the gun boxes, then the ugly one took a box out of his sheepskin vest pocket and opened it. It was full of bullets—not real bullets—but twists of paper full of black powder with these odd-looking foam tops he called Wonder Wads. He said he'd made them himself. They didn't even look like real bullets, so I don't think he brought the wrong ones by mistake. He and the cute one loaded all fifteen guns. When they were through, the hairy guy had each of us initial the box top as proof that we witnessed him load the guns. That was it."

"Did anything else happen?"

Lizzie crinkled her brow in thought, then shook her head. "We all stepped into the hall. Janet pulled the door shut, locked it, and put the key ring in her pocket. She said she needed to go up to the office for a few minutes. I don't like hanging around the building after dark—because of the ghosts—so when she said she didn't need me to stay, I left with the reenactors."

The "ghost" reference stopped my thought process in midstream. "What ghosts?"

"It's silly, I know, but stories have been going round for years that the campus is haunted. Some of the buildings were used during the Civil War as a hospital, and so many men died here that they had to be buried on campus."

"Is that why you thought I was a ghost when you saw me in the basement?"

She nodded and looked a little embarrassed. "The Sisters of Charity set up an operating room in the basement. Students say the ghost of a nun in a blue habit appears there sometimes. She's supposed to have died here."

Skepticism must have showed on my face. "I know," she said. "It's probably just stories the guys make up to give the girls a good scare."

"Guys? I thought this was a women's college."

"At this point in time, they'd accept anybody who was breathing." She laughed. "Actually, Tori, men have been on campus since World War II."

I tried to bring the conversation back around to the former congressman's death. "Who else had access to the room? Custodians? Students? Faculty?"

"There were only two keys, and Janet always kept them with her. I didn't even have one."

"And she opened the door on Saturday so the soldiers could get their guns out?"

"Right."

"What about after she unlocked it on Saturday morning? Could someone have gotten in then and reloaded the guns?"

"She didn't unlock the door until Mack got there. Then Woody passed the guns out to the men while we watched. There was no possible way for anyone to have tampered with them."

"And she had both the storeroom keys with her all night? This doesn't look good for Janet, does it? Suppose I start by going through your file? See if I can't pull out the names of some people to talk to."

She led me into her office in the other half of the garret. It was slightly larger than Janet's domain, with a lot more actual work equipment, including a cluttered desk, a large drafting table, a light box, and lots of things with flashing lights I didn't even recognize. In contrast to the cyber-age electronic equipment were the old-fashioned slate blackboards covering the walls from the waist-high chair rail to the ceiling. On each was a chart outlining the progress of the different projects the PR department was working on.

"Impressive," I remarked, pointing to the boards.

"The only way I can keep up with what we're doing and make the deadlines is to put up a time line for each project. I tried to do it on the computer, but this seems to work better for me." She walked over to one of the boards and proudly explained, "This is the time line for the view book."

"What's a 'view book'?" I asked.

"Propaganda we send out to prospective students, telling them how wonderful our campus is and what a charming place Lickin Creek is to live in. Hopefully, it will encourage them to visit, and when they come we will try to persuade them to choose our small, very expensive, nearly-out-of-business women's college over one of the Seven Sisters."

"Sounds like quite a challenge."

"To say the least."

I noticed a date had been checked off, indicating the faculty had been reminded to send information. The dated column where receipt of the information was noted was nearly empty, even though the date had passed.

Lizzie shrugged. "It's hard to get them moving on anything. They don't realize the amount of lead time it takes to put something like this together. They seem to think spring is too far away to worry about. Let me get you the reenactment folder."

This should be pretty much like following leads for a news story, I thought. Lizzie placed a thick file folder on the desk. I thumbed through it. "You're very thorough," I said.

"I keep everything," she said. "Janet and I call it the COA approach to public relations and marketing— that's short for Cover Our Ass, in case you couldn't guess—we even save the doodles we make while talking on the telephone." She handed me a notebook and a pen. "You know what you're looking for, I guess. You can use Janet's desk if you like. I'll get to work on the ads for the night classes. Holler if you have any questions."

I carried the file into the outer office and went through the papers, one by one, making a notation in my notebook whenever I came across the name of someone I might want to interview. Naturally, the men who'd loaded the guns were first on my list.

CHAPTER 4

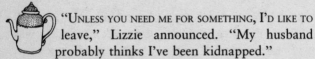 "UNLESS YOU NEED ME FOR SOMETHING, I'D LIKE TO leave," Lizzie announced. "My husband probably thinks I've been kidnapped."

"I only need a few more minutes," I said. "Is it all right if I stay here alone?"

"Suit yourself. I imagine everybody's gone home by now, but you can get out through the front door by just pushing on it."

With her departure, I was left alone in the attic. The building was so still, I realized I was probably the only person there. After a short while, I gave up and tossed the folder into the top desk drawer. Perhaps it was Lizzie's silly story about ghosts on campus, perhaps it was knowing I was alone, but I found myself jumping with each creak and moan of the old building.

As I was pulling the brass grille of the elevator closed, I thought I heard a sound coming from the direction of the PR office. I stopped and listened but heard nothing. "Anybody there?" I called. There was no answer. Then I heard it again, a creaking noise that sounded as if someone was stealthily opening or closing a door. Thoughts of ghosts ran through my mind. But even more frightening was the thought that a real person might be sneaking up on me in the dark hallway. I jammed my finger against the down button and breathed a sigh of relief as the ancient elevator jerked and began to move. As it slowly bounced downward, I prayed it wouldn't get stuck. All I needed was to be locked in the building all weekend with a ghost or something worse.

Outside, I stood on the porch for a few moments, thinking about what I should do next. The yellow police tape was still up, but the mock grave had been filled in and was covered with grassy sod. The investigation, if any, had moved to another level. If Garnet were still the chief of police, I'd be able to ask him what was being done, and after he grumbled a little he'd tell me. But he was gone, and I was on my own.

Now what? I wondered. I certainly didn't want to go home and continue last night's mind-numbing discussion with Ethelind about figures of speech in *King Lear*. What I could do was get started on my interviews, I thought. I opened the notebook and studied the list of names. There were two reenactors who'd loaded the guns, and I needed to talk to both of them. For one, I had only the number of a post office box in a nearby village, for the other, the address of a shop in Gettysburg. Unlike Lickin Creek's, most Gettysburg shops were open on Sundays. I could zip across the mountain and be in Gettysburg in fifteen or twenty minutes. At least I'd be doing something constructive with my time.

The "company car," a white Chevy Cavalier from the vintage year of 1985, stood alone on the far edge of the deserted parking lot. It was great having wheels of my own, but every time I got in it to go somewhere, I said a little prayer that this would not be its last trip. Today, it took its own sweet time about starting.

"Please, please, please . . ." I muttered under my breath. The engine coughed, then turned over.

I left Lickin Creek behind me and headed over the mountains on the narrow, winding road that would take me to Gettysburg. I drove through several small villages, hardly more than a few buildings at a crossroads, and past neat little farms where the brick houses were dwarfed by the nearby barns. Twice, I crossed rivers on old stone bridges. Or more likely it was one meandering river that I crossed twice. There were few cars on the road, and I made good time.

Soon, I was in the center of town, waiting at Lincoln Square for a break in the traffic. All the stores I could see were open, and the sidewalks were full of people, some of whom wore clothes of the Civil War era. I glanced down at my page of names on the front seat beside me and read the address of the shop I was looking for. Lizzie had told me it was only a few blocks off the main street, not far at all from the square.

Taking my life in my hands, I cut into the circle. Four streets branched off from it like the spokes of a wheel, and from each street came a steady stream of cars which swept me all the way around the square back to where I had started. As I went round again, I wondered if there was any way to escape, or was I doomed to ride forever around the center of Gettysburg? Finally, I ignored angry honking from the car behind me, squeezed between a pickup truck pulling a camper and an SUV, and managed to exit the circle. I drove for a few blocks and then turned left.

Tall, narrow brick town houses lined both sides of the one-lane, one-way street. Several had been converted to shops, and in front of one of them was a hanging sign with raised gold letters that said THE OLD CAMP GROUND. That was what I was looking for.

I found a parking spot about two blocks up the street and got out of the car, feeling almost as though I'd stepped back into the last century. Walking ahead of me were two women in hoopskirts carrying string bags. A bearded soldier in a gray Confederate uniform stepped out of a bookshop and nodded pleasantly to me. The mood was broken when two teenage girls with spiky purple hair whizzed past me on roller blades. I paused for a minute to look into the windows of the bookshop and wished I had time to stop. Reluctantly, I decided I couldn't. Not today. Time has no meaning for me once I get into a bookstore. As I turned away, I had the uncomfortable sensation that someone was watching me. I looked around, but the street was now empty.

Across the street was another shop with a hanging sign that spelled out DREAMGATE in gold letters. To the left of the door was a dusty window, full of Celtic jewelry and crystal suncatchers, and through the window, I thought I saw a furtive movement, as if a person had been there, then stepped back. For a moment I was unnerved, then I decided my imagination was carrying me away. There was no reason for somebody to be spying on me; it was only a customer who had just entered the shop—or maybe the owner was straightening up the window display.

THE OLD CAMP GROUND had a single window, and all that was in it was a small sign that read SUTLERY, ANTIQUITIES, GUNS, AUTHENTIC COSTUMES, AND CIVIL WAR SOUVENIRS. Another sign, on the door, said OPEN, PUSH HARD.

I pressed down on the latch, put my shoulder to the door, and pushed with all my might. The door swung open easily and I tumbled inside, landing on my knees. I quickly got on my feet and brushed the dust off my skirt. I wasn't hurt, just embarrassed and hopeful that nobody had seen my ridiculous entrance. The contrast between the bright day outside and the dim interior caused me to stop and blink. As I waited for my eyes to adjust to the darkness, I heard a deep chuckle, then a man's voice saying, "Afternoon, miss. Nice of you to drop in." So much for my hope that nobody had witnessed my fall. The room slowly began to materialize, first a waist-high glass case to my right, full of small objects for reenactors like tin cups and enamel cookware, then shelves stacked with boxes, and finally, in the back of the room, a number of lifelike mannequins dressed in clothes of the Civil War period.

"Hello?" I said, looking around for the source of the voice.

What I'd first thought was a mannequin, sitting in a rocking chair, stood up. I gasped in surprise. "You really startled me," I said. As the figure moved toward me, I was even more startled, for the man was at least six and a half feet tall and had to weigh close to three hundred pounds. He wore a blue Union Army uniform, and the lower half of his face and most of his chest were hidden by a bushy, sandy-colored beard. And most startling of all, an enormous rifle rested in the crook of his left arm.

"Sorry, miss. Didn't mean to scare you." His stentorian voice was better suited for the Broadway stage than a dusty shop in Gettysburg.

"Are you the owner?" I groped in my memory for his name, "Wood . . . Uh . . . Woody . . . ?" I couldn't recall his last name.

He unlocked the glass doors of a gun cabinet and placed the gun inside along with a dozen others, then locked the case, pocketed the key, and moved toward me with surprising grace for a man of his size. Nothing jiggled; his bulk was all muscle. "Woody Woodruff." He smiled down at me, and his blue-green eyes sparkled as he extended a hand the size of a roasting chicken, which I shook. Woody Woodruff seemed to be trying to exude a sexy animal magnetism, and he was failing miserably.

"What an interesting shop," I murmured to cover up my discomfort. Why I feel uncomfortable when a man, any man, pays attention to me, I just don't understand. In this case I was totally dumbfounded. Woody wasn't at all attractive. Especially in his silly blue costume.

"You don't look like most of the gals what come in here," he said.

"And how do they look?"

"Long hair, rimless glasses, sandals, ethnic jewelry. Reenactors look kind of like hippies, only with a purpose in life. And they're usually younger."

Younger! I was only a little past thirty, just enough to feel the first pangs of self-consciousness about my age. Soon I'd have to wear bathing suits with skirts and pad my bunions with moleskin, and people would call me *ma'am*, and life as I knew it would be over. I realized Woody was staring at me, as though waiting for me to comment on what he'd just said.

"Oh," I said, demonstrating the agility with words that made me such a brilliant writer. I pulled my aging self back to the moment and, thinking it best not to tell him I was a reporter, said I was from the college and needed to ask a few questions about Mr. Macmillan's death. He led me to the back of the store where there were two rockers and gestured for me to sit in one.

"Want a soda?"

"Diet, please." I opened my notebook while he disappeared through a pair of curtains. He was back in a minute with two ice-cold cans.

"I got a Coke machine in back," he said, handing me a soda. "Didn't want to spoil the ambience by putting it in here." He sat down and looked intently at me. "I been over this several times." He raised the Coke can to his lips and drank. "I talked to that weird little police chief from Lickin Creek twice yesterday. He couldn't seem to think of what to ask me the first time, so he come back later with more questions."

At first I thought he was referring to Garnet and was offended, but then I remembered Luscious Miller was now the acting police chief, and *weird* described him well. Luscious was a nice guy, but really out of his league in Garnet's job. I could picture him stumbling through an interview, going home and wishing he'd asked better questions, then coming back to stumble through another. Poor Luscious—I knew no one had wanted Garnet to stay in Lickin Creek more than he.

"But I'm not with the police, you see, so I have no access to their report."

He still looked doubtful.

"We—I mean the college—want to keep this as quiet as possible and find out what happened."

"What happened"—he grinned—"is that Mack Macmillan bit the bullet—fifteen of them to be exact." He swigged down the last of his soda and belched.

I restrained from shuddering at his rude behavior and said, "I know that, Woody. But how? You loaded the guns the night before, didn't you . . . ?"

"Yeah—but not with lead. Just black powder and foam Wonder Wads to hold it in place." He glared at me as if daring me to contradict him.

"Were you alone at the time?" I knew he hadn't been but wanted to hear his version.

"There was four other people in that room with me. That PR gal from the college let us in and stayed with us like she was scared we'd steal some of her precious paper clips."

"That was Janet Margolies," I told him.

"Yeah—Janet—the pregnant one. And her helper-gal. Then there was Darious—he loaded half the guns—with the ammunition I brought with me."

"His last name?"

"DeShong." He spelled it, and I wrote it down. That was the man for whom I had only a post office box.

"Have you known him for long?"

"Met him last summer. We done maybe a half-dozen reenactments together. Fairly dependable. Usually shows up like he says he will. That's why I asked him to help out."

"Why were you in charge, Woody?"

"I'm the commanding officer of the company what was invited to stage the execution. Executions is our specialty. As CO, loading the guns is my job. Looky here, miss, I take my responsibilities serious. My reputation can be ruined by this. I might never get asked to do another execution."

"The college doesn't blame you at all, Woody," I said, trying to soothe him.

"I wanna find out what went wrong—maybe more than anybody."

I looked at my notebook and thought for a moment about what to ask next. Lizzie had told me Woody had taken the box of ammo out of his vest pocket. "Woody, when you took the guns to the college, did you take the exact number of cartridges you'd need? Or were there some left over?"

"There was lots left over. I only make them up about twice a year."

"Could I see the box, please."

"Sure." He crossed the room with three giant steps, opened a drawer in a rolltop desk, and pulled out a box. "Here's what we didn't use." He handed me one.

To me, it looked like a dirty twist of paper with an earplug glued on top.

"What does the foam thingy do?" I asked.

"It holds the powder in place. In the old days, soldiers would fill a piece of paper with black powder, then put a ball on top. The ball was what did the killing. See—here's a real one. It don't even look like the ones I made. Nobody could mistake mine for the real thing. I load them myself, and I ain't never had no accident."

"How do I know this was the box you had in the storeroom?" I asked.

His mouth smiled, but not his eyes. "You're tough, Tori. Lucky for me I don't fool around when it comes to guns and ammo. Take a look-see at the box top. I had everybody there initial it."

I took the box from his outstretched hand, ignoring the way he let his fingers linger on mine. "W. W.— that's you, I suppose?"

He nodded.

"J. M. is Janet Margolies, I assume. L. B.—that's Lizzie Borden."

"Hell of a name. And D. D. is Darious DeShong."

"Who was this E. M.?"

"That was Mack. His real name was Edward Macmillan. He liked to be called Mack because it made him sound like one of the boys."

"Who actually loaded the guns?"

Woody shook his head. "Darious and me. Want another Diet?"

"No thanks. Can you recall anything unusual happening?"

He shook his head again. "After we was done, we left the room. Janet locked the door behind us. Darious and me got in my truck, and I drove him home. That's all."

"Are you sure it was locked?"

"I tried it myself. Them guns is my responsibility."

"Was there any other way in? A window, maybe?" I asked.

He shook his head. "Nope. It was just a big closet. One door. No windows."

It was like a John Dickson Carr locked-room mystery. Door locked. Two keys, both in Janet Margolies's possession. No evidence of the lock being picked. No other entrance to the storeroom. How on earth could the switch have occurred? "What about on Saturday when you went to get the weapons? Did anything look different?"

"Nah. Janet opened the door. Her secretary was with her. Darious and me went in, got the guns, and passed them out to the men. They was standing in the hallway."

"Did you see any discarded blanks, I mean Wonder Wads, lying around?"

"Of course not. The storeroom looked exactly like it did when we locked it up on Friday night."

That meant whoever had reloaded the guns had taken the original ammunition away with him, or her. I wondered if it would ever turn up.

"Please think back—did anything unusual happen?"

"We had a long wait before Mack showed up. About an hour late. Janet looked pretty damn mad, but there weren't much she could do about it." He shrugged. "Guess when you're a big shot, you don't mind keeping people waiting."

"What did you and your men do while you were waiting for him to arrive?" I asked.

"We just hung around the hallway. Drank a Coke. Ate some pretzels one of the guys brought with him."

"You didn't go into the storeroom?"

"I already done told you, Janet didn't unlock it until Mack showed up. And I know it was locked because I tried to open it when we first got there."

"I understand Macmillan was a Civil War expert. Was he a collector, also? Did he ever come here to buy things from you?"

Woody chuckled. "I don't sell the type of things Mack Macmillan collected. Couldn't afford to stock them."

His eyebrows grew together. "Wait a second—I done near forgot—there was a little problem. After Mack finally showed up, Janet couldn't get the door open. Then she tried another key, and it worked okay."

"Wait a minute," I said. "You mean one of the keys couldn't unlock the storeroom door?"

"Uh-huh," Woody replied with his usual eloquence.

Hmm, I thought I'll have to talk to Janet about this. I snapped my notebook shut, stood up, and extended my hand. "Thanks a lot, Woody. If you think of anything else, please call the public relations office at the college. If I'm not in, leave a message with Lizzie." I knew I wouldn't be there, but I was also sure Lizzie would let me know if he called.

He grasped my hand with both of his and stared intently into my eyes. "I don't think you understand how careful we'uns always is—so nobody gets hurt."

"I'm sure you are," I commented, trying to free my hand from his grip.

"Maybe you'uns should take part in a reenactment. See how we do it."

"That would be really nice," I said, surreptitiously wiping my hand on my dress. I looked for a way to get past him to the door. He stepped aside before I decided how to make a run for freedom.

At the door, I thought of one more question. "Can you tell me where Darious DeShong lives? The only address I have for him is a post office box in Lickin Creek."

"Try the Hostettler farm out on Orphanage Road."

"Do you have his telephone number?"

"Darious with a phone? Hah!" He pulled the door open and stood aside. "Do you have an Esso?" he asked.

"Esso?" I repeated, feeling confused. Wasn't that a gas station?

My face must have looked totally blank, because he chuckled and said, "S.O. . . . Significant Other . . . person you got something going with . . . a boy-friend."

If I didn't, I certainly wouldn't want him to know. "Yes," I said. "I do have an . . . S.O."

"Took you a little while to answer. You telling me the truth?"

"I have to go now." As I pushed past him, I felt warmth radiating from his body.

"I'll call you," he yelled at my back.

In my car, I rolled down the windows and exhaled loudly. What had he been thinking? The creep had been coming on to me through the whole interview. Who did he think he was—Brad Pitt? Did I really come across as a lonely single woman looking for a man? I turned the ignition key on the Cavalier more forcefully than I needed to, said my usual please-let-it-start prayer, and pulled out into the empty street.

Maybe, I thought, as the car rolled back into the twenty-first century, I should wonder why he thought I was available. Did I unconsciously project a man-hungry aura? Good God, I hoped not.

Deciding to put off my visit to Darious DeShong, the other reenactor, for another day, I headed back to Lincoln Square where I noticed a couple of restaurants. It was getting late, and I had missed lunch. The place I chose was called the Pub and Restaurant. Inside, the walls were painted dark blue, with a frieze around the top depicting babies and young children with wings. A pleasant young woman in a blue shirt and beige shorts led me to a booth, trimmed with red and gold, near the window, where, through a potted fern, I had an excellent view of an endless stream of cars and trucks racing around the traffic circle.

"What'll it be, hon?" the waitress asked. I'd almost become used to waitresses calling me *hon,* and so I barely cringed. I studied the menu for a minute. It featured a nice selection of salad plates, but phooey on that. I deserved something far more substantial after the difficult day I'd experienced.

Since I was really planning to start my diet Monday, I decided to go all out and ordered a Reuben with french fries and coleslaw. My plate was nearly clean when my waitress approached the table. "No dessert, just the check," I told her, and felt positively virtuous.

"No, ma'am, I was asked to give you a message."

Ma'am, she called me *ma'am.* That was even worse than *hon.* It really was the beginning of the end when a waitress, only slightly younger than myself, called me ma'am!

She didn't seem to notice my distress and pointed to the doorway, where a black figure was silhouetted against the sky. "Lady there says she wants to talk to you." I took the check from her hand and headed toward the counter.

The figure, a woman, stepped forward. She wore an ankle-length black gauze dress and lots of clunky silver Celtic jewelry. Her blond hair hung straight to her waist and was crowned with a wreath of white flowers. Despite the New Age outfit, suitable for a teeny-bopper, I guessed her to be older than me by several years.

"Tori Miracle?" the apparition asked.

I acknowledged that was my name.

"My name's Moonbeam."

"Yes?" I asked.

"I have a shop here in Gettysburg."

"Dreamgate?"

She nodded. "I saw you go into Woody's sutlery."

"I'm really in a hurry," I said, and made an attempt to step around her.

She deftly blocked my escape. "Woody's my friend. A really good friend."

Did she mean boyfriend? I wanted to offer her my deepest sympathy, but I kept still and waited to hear what was coming next.

"I didn't think you looked like one of his regulars, so I went over to his shop to see what you were doing there. We look out for each other."

Oh man!

"He said you're looking into Mack Macmillan's murder."

Murder. Moonbeam was the first person who had used that word. I wondered if she knew something. "That's absolutely correct," I said. "Is there something you can tell me about it?"

She shook her head, sprinkling flower petals on the floor. "Not really." She changed the subject abruptly by saying, "I'm psychic, you know." She appeared to be both jealous and wacky, a dangerous combination.

"I sense that you are troubled."

"Who isn't?"

"I can help you." Little silver bells tied to her ankles by string—probably hemp—tinkled as she moved.

"You can help me find out who murdered Mack Macmillan?"

Her blue eyes widened with surprise. "No. I meant I could help *you*." She handed me a little lavender card covered with moons and stars and small print. "Come to my shop, soon. I'll do an evaluation and determine what kind of treatment you need."

"Thank you, but I'm not really into aromatherapy, or Reiki, or Rolfing, or feng shui, or . . ." I stopped reading from her card because, with a tinkling of her bells, she spun away and was gone.

I glanced at her card. *Moonbeam Nakamura,* it said, *holistic healer of mind, body, and spirit.* It struck me as very odd that I'd met two people named Nakamura in one day. Nakamura was as common as Smith or Jones in Japan, but certainly it was rare in south-central Pennsylvania. Determined to find out what the connection was between Moonbeam and Professor Nakamura at the college, I dropped her card into my purse.

The air was cool and the sky was darkening when I pulled into the circular driveway in front of Ethelind's dilapidated Moon Lake mansion. The gloomy thought hit me that it was probably too early for her to have gone to bed. My only hope was to sneak up the back stairs with Fred and Noel before she heard me. When I moved in a few weeks ago, I'd thought she was leaving right away, but she stayed on—and on—and on.

Hoping to get in without attracting her attention, I tried to close the car door quietly, but the front door to the house popped open and Ethelind's shrill voice pierced the evening air. "Tori? Is that you? Are you okay? It's so late!"

"Everything's fine, Ethelind," I replied.

"I've got the Parcheesi board set up for a game," she called.

I marched toward the house feeling like a "dead man walking."

CHAPTER 5

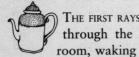 THE FIRST RAYS OF EARLY MORNING SUN STREAMED through the louvered window of my bedroom, waking me.

As quietly as I could, I went downstairs and entered the kitchen. Noel, my dainty little gray and white tabby, lay sprawled on the oaken kitchen table between the salt and pepper shakers.

"Hi, sweetie." She rewarded me with a gentle purr for stroking her back. "Where's Fred?" I whispered. I was speaking softly because the last thing I needed was Ethelind demanding to know where I was going. It was as if I were a teenager again, having to explain my every move.

"Well! Good morning, young lady." Ethelind's voice boomed in my ears. She stood in the doorway that led into the front of the house with one of her disgusting brown cigarettes stuck to her lower lip and Fred goofily draped over her left shoulder. "I've been up for hours," she announced. Fred turned around and blinked twice as if he also wanted to chastise me for sleeping late.

I removed Fred from her shoulder. "He's got chronic bronchitis," I told her. "He shouldn't be exposed to

cigarette smoke." Fred added emphasis to my statement
by sneezing twice. It helped make the point.

"I've heard of people being allergic to cats, but I've
never heard of a cat being allergic to people."

"Not people, just cigarettes."

She tossed her cigarette into the sink and ran water
on it. "Good thing I'm due to leave in a couple of
days."

I'd heard *that* before!

I busied myself with filling the cats' dishes with Tasty
Tabby Treats. Both cats came running over, thanked me
by gently winding around my legs a couple of times,
then began to gobble their food as if they hadn't seen
anything to eat in a week.

"Got to get to work," I muttered, trying to sound
cheerful.

"Will you be here for dinner tonight?" Ethelind
asked. "I fix a damn good toad-in-the-hole."

Toad-in-the-hole was the British equivalent of
Greta's scalloped weiners. I didn't care for either. "I
think I have to work late. Sorry."

Disappointment showed in her face, and I felt bad.
Well, a little bad. I vowed to spend a whole evening
with her before she left—if she ever did leave.

I had dressed this morning in what I hoped was appropriate fall office attire: brown slacks, a lightweight
pumpkin-colored sweater, and gold corduroy blazer.
With the addition of my gold hoop earrings and a couple of chains, I thought I looked quite stylish. Even Cassie couldn't find anything wrong with this outfit.

The cats were in the sink playing catch with the cigarette butt Ethelind had tossed into it and didn't even
glance up as I left. I'll be home early, I promised them
silently as I made my escape from the smoke-filled
kitchen.

When I walked into the office, Cassie looked up from a stack of papers, rubbed her forehead as though suffering severe pain, and groaned.

"What's wrong?" I asked. I hung my blazer on the back of my chair and sat down.

"This." With each hand she waved a piece of paper at me. "Subscription cancellations. Dozens of them."

"But why?"

The phone rang, and Cassie snatched it up. "Are you sure you want to do this, Mrs. Layman? Please don't forget we put your grandson's picture on the front page last year . . . yes, I know the article was about the symphony, but he was first violin . . . I promise you it will never . . . yes, I know Miss Mullins would never have . . . I'm sorry you feel this way . . ."

She hung up and glared at me. "It's been like that all morning. The *Chronicle* is doomed. You might have told me that the reenactment was going to be an execution, Tori."

It had crossed my mind when I attended the first planning session, but somehow I thought she wouldn't have approved, so I had kept quiet. "Are you telling me the *Chronicle* is going down like *Titanic*, just because we cosponsored Saturday's event? I can't believe that."

She waved another paper at me. "Here's the proof. They might have put up with something like this if P. J. had been in charge, but you . . . let's face it, Tori, you don't have the best reputation in town."

I was shocked. "What do you mean? Surely, they've forgiven me for burning down the Historical Society. Everybody knows that was an accident."

"They might say they've forgiven you, but then you ruined the Apple Butter Festival, and they haven't had time to forget that. And of course there's the matter of the clinic closing, too."

Tears brimmed in my eyes, and I had to blink to keep them from falling out. "That's really unfair," I mumbled into a Kleenex. "I was only helping out. And I'll kill you if you say something smarmy like, 'who said life is fair?'"

To hide my distress, I pulled the cardboard box I'd brought from home out from under my desk and looked through it.

"What are you doing?" Cassie asked.

"This office is really drab. It'll look better once I hang up a few personal items." I took a faded old photograph down from the wall above my desk. "Just look at this ugly frame. It's all chipped."

"It's a photograph of the paper's founder," Cassie said.

"We'll put it back up before P. J. returns." I climbed up on the desktop and hung a framed poster on the hook. It was from the Philomathean Society's show of W. W. Denslow's children's illustrations, a real favorite of mine.

"Where did that come from?" Cassie asked.

"I had my neighbor send my stuff. Figured if I'm going to be in Lickin Creek for six months, it would be nice to have my own things here."

After a few adjustments, I was happy with the way the picture looked. The bright green color added a cheerful note to an otherwise drab room. Before I could climb down, the door burst open and President Godlove from the college entered. Even in his sharp gray suit, cream colored shirt, and subtly striped silk tie, he reminded me of a military officer as he stood stiffly in the doorway gazing with disapproval at me.

"I've been trying to get you on the telephone for ten minutes," he said. He stared at my desktop. "No wonder. The phone's unplugged."

"I must have caught my foot in the cord when I climbed up here," I admitted.

He looked up at me and shook his head.

"What can I do for you?" I asked, once I had my two feet on the floor.

"Are you planning on going to Mack Macmillan's funeral this afternoon?"

"I hadn't planned to."

"It could smooth things over for you. Show the community that you're really sorry this happened."

"I don't see how I could possibly get away." I picked up the day's calendar and read, *Cover the Chicken and Stuff benefit lunch at the Rec Center* . . . Maybe that wasn't a good example. "There's a guest speaker at the monthly meeting of the Caven County Realtors' Society. And the AMVETS has a new flag." I didn't mention that I also hoped to track down the other reenactor, Darious DeShong.

"Tori, I can get one of our freelancers to handle all of today's hot news stories," Cassie said. "I agree with Dr. Godlove. You really should go to the funeral. It might even get us back some of our disgruntled subscribers."

"All right. What time and where?"

"Two o'clock," the college president said. "At Arlington National Cemetery."

"Please tell me you don't mean the one in Washington, D.C.!"

"That's the one. If you leave by ten, you'll be there in plenty of time." He stopped in the doorway on his way out. "I'd give you a ride, but my car's already full with the trustees."

"Be sure to keep track of your mileage," Cassie said. "If there's any money left at the end of the month, we can reimburse you for the gas."

Being the editor/publisher wasn't all I'd hoped it would be.

"I nearly forgot, you had a phone call this morning." Cassie rummaged through the mess on her desk. "Here it is. Dr. Washabaugh. Again."

"I'll call her first thing tomorrow," I said.

Cassie said, "Call her now, Tori. Why are you procrastinating on this?" She began pushing buttons on her telephone.

"Procrastination is one of the character defects which make me so lovable," I said.

She ignored me and said into the receiver. "Dr. Washabaugh, please. This is Tori Miracle returning her call." To me she said, "She'll be on in a minute. You can take it on your phone. Yes, yes, she's right here." She glared at me until I picked up the phone on my desk.

"This is Tori," I reluctantly said to the invisible person on the line.

"I've been trying to get hold of you for a long time." Dr. Washabaugh sounded aggravated. "Didn't you get any of my messages?"

"Sorry. I've been really busy."

"Can you come to my office this afternoon? I want to go over your test results with you."

"Can't make it today," I said.

"Tomorrow morning, then."

I felt a growing sense of alarm. "What is it? Can't you tell me now?"

"It would be better if we did this in the office. I'll see you at eight."

I held on to the receiver for a long time after I heard the disconnecting click.

"Something wrong?" Cassie asked.

I hung up and shook my head. "No. Just routine

stuff. Are you sure you can handle everything this afternoon?"

"Of course I can."

"I know you can. Which makes me wonder why P. J. didn't ask you to take over the *Chronicle*."

"She did, Tori."

"Why didn't you . . . ?"

"You'll find out."

The drive to Washington on the interstate was long and boring, making me wish once again the *Chronicle* could afford a tape player for its car. Or even a radio. Air-conditioning would be nice, too, I thought, as my face was bombarded by dirt thrown through the open window by the parade of tractor trailers speeding past me. At long last I drove through the impressive entrance to Arlington National Cemetery, parked at the modern visitor center, and picked up a funeral pass.

"There's a bus to the grave site," the woman at the desk told me. "It's parked out front."

I paused for a moment outside to admire the beautiful vista before me of rolling hills marked with small white grave markers and impressive monuments. On the hill stood Arlington House, once the home of Robert E. Lee and Mary Custis, the great-granddaughter of Martha Washington, and, since the Civil War, a possession of the United States government. I'd been to a beautiful wedding there once, a long time ago.

I found a bus marked SSGT EDWARD MACMILLAN and climbed the steps. "Is this the right bus?" I asked the driver. "I'm looking for Congressman Macmillan's funeral."

"This is it," he told me. "Here, we go by the departed's military rank."

As I walked to the back of the bus, I recognized a lot

of people from Lickin Creek. I've come to the conclusion there are only fifty people living in the town, and they go to everything as a group. They all were in gray, black, or navy blue. I was dressed all wrong, as usual— my gold corduroy jacket stood out like a lighthouse beacon in a storm.

A plump lady with a stiff white bonnet on her bun of gray hair patted the seat next to her. "Sit with me, Tori. If I'd known you was coming we could have rode together."

She was Garnet's aunt Gladys. One of them anyway. At family gatherings it always seemed as if all the women were Aunt Gladys and all the men were Uncle Zeke.

I'd barely had time to sit down on the hard brown vinyl bench seat next to her before she said, "My, what pretty earrings, Tori. You look like a gypsy."

The bus lurched to a start, and a few minutes later we were disembarking at the grave site.

Rows of metal folding chairs faced an open grave, hauntingly reminiscent of the one recently dug on the lawn of the Lickin Creek College for Women. Aunt Gladys insisted on looking at the white marble grave marker, so I went with her. The carving on the stone said, *SSGT Edward Macmillan. D.O.B., March 27, 1924. D.O.D.—.* His date with death had not yet been filled in. On the back of the stone were more words: *Ramona Macmillan, D.O.B., December 12, 1926. D.O.D., April 9, 1966.*

"He was married before?" I asked.

Gladys nodded and dabbed at her eyes with a lace-edged handkerchief. "Lovely woman. Died of cancer. Smoker, of course." I was sure no cigarette had ever soiled Garnet's Aunt Gladys's lips. She added, "She was an Unterberger, you know," as if that should mean something to me.

We took seats in the last row and rested our feet on the green artificial grass carpet beneath the chairs. Soon Dr. Godlove arrived, accompanied by several people who must have been the college trustees. He nodded and passed by me to take a seat in the roped-off section down front. Exactly at two o'clock, the sound of a band playing a Sousa march prompted us all to turn around.

Over the crest of a hill came an impressive parade, an army band, an honor guard of soldiers in dress uniform, a riderless horse, and a caisson, on which lay a coffin covered with an American flag. Walking behind the coffin were several mourners, including one who I assumed was the widow since she wore a long black veil, à la Jackie Kennedy, that hid her hair and face.

The mourners took their seats in the front row, and an army officer stepped forward. From the little silver cross he wore on his uniform, I guessed he was the chaplain. He gave a subtle signal with one hand, and a sharp-looking soldier stepped up to the caisson, lifted the flag on top of the coffin, opened a little door in the rear of it, and removed a small flat metal box. Everyone stood as he carried it to the grave site, where he solemnly laid it on the artificial turf.

"What's that?" I asked Aunt Gladys.

"That's Mack. He was cremated."

I'd never seen a box of cremated human remains before, and I was surprised that it was so small. How could a person be reduced to so little?

The service went quickly. The chaplain said a few words about the congressman's military service in World War II and his long tenure as a congressman, then offered a prayer. The band played taps, and the honor guard raised their rifles and gave the departed man a twenty-one-gun salute. Ironic, I thought, considering the last thing he'd seen was fifteen rifles aiming directly at him.

The flag from the coffin was folded into a neat triangle by several soldiers, one of whom passed it to the chaplain, who then handed it to the widow. That was the signal for everyone to stand and rush forward to offer condolences to Mrs. Macmillan. I stood in line and waited my turn, wondering what I was going to say to her.

From behind I admired her trim, athletic figure. She had to be a lot younger than her husband, I figured. Nobody could look that good in their seventies, even from the back.

It was almost my turn. She extracted herself from a bear hug given her by one of the Lickin Creek contingent and turned to me. I reached out to shake her hand, then stopped with it hanging awkwardly in midair.

She had raised her veil in order to hug and kiss the well-wishers. Other than her lips and eyes, Mrs. Macmillan's face was totally covered with a tan elastic mask. A black hole marked the place where her nose should be.

The lips smiled and said, "Thank you so much for coming today."

I completely forgot what I thought I should say. "I'm so sorry," I stammered, not sure whether I meant sorry about her husband or sorry about her face.

"Thank you so much . . ." she murmured automatically, and reached past me to take Aunt Gladys's outstretched hand. I walked slowly back to the bus. What dreadful thing had happened to her face, I wondered?

Gladys joined me on the bus and fanned her pink face with a memorial leaflet. "Can't believe this kind of weather so late in October. Throws the animals off their feed. Not to mention what it does to the fruit crops. I recall back when I was a kid, we didn't have none of them cloud seeders keeping it from raining then, and the weather was always . . ."

"Aunt Gladys," I interrupted. "Do you know why Mrs. Macmillan has to wear the elastic mask?"

"Of course," she said, wiping her forehead with a lace handkerchief.

Since she'd apparently answered my question to her satisfaction, I tried another tack. "Why does she wear it?"

"Oh, I'm sorry. I keep forgetting you aren't local, Tori. It was an accident last summer. The Macmillans had a big barbecue at their farm for the horsey set. The charcoal didn't seem to be burning, so Charlotte sprayed it with lighter fluid. Naturally, it flared up in her face." Gladys shuddered. "Horrible burns, I understand. She was a patient at Hershey Medical Center for a long time. Then when she came home, she had to wear that mask. Something to do with keeping the skin from scarring more badly. Such a shame. She was a beautiful woman."

I repressed a shudder. I could imagine nothing more painful than a severe burn. "A few weeks ago, at the college, I heard someone say Mrs. Macmillan was settling a crisis at the stable. Is she a horsewoman?"

"Oh my, yes indeed. And a famous one. The college is lucky to have someone like Charlotte running its equestrian program. She was a famous horse trainer before marrying Mack. He bought a horse farm in Gettysburg for her, right next to the battlefield. Besides teaching riding at the college, she gives lessons at her farm. Also does volunteer work. Brings handicapped kids to the farm to ride for free."

"She sounds like a remarkable woman."

"She is, Tori. It was a blessed day when *she* came to our community." She peered at me through the midsection of her trifocals, and I felt she was comparing me to the saintly Mrs. Macmillan. And I didn't even come in a close second.

CHAPTER 6

"MORE COFFEE, DEAR?" ETHELIND SMILED AT ME across the table, revealing large, stained teeth. Fred sprawled on her lap as if he didn't even notice the poisonous nicotine fumes rising from her fuzzy green bathrobe.

At least Noel showed better taste. She lay across my knees, with her little white paws tucked neatly beneath her, and allowed me to scratch the space between her ears.

"No thank you." I didn't really care for her private blend of Kona and tobacco.

Ethelind had happily had me all to herself last evening. I'd had enough Shakespeare, Parcheesi, sweet sherry, and chamber music to last a lifetime.

I went upstairs to get ready for my doctor's appointment by shaving my legs and showering. Somewhere, I read that women are more apt to shave their legs for a visit to the doctor than before a date; that was definitely true for me.

Before I got dressed, I called Cassie to make sure I was wearing the appropriate apparel for whatever she had arranged for me to do today. No more showing up at funerals looking like a clown or a gypsy queen in orange and gold.

"Everything's under control here, Tori," she said. "I'm going to contact all our advertisers this morning to try to convince them not to cancel their contracts with us. There's really no need for you to come in; I can easily cover the YMCA swim meet this afternoon. Dr. Godlove called this morning to thank you for going to the funeral. He wants to know how you're coming along with the investigation."

"What does he think I am—a PI?"

"It wouldn't hurt for you to find out what went wrong," Cassie said. "It might even help your reputation—and the *Chronicle*'s. I've got Luscious's police report here on my desk, Tori. He and the coroner are calling it an accident."

"Accident my foot! That ammunition was deliberately switched."

"Why don't you find out how?"

"I will!" After I hung up, I realized I'd been manipulated again.

Dr. Washabaugh's office was located outside of Lickin Creek on the Gettysburg Road. The middle-aged receptionist put aside her harried frown to greet me as if we were old friends with a cheerful "Hi, Tori."

"Hi, yourself. Sorry, I don't remember your name."

"It's Vesta. Vesta Pennsinger. I'm from Lickin Creek too."

I liked the way she said "too," as if she regarded me as a native. Then she ruined it by saying, "Guess the *Chronicle*'s in a lot of trouble. Do you think you're gonna be sued?"

"What on earth for?"

She shrugged. "I don't know. Seems like every time someone gets killed, someone else gets sued."

I hadn't even considered the possibility of legal action being taken against the paper. No wonder Cassie was worried.

The door to the inner sanctum opened and Dr. Washabaugh stuck her head out. "Tori? You're late."

"No I'm not. It's only . . . nine-thirty."

"My office hours start at eight. Come in, please."

"Yes, ma'am." Just as if I'd been summoned to the principal's office, I hung my head and shuffled through the door. Behind me, I heard a snicker from Vesta. Dr. Washabaugh looked sharply in her direction and squelched any more hilarity.

She took forever to open my file folder and read through it. I swung my foot nervously and chewed the cuticle off my little finger until it bled.

"All your lab tests were fine, Tori. Your cholesterol was a little high, 210." She regarded me over the top of the folder. "Nothing that you have to worry about. Maybe you could watch your fat intake and lose a few pounds."

Hatred and loathing of Dr. Washabaugh nearly overwhelmed me. Lose a few pounds indeed! "According to all the charts," I said, "my weight is perfect. I'm just four inches too short."

Her lips didn't even twitch. She must have missed the lecture on "dealing with patients' humor" during med school. She resumed flipping through the papers.

"Look, Doctor, you didn't call me in here at dawn to tell me I needed to lose a few pounds. Why don't you get to the point?"

This time a trace of a smile crossed her face. "You call nine-thirty in the morning dawn? I made hospital rounds this morning before I opened this office at eight. That's dawn! Okay, Tori, here's what we need to talk about. Your mammogram . . ."

So much blood rushed through my ears that I couldn't hear anything she said after that.

"What are you trying to tell me?" I gasped. "That I have cancer?"

"Didn't you hear anything I said? Probably not. But there is a suspicious mass that we need to check out. I recommend a biopsy."

While I sat in a near stupor, she explained it would be a simple outpatient procedure under local anesthesia. If I wanted, she'd give me a tranquilizer to take before I came in.

"And if you find something?"

"There's no need to worry about that now. We'll have to wait and see."

I rubbed my right breast. It felt fine to me. "Mastectomy?"

"Even if I find a malignancy, I don't know if anything that drastic will be needed. There are options . . ."

"Cut my breast off?"

"Stop it, Tori. You're letting yourself get all upset for no reason. It may be something as simple as a cyst. If it's cancer, we could possibly get by with a lumpectomy, followed by chemo. I'll check with the hospital for a date, then call you."

"Bye-bye, now," Vesta called as I staggered out of the office. I didn't answer, for my head was spinning, full of the frightening words I'd just heard. Suspicious lump, cancer, mastectomy, biopsy, operation, chemo. To those words, I added the unspoken ones. Disfigurement, nausea from chemotherapy, and quite possibly an early death. If I hadn't put my checkup off for five years, would this have happened? One thing I knew for sure, I'd never let another year go by without one.

Somehow I found myself sitting in the front seat of

my car with no recollection of walking from the building to the parking lot. There was no way I could go on like this until I heard from the doctor. I had to find something to do to keep myself from worrying about it.

Back in Lickin Creek, I drove directly to the Lickin Creek College for Women. Getting back into the investigation of Mack Macmillan's death might be what I needed.

Instead of parking miles away in the visitors' lot, I took a chance and parked in the faculty lot adjoining the administration building. After all, I figured, I was here on semi-official business.

I rode the clanking elevator to the attic and entered Lizzie's office, where I found her working at the computer. "Morning," she said. "Cuppa coffee?"

I remembered her coffee from Sunday. "No thanks. What are you working on?"

"Press releases. The college expresses sympathy to the widow of Representative Macmillan on the occasion of his tragic accidental death—blah blah blah. When I'm finished with them, I've got to go through all these newspapers and clip any mention of the college for the scrapbook. Three more students left this weekend. You'd think we had a psycho serial killer on campus from the panic this has generated."

"Sorry to hear that. The paper isn't doing too well, either."

"One good thing came out of all this," Lizzie said. "At least Professor Nakamura won't be retiring soon. He's everybody's faculty favorite."

"What made him change his mind?"

"He announced his retirement when Mack became the chairman of the board of trustees. Said he couldn't work with the man. Now he won't have to."

"Do you know why he felt that way?"

Lizzie shook her head. "Uh-uh. He never said why— just that it was personal. We all thought it was kind of odd, him being a Quaker and all. I thought they were supposed to love everybody."

I made a mental note to talk to Professor Nakamura soon. "So—let's do something. Can you show me the storeroom where the guns were kept?"

"Sure." She reached in her top desk drawer and pulled out a key ring. "Janet had the keys with her when she went to the hospital, but her husband brought them back yesterday."

I headed toward the elevator, but Lizzie stopped at the head of the stairs. "If you don't mind," she said, "I really don't trust that thing."

By the time we reached the basement, my knees were shaking. Lizzie looked okay, though, so I didn't complain. She clicked a switch, but the single bulb hanging from the ceiling didn't do much to light our way.

"Watch your head," she warned. "Some of these pipes are really low." She ducked a few times, but I didn't have to. It was one of the few times being vertically challenged was an advantage.

At the end of a long hallway, she stopped before a metal door. Some yellow police tape lay on the floor. "Here we are," she announced. Nothing happened when she turned a key in the lock.

"Just like Saturday, right?" I said. "Woody told me Janet had to try two keys to open the door." Lizzie nodded as she shoved with her shoulder as she again turned the key, but the door still didn't open. "Hang on, I'll try the other one." This time the door opened without a hitch.

"Let me see those keys," I said. She handed me the ring with two keys on it. They looked very similar, the one that had worked and the one that hadn't; they were from the same manufacturer, were the same brass color, and basically were the same shape. But when I put one against the other, it was obvious there was a slight variation.

"I wonder how that happened. We've never had a problem before . . . not until Saturday . . . The day of the reenactment."

When I pointed out to her that they were both Kwikset keys, she said, "That's not surprising. The college has a contract with a local locksmith, Lucy Lock-It. That's probably the type of lock she always uses. See, here's the key to our office—it's a Kwikset too."

"Let me try that one."

"You can, but there's no way it could be the storeroom key. See—it's silver—and the storeroom keys are brass."

I tried it anyway, but she was right. It didn't even go halfway into the lock.

"Told you so," Lizzie chortled.

We entered the storeroom, hardly more than a closet, with metal shelves along each wall. There were no other doors, nor was there a window. The floor, walls, and ceilings were of solid concrete. Whoever had replaced the blanks with real bullets had come through the door. Lizzie showed me where the guns had been left overnight. We looked on and under every shelf, but there was no sign of anything unusual, nor was anything out of place.

Lizzie grabbed a box of ballpoint pens from a shelf before she locked the door behind us.

"Now what are you going to do?" she asked as we walked down the hall.

"I should talk to the widow, Mrs. Macmillan. Can I get her address at the front desk?"

"You can, but she's probably here at the college to-day. You'll find her at the stables."

"She wouldn't be here the day after her husband's funeral, would she?"

"Sure she would. Horses are her life."

We climbed the stairs to the first floor, where Lizzie waved good-bye before continuing her upward trek. I was more than grateful I didn't have to go to the attic with her. If there ever was a next time, I'd make an excuse about a bad knee or something and take the elevator.

Outside, I asked a young man dressed in Desert Storm combat gear, right down to the combat boots, if he could tell me how to find the stables.

"Yes, ma'am, go down the hill across the creek, turn right and follow the signs."

When he answered, I realized he was a young woman. Hanging around the campus was making me feel older by the minute. Next thing you knew, I'd probably be saying things like "In my day . . ."

As I crossed the foot bridge spanning the Lickin Creek, I paused, as I had a few days earlier, to admire the view. But today the mountain ridges loomed darkly against the sky and there were no ducks on the water, only a Styrofoam cup bobbing along on the surface. A little voice in my head kept repeating over and over, *The world's never going to look beautiful to you again, because you've got—*

"Shut up," I said sharply, startling two young women who were passing me. The voice quieted and I continued on my way, smelling the stables several mo-ments before I actually saw them. It wasn't an unpleas-ant odor, but a mixture of warm earth and straw. A group of girls worked outside the longest building, painting, hosing down the sidewalk, and deadheading geraniums.

"Charlotte's inside," one of them said in response to my asking where Mrs. Macmillan was.

"Don't you find it odd that she's here so soon after her husband's death?" I asked the girl.

She looked surprised that I would ask such a question. "Of course not. We have a competition coming up in a few weeks. She's got to help us get ready for it."

I entered through the open door and recognized Mrs. Macmillan immediately. Even though I'd seen her only briefly at the funeral, the elastic mask covering her face was unforgettable. My imagination conjured up visions of Vincent Price in *House of Wax* and Lon Chaney in *The Phantom of the Opera*. What was she hiding under it? Since she was without the veil she'd worn to the funeral, I could see some shiny blond hair swinging loose around her shoulders. Today she wore faded blue jeans, white T-shirt, and a bedraggled beige cardigan. She looked no older than the college girls around her. Ivy Leaguer, I'd bet my life on it.

When she noticed me standing by the door, she excused herself and approached. "Is there something I can do for you?" she asked.

"I'm Tori Miracle. President Godlove has asked me to look into your husband's . . . uh . . . accident."

"Don't beat around the bush. My husband is dead. You can say the word." Her blue eyes looked calmly at me through the holes in her mask.

I decided right then I admired her for her forthrightness. "Okay, I'm sorry. I've been asked to look into your husband's death. Try to find out exactly how it occurred."

"I'm so glad to hear that. That new police chief seems to think labeling it an accident is going to put an end to my questions. I want to know how . . . and why . . . this happened. Someone was to blame, and I want to know who!"

"Do you have any ideas?" I pulled my notebook out of my purse and opened it.

"I certainly do. Those men from Gettysburg who loaded the guns. I think you ought to begin with them."

I didn't tell her I already had. "That's a good idea, Mrs. Macmillan."

"Please call me Charlotte."

"Charlotte, do you know why Professor Nakamura disliked your husband?"

"That's news to me. We had very little contact with him. As a matter of fact, I've been teaching here for a year and can only remember talking to him once, at the president's Christmas party. What gave you the idea he didn't care for Mack?"

"I was told he turned in his resignation when your husband was named chairman of the board of trustees."

She smiled wryly. "Ken Nakamura has got to be seventy-five or eighty. I'd say it was about time he retired."

"Were you at the reenactment when your husband was—"

"Killed? You can say that word, too. No, I was at Penn National. That's the racetrack near Hershey. A friend of mind had a horse running, and she asked me to go along with her. We were planning to be there from Friday afternoon until Sunday. But of course I came home Saturday as soon as I heard what had happened."

"What is the name of your friend?" I asked.

"Minta Sue—" She stopped and put her hands on her hips. "Good grief, young lady, are you asking me for my alibi? Are you suggesting I had something to do with my own husband's death? Well, I can assure you I was at Penn National, Friday and most of Saturday. There are plenty of people who can tell you they saw me at dinner and the parties afterward. And the stable hands will tell you that Minta Sue and I spent the night in the stable with her horse." A few tears stained the front of her mask. "Now look what you made me do," she snapped, dabbing at the elastic with a tissue. "It's going to be all spotted. Shall I give you some names?"

"Yes, please." At times like this, when I had to break into other people's private tragedies, I hated myself and the entire journalism profession. At times like this, I wish I'd done what my mother suggested and gone to library school.

She rattled off a bunch of names. "Sorry I don't have their phone numbers memorized, but . . . Do you ride?"

I nodded, a little surprised at the sudden change in topic.

"Then why don't you come over to my place Saturday and ride with us? Some of them will be there. You can talk to them then." She sniffed once or twice, but the tears seemed to have stopped.

"What about the stable hands you mentioned?"

She sighed and snapped out a few more names, which I wrote down in my notebook.

She looked down at the tiny gold watch on her wrist. "Excuse me, I have to get changed for my class."

One thing I could do today was interview the second reenactor, Darious DeShong. I had his address in my notebook and some typical Lickin Creek directions on how to find the Hostettler farm where he lived. "Head west, till you get to the fruit stand, the one what sells the good peaches not that other one, turn right at the second or third stone house, drive a couple of miles and after you pass the place where the dairy used to be, turn left . . ." Surprisingly, I'd actually become accustomed to following directions like these and figured I'd have little trouble finding the place. It would have been nice to have been able to call ahead to make sure he was there, but Woody had made it clear Darious didn't have a phone. I'd just have to chance it.

When I returned to my car in the nearly empty faculty lot, I found it had been ticketed by the campus security police for illegal parking. I jammed the ticket into my purse. President Godlove owed me something for roping me into this. At the very least, he could fix a parking ticket.

CHAPTER 7

I DROVE WEST, WITH THE AFTERNOON SUN SHINING brightly in my eyes. The peach stands were all closed, of course, for it was well past peach season. But I guessed that the second one was probably the home of the "best" peaches, because that's what the sign out front said. I turned right, I turned left, I backed out of someone's driveway, I tried again, and soon I found myself at a black mailbox with the name Hostettler printed on it in white letters. Set back from the road was a brick farmhouse, looking like many others I'd seen around Lickin Creek. It stood two stories high, had a small balcony with a white railing opening off a second-floor room, and a small front porch. I also noticed it had no power lines going out to the road, which meant it was most likely owned by an Amish family.

I knocked on the door. Waited. Knocked again. Heard a dog bark. Then the door opened and a slender middle-aged woman smiled out at me. She wore a long, full-skirted purple dress with a black apron over it. Against the black background, I could see the glint of the straight pins that held her clothes in place. I'd heard once the Amish don't use buttons. And they always wore the pins pointing inward so they wouldn't scratch the babies. She had blond hair, pulled straight back, and a rosy complexion that could only come from drinking milk and eating healthy foods. Although I didn't think she looked old enough to be married, a toddler peeked out at me from behind the skirt. She bent to stroke his head, and I saw the net bonnet covering her hair in back. She dried her hands on a blue crocheted dishrag and said, "We do not want any more magazines."

"I'm not selling anything. I'm looking for someone I was told lived here. A Darious DeShong."

"Oh yes, the Englishman."

I knew the Amish and other Plain People liked to refer to the rest of us as the English, so I didn't really expect to find someone from Great Britain on the farm.

She gestured to her left. "He rents the old barn from us. Down in the hollow. The road needs work. You will have to walk, but you can leave your automobile here."

"Thank you. Is it safe to go down there?" From a distance came the sound of more dogs barking, and I was hesitant about marching alone into the Pennsylvania Dutch equivalent of a wolf pack.

"The dogs will not bother you. They are all penned."

Feeling reassured, I thanked her again, and walked behind the house The barn was at the foot of a hill, and as I started down the footpath the barking grew more frantic. To my left I saw several rows of cages, and walked over to take a peek. What I saw there was nearly undescribable. The dogs, mostly little white puppies, were covered with their own filth and many had large open sores. The runs were so dirty, I knew they couldn't have been cleaned in more than a week. I made a mental note to report this to someone.

The barn was about a hundred yards away from the dog runs, and it was immense. The largest I'd seen in the area. Its faded, red-painted walls rose three stories above a stone foundation at least ten feet high. There were louvered windows on each level, once painted white, now gray and peeling. High up on the top level was a door. What use, I wondered, was a door that opened forty feet above the ground? It certainly was a case where the warning "watch that first step" had real meaning.

As I drew closer I saw one end of the barn had been painted with a giant advertisement for Mail Pouch chewing tobacco. I also noticed that there was a power line running into the building. Evidently Darious De-Shong did not share the Amish farm owner's distrust of electricity.

I walked around two sides of the barn, looking for a way in. There had to be a door in the stone wall somewhere. I couldn't believe Darious swung open the huge double doors on the end of the barn every time he wanted to go in and out.

In back, I finally came upon a wooden door. Before I knocked, I put my ear to it trying to determine if anyone was inside. I thought I heard music, but it was so faint, I couldn't tell what it was.

I knocked, I pounded, and finally I yelled, "Hello," as loudly as I could. Just as I was about to give up, the door opened a crack, and I could see and smell a lighted cigarette.

"Yeah?"

"I'm looking for Darious DeShong."

"Yeah?"

I tried another approach. "Are you Darious De-Shong?"

"Yeah."

I was making progress. "My name is Tori Miracle. I'm looking into Mack Macmillan's death. Woody

Woodruff gave me your address and said you'd be glad to help me out." That was a fib, but just a little one. After all, why would Woody have given me Darious's address if he didn't think the man would be willing to answer questions?

The door opened a little wider, just enough for the man to squeeze through. Before it closed behind him, I heard music again.

I was now able to get a good look at him, and I have to admit I liked what I saw. He was about six feet tall, and had a mop of curly blond hair much like Roger Daltrey in the movie *Tommy*. Eyes the color of dandelion leaves were fringed by long, dark eyelashes, and his skin was a rich golden brown, reminding me of Garnet, who always looked tan. He wore tight jeans, very tight I couldn't help noticing, a white dress shirt unbuttoned halfway to the waist, and white high-top sneakers.

While I was admiring—I mean studying—him, he appeared to be looking me over. His gaze moved slowly from my head to my feet, then back up to meet mine. His smile revealed the whitest, most perfect teeth I'd ever seen off a movie screen.

"Tori. Pretty name for a pretty girl."

Oh God, there was that inane giggle again. Would I ever learn to control it?

"Can you keep a secret?" he asked.

"Not if it has anything to do with Mack Macmillan's death," I replied in all honesty.

"It doesn't. If I let you in, will you promise me you won't tell anybody what you see here?"

"Cross my heart and hope to die."

He opened the door. "Come in," he said.

As I stepped across the threshold the music grew louder, and I realized what I'd been hearing was a calliope playing "In the Good Old Summertime." Odd choice of music for a man of about my age to be listening to, I thought.

The room we were in was very small, no more than ten feet square, with a lot of old gear hanging from hooks on the walls. I recognized rakes, shovels, and harnesses, but there were many things there that I'd never seen before. Lined up on the dirt floor against the walls were old crocks, farm machines, and wooden crates. A small wooden staircase of only four steps led up to another door.

"Give me a minute," Darious said. He ground out his cigarette, opened the door, and disappeared into the black void on the other side. The door closed behind him. After a short interlude it opened again, and his voice called out, "Come on in."

I climbed the steps and cautiously entered the dark, silent interior of the barn.

"Stop right there."

I was glad to stop. I don't like dark places. They could be full of snakes, or bats, or rats, or maybe even something worse.

The calliope began to play again. This time I recognized the music as "After the Ball Is Over," and it was quite loud, as if I were standing close to the source.

"Now!" Darious said. And suddenly, looming up before me, all was flashing lights and swirling colors. It was all out of focus, as my eyes made the sudden transition from darkness to light, and I grew giddy as I tried to figure out what I was seeing. Then a horse went spinning past me, his front legs raised as if he were about to jump, and I realized I was seeing a carousel.

One after another, the animals leaped, spun, jumped, and twirled. Horses, giraffes, bears, unicorns, sea monsters, all covered with glass jewels and gilt and flowers, paraded past me, then disappeared into the darkness only to reappear a few moments later. I felt as if I'd been transplanted to another world: a fairyland or perhaps the Twilight Zone.

"Do you like it?" Darious had come close to me as I stood transfixed by the vision before me, and now when he spoke I could feel his breath on my ear. It gave me goose bumps, a sensation I didn't find unpleasant at all.

"It's breathtaking," I said, reluctantly moving an inch or two away from him.

"Would you like to ride?"

"Please!"

He took my hand and helped me jump onto the moving platform. He then led me past several spectacular horses to a sea horse, painted with the luminous shades of blue and turquoise usually found in tropical seas. "The hippocampus. It suits you. I can imagine you as a sea nymph, rising naked from the coral sea."

There was that giggle again. I tried to pretend it hadn't come from me and settled myself in the gilt saddle, then looked around in amazement, at the wild-eyed pinto pony next to me with one foot perpetually raised, at the tiny lights twinkling overhead, at the center of the carousel where sparkling mirrored panels reflected the animals and lights to eternity. I turned to see where Darious had gone and saw him sitting behind me in a golden chariot, a modern-day version of Apollo the sun god. As my mythological creature moved up and down on its brass pole, I surrendered to the sensation and let the carousel whirl me back to the magical world of childhood. It was a happy place where I'd never heard of cancer, my brother still lived, and a relationship was simply something to be enjoyed, not worked at.

When the music had faded and the carousel slowed down, I reluctantly returned to the present. Darious was right there at my side, helping me to dismount.

"What did you think?"

"There aren't enough words to describe it. Where did it come from . . . how did it . . . did you . . . ? What I mean is, how can something this wonderful be in a broken-down old barn on an Amish farm in south-central Pennsylvania?"

"It's my one passion," he said, staring down at me in a way that made me hope he had room for more than one in his life. "I've been working on it for years. Restoring the animals one by one. It's a slow process, but I was lucky to find a carousel that hadn't disintegrated too badly. Want to see my workshop?"

I nodded and followed him to the back of the barn. I moved slowly, afraid of stumbling on something, because the only light in the vast space came from the carousel itself. There wasn't even any daylight coming through the windows. "Why don't you put in some lights?" I asked. "You've got electricity. Or at least open some windows."

"They're boarded up. I don't want anybody to see inside. Obviously you have no idea what a carousel like this is worth. Besides, I like it this way."

We stepped inside a large room, made bright by the fluorescent lights hanging from the ceiling. We were surrounded by carousel animals in various degrees of disrepair. Darious stroked the carved mane of a statuesque horse. "One more coat of varnish on this beauty, and he'll be ready to join his friends on the carousel."

"What do these letters stand for?" I asked, pointing to the monogram on the figure's saddle.

"PTC stood for the Philadelphia Toboggan Company. It was founded in 1903 and was one of the most important of the carousel manufacturing companies. This particular carousel is an early one, probably most of the carving was done in 1904."

"Aren't carousels hard to come by? Where did you find this one?"

"That, dear Tori, is my secret."

"There can't be many as complete as this."

"I'm afraid you're right. In the golden age of carousels, 1905 to 1925, there were thousands of them. Only about three percent have survived."

"What happened to the others?"

"Fire, mostly. Neglect. Natural disasters. But I'd say there are probably still a few more carousels rotting away in barns, waiting to be discovered."

He moved over to a bench where a creature lay on its side. Even my untrained eye could see it had been sloppily painted. "I'm going to start stripping this baby next. It looks like it's got a dozen layers of paint over the original."

"Do you use chemicals?"

Darious shuddered. "No. I use a heat gun to melt the enamel. It gives me more control, and I don't have to worry about damaging the wood."

For the next hour he proudly showed me animals in various stages of restoration. Some had been badly rotted in places, and he'd had to carve replacement pieces. With others, he'd blended oil paints to fill in worn areas. He showed me where he had applied real gold leaf to a horse's mane. The nearly finished figures didn't look new, they still showed signs of imperfections, but he assured me that he did that on purpose so they would retain their antique appearance.

It was all so fascinating, I would have stayed hours longer listening to him describe his work. But he put an end to it by saying, "I'm sorry, Tori, but I've got an appointment I have to keep."

"I need to get going anyway."

He walked me to the door. While I stood blinking in

the sunlight, he asked, "Will you come back for another ride?"

"Just try to keep me away!"

I drove back to town, humming, "In the good old summertime, in the good old summertime . . ." It wasn't until I turned into Moon Lake that I realized that while I had learned a lot about carousel restoration, I had not asked Darious DeShong any of the questions I'd gone there to ask!

CHAPTER 8

IT WAS SUCH A GLORIOUS FALL DAY THAT I DECIDED to walk the half a dozen blocks to the office. Three blocks later, I was sorry. Twice, I'd stumbled over rough places in the sidewalk where tree roots had heaved the pavement up. And it was hot, much hotter than an October day should be.

I passed a church with a bulletin board out front that said REPENT IT'S HOT IN HELL. Not much hotter than this, I bet. Under my gold corduroy blazer, my beige T-shirt was already sticking to my back.

At the corner of Maple and Elm, which was the beginning of the downtown commercial district, all three blocks, I came to the Lucy Lock-it Shoppe. Through the plate-glass window I saw the owner, Lucy, talking to a single customer. This would be a good opportunity for me to ask her some questions about the locks at the college and the key that didn't open what it was supposed to.

The shop was barely big enough for the three of us, but thankfully the paying customer soon left with his new key.

"Have a safe day," Lucy called to his departing

back. "Hi, Tori," she said with a cheerful smile. "Do you have some more keys need made?"

"As a matter of fact, I found the missing ones, so now I have two sets." The day after I'd started work at the *Chronicle,* I'd lost my entire key ring, including the keys to Garnet's house and P. J.'s car, and the office key that Cassie had given me with obvious reluctance. In response to my panicky call, Lucy had visited the Gochenauer residence and the office and made me a set of new keys. The next morning, I'd found the original ring under the bed, along with a small wedge of cheese, Garnet's favorite tie tack, two of Greta's scarves, and a lot of dust bunnies. Fred lay next to his hoard, looking smug. "Some hunter you are," I'd said, scooping the things out. "I wonder how brave you'd be if they could fight back."

From the back room came the whine of a machine. "I have a lot of work to do," Lucy said.

I took the hint and got right to the point. "It's about the Lickin Creek College for Women. I understand you have a contract to do all its locksmithing."

"Right. Not too unusual, considering I'm the only locksmith in town."

"Do you recall putting a lock on a basement storeroom for the PR department?"

"Storeroom—is that what they call it? More like a closet if you ask me. Yes, I did. About three months ago. Why do you ask?"

"I was wondering about the keys. I was over there yesterday and one of the two keys didn't work in the lock."

"Then you used the wrong key," Lucy said.

"But I couldn't have. They were the only keys on the ring labeled storeroom. I just wondered if you might have made a little mistake and given Janet Margolies the wrong key when you put the lock on."

She bristled, and I realized I'd offended her professionalism. "Look, Tori. I don't make mistakes. The lock came packaged with two keys. I put the lock in the door. Made sure both keys worked. Handed them to Janet. End of my involvement. Got it?"

"Okay. Thanks."

Without saying so much as "you're welcome," Lucy spun around and disappeared through the beaded curtain that concealed her workshop area from the public part of the shop. Who recently said that I often left my tact at home?

I was so anxious to escape the heat of the street, I didn't even pause to take my ritual swipe at the smudges on the brass plaque next to the *Chronicle*'s front door. When I hung my blazer on the hook behind the door, Cassie looked at my damp T-shirt and asked, "What did you do, swim over?" She, of course, looked terrific and cool in a cotton shirt of fall colors.

I collapsed into my chair and fanned myself with last Saturday's newspaper. It didn't help. "Wish we had air-conditioning."

"We don't need it in Pennsylvania," Cassie said.

"Save that propaganda for the tourists. I know better. What's on the agenda for today?"

Cassie opened the calendar that lay on her desk. "A ribbon cutting at the new pizza shop on Main Street at eleven-thirty—you might be interested in covering that event, they're offering all the free pizza you can eat. A pro-life rally at Saint FX School—students in grades five through eight will hold up signs on the steps of the school during their lunch break. And there's an ice-cream social and craft show at the Sigafoos Retirement Home this afternoon."

"I can do them all in one fell swoop," I said. "And if I can get the camera to work, I'll even take some pictures."

"Be sure and get one of Marvin Bumbaugh, the borough council president, cutting the ribbon at the pizza shop. He's been complaining we don't give him enough press."

"We had two 'grip and grins' last week, if I recall. One of Marvin and the new director of the Scene of the Accident Theatre and another of Marvin and the president of the downtown development council."

"I know. I know. But please keep him happy and quiet and take his picture again. We need all the good will we can get." She pointed to a stack of mail on her desk.

"More cancellations?"

"I'm afraid so. We may have to cancel the paper route on Lepper Road. We only have one subscriber left out there, and she's on vacation. One other thing, you got an invitation to a baby shower for Janet Margolies. I put it on your calendar."

"Thanks." I browsed through the wire releases, looking for items of local interest. "Do you think our readers will want to know that opening the Susquehanna floodgates dumped a ton of nonbiodegradable trash into the Chesapeake Bay?"

"Maybe. We can use it as a filler if we don't get enough local stories. But with Macmillan's death taking up the entire front page, we probably won't need it." She cleared her throat and looked sideways at me, and I was sure I knew what was coming.

"Tori, I heard you're scheduled to have surgery Friday morning. Is there anything I can do?"

The Grapevine had been working overtime. Rumors flew at lightning speed in Lickin Creek, but this was amazing. I only learned yesterday I was to have a biopsy done on Friday morning, and Ethelind was the only person I had told about it.

"Who told you?" I asked.

She shrugged. "I don't really remember. I think it was someone at the grocery store last night. Is it very serious?"

I shook my head. "Just a simple outpatient procedure. I'll probably be here by ten to help you proof the paper."

"The Creekers are playing Chocolatetown tonight. If you like, I'll cover it."

"I'd appreciate that." Cassie knew how I felt about high school sports. She also knew I never got the names right.

The phone rang, and Cassie answered, listened for a moment, then gestured for me to pick up the extension on my desk.

I immediately recognized the voice of Luscious Miller, Garnet's temporary replacement. I couldn't bring myself to even consider that he might become the permanent Lickin Creek police chief.

"What's up?" I asked.

"Big robbery, Tori."

In Lickin Creek? What's there to steal? I picked up my pencil. "Tell me about it."

"Someone broke into the volunteer fire department's headquarters last night."

"And?"

"And stole their trumpet collection."

I put my pencil down. "Could you explain to me why a fire department would have a trumpet collection? Do they have a jazz band or something?"

His exasperation was audible. "Not that kind of trumpet. These were antiques—fire chiefs' trumpets, like megaphones. In the old days the chiefs used them to give their men orders at fires. The chief says they are irreplaceable. And very valuable. He gave me some photos of the collection. Maybe if you'uns ran a couple in the paper, somebody in a pawn shop would recognize them."

"Good idea, Luscious. I'll drop by and pick them up this afternoon."

"Major crime wave, Cassie," I said after hanging up. "The fire department's trumpet collection was stolen."

"No need to be sarcastic, Tori. I've seen the collection. It's priceless."

"I stand corrected. Guess I'd better get going if I want some free pizza."

"See you later." She didn't look up.

Reluctantly, I put my blazer back on and went outside. Lickin Creek's Main Street sparkled today. The bright autumn sunshine cast a soft golden glow over the charming Early Victorian pastel brick buildings with white gingerbread trim. If you didn't look too closely, you wouldn't notice the flaking paint or realize that at least half the stores were empty and most of the others sold used books or secondhand furniture. At the Pizza Joint, Marvin Bumbaugh was impatiently waiting for me. I snapped two pictures of him outside the shop, holding an enormous pair of ceremonial scissors that didn't work, and one of him cutting the red, white, and green ribbon with his pocket knife. After that the entire crowd of six spectators and I entered the shop for free pizza.

Still savoring the flavor of pepperoni, I walked to the next block, where several dozen preteens were waving their pro-life signs in front of the parochial school. Once I'd taken a couple of pictures and written down all their names, they went inside, leaving me on the street with nowhere to go until time for the ice-cream social.

I didn't feel like returning to the office, since there really was nothing for me to do there. And I'd had so much pizza at the Pizza Joint's grand opening, I couldn't even go to lunch. Then I thought of the Lickin Creek Public Library, always dark and cool, and always a good place to kill some time, especially on a hot day like this. I was particularly fond of Maggie Roy, the overworked but always pleasant librarian. Since my best friend Alice-Ann MacKinstrie had gone to Seattle to stay with her mother after the tragedy at the Apple Butter Festival, Maggie had become my closest friend in town.

I climbed the granite steps of the library building. Carved in stone above the double doors were the words POST OFFICE. Maggie once told me the building had been purchased by the Friends of the Library in the early 1950s, when the post office moved to newer and more efficient, but less interesting quarters. While it might have been an adequate size back then, it was now bulging at the seams, and there was no relief in sight. As is so often the case, whenever the borough council or the county commission needed to save money, they cut the library budget.

Maggie was standing on a stool arranging objects in a glass wall case when I walked in. I greeted her and she smiled and jumped down.

I recognized some of the things in the display case as daguerreotypes, but the cases weren't the usual leather and metal ones I was used to seeing. "What kind of display are you making?" I asked.

"It's a collection of jewelry and daguerreotype cases made of gutta-percha," Maggie told me. "From the collection of Gerald Manley." When I looked blank, she continued. "He's the borough's unofficial historian. I'm going to put up a display of Civil War books to go with it."

"I hate to sound stupid, but I guess I am when it comes to Civil War collectibles. What is gutta-percha?"

"It's a compound that's a lot like rubber but with more resin in it, made from some sort of Malaysian tree, I think. The Victorians were very fond of it." She held up a gray hexagonal bracelet set with seed pearls so I could admire it, then slipped it on her wrist. "This is my favorite. It fits really well. I do wish Manley would sell it to me." She took it off and reluctantly placed it on the bottom shelf. "Manley tells me the daguerreotype cases are very popular with collectors, especially if they have pictures of uniformed soldiers in them like these. By the way, your book went out twice last month. Have you had lunch?" She looked disappointed when I said I had.

"In that case I guess I'll eat my nonfat yogurt. Want to watch?"

After she locked the case, I followed her through the door that said STAFF ONLY into the small, cluttered workshop she liked to call her office. She removed a cup of strawberry yogurt from the tiny refrigerator, and we moved aside some plastic book covers and sat down facing each other across the paper cutter.

"I don't understand it," she moaned, opening the cup. "I eat like a bird and can't lose a pound. Want some homemade cookies? They're really good—one of the staff brought them in."

"No thanks," I said, then noticed they were peanut butter cookies.

"How's your fiancé?" I asked. He'd been in a bad accident last month when his van went off the Deer Tick Ridge Road.

"He's fine. Back at work already. How's your arm?"

I rubbed it where the break had been. The soft cast was off now. "Neatly healed. Aches a little when it's damp out."

"My grandmother gave me a recipe for a poultice that really helps with arth-ur-itis."

"My doctor gave me a prescription for an anti-inflammatory. And I don't have arthritis." I changed the subject to something that had been on my mind since yesterday afternoon's visit to the Hostettler farm. "Do you have any books or magazines about carousels?"

"You mean like merry-go-rounds? Probably." She looked ruefully at her half-empty yogurt cup.

"I'll check the catalog while you finish lunch," I said, to her obvious relief.

"If you find something, bring it back here," she called as I left the room.

I thumbed through the card catalog, glad that the library was too underfunded to afford computer cataloging. There's something about reading the cards that I like.

In about ten minutes, I was back in Maggie's office with a small pile of books, which I spread out on the worktable. While she finished the last of the peanut butter cookies, I flipped through the pages of one.

"Look at these pictures," I raved. "I had no idea carousel animals were such works of art. There's all different kinds. Standers, prancers, jumpers . . ."

Maggie leaned over, but didn't touch the book for fear of getting grease on it. "And menagerie figures— look at that sea horse. Isn't it beautiful."

"Hippocampus," I corrected her, thinking of the one I'd ridden yesterday.

I turned some pages in a magazine devoted to carousel horses, while she looked on. "Amazing! Will you just look at some of the prices people are paying." Maggie pointed at a picture. "It says this carousel sold for one million dollars in 1989."

"How about this, Maggie? Here's a single horse made by Marcus Illions that someone paid forty thousand for." Thinking of all that money made us both sigh.

"Have you ever ridden one, Tori?"

I almost blurted out Darious's secret, but remembered just in time I'd promised not to tell anyone. "Only a small reproduction one at the mall."

"Why the sudden interest in merry-go-rounds?"

"No particular reason. I think I must have seen a picture from the wire service that made me wonder about them."

"There are two really gorgeous old ones at Knoebel's Groves Amusement Resort near ShamoKin. You ought to get Garnet to drive you down there someday. Oops! Sorry. I forgot he's gone."

I nodded. "He'll stay in D.C. for a few weeks while he brushes up on his Spanish at the Foreign Service Institute, so I'll probably get to see him on weekends for a while. I've got to get back to work, Maggie. Do you want me to reshelve these books?"

She shook her head. "That's a job best left to the professionals."

I couldn't tell whether or not she was pulling my leg.

Maggie walked with me to the front door, and there I noticed a piece of paper had been taped to the glass announcing that the start of the sign language classes taught by Charlotte Macmillan had been postponed for a week.

"Sign language is something I always thought I'd like to try," I said. "Is Mrs. Macmillan good at it?"

"My, yes. Charlotte taught signing before her marriage."

"I thought she was a horse trainer."

"That, too. She met her husband when he came to her to learn how to sign after he suddenly lost his hearing."

"She's a lot younger than Mack. I wonder what she saw in him?"

"Who knows what attracts one person to another. Maybe Charlotte had a thing for powerful men. He was still in Congress when they met.

"Give some thought to signing up for our classes, Tori. They're free."

We hugged good-bye, and I walked down the street to cover the Sigafoos Retirement Home's ice-cream social and craft sale to raise money for a senior citizens' center.

I bought a crocheted doily, snapped a few pictures, wrote the subjects' names down in my notebook, and headed to the One-Hour Photo Shop, where I dropped off my roll of film. According to a long-standing agreement, the owner would drop the prints off at the *Chronicle* office on his way home.

By now, I really wished I had my car, but I only had a couple of more stops to make, so I pushed on. When I appeared at Hoopengartner's Garage on foot, I was subjected to curious stares by the locals who hung out in front of the station.

"Fill ya up?" one wag asked.

"Very funny," I muttered and continued inside. With tongue firmly clenched between her teeth, the teenage receptionist *du jour* was concentrating on applying black fingernail polish and barely glanced up. "He's in," she muttered.

The Lickin Creek Police Department rented the back room of Henry Hoopengartner's garage. Since the garage offered round-the-clock towing service, there was always someone there to answer the phone, which saved the borough council the money it otherwise would have spent on a dispatcher.

Luscious Miller, red-faced and distracted-looking as usual, was sitting at the back desk where Garnet usually sat, but he leaped to his feet when he saw me enter. He had three thin strands of blond hair carefully combed over his forehead to hide his receding hair line, and the blue and white uniform of the Lickin Creek Police Department made his long, lanky body look like a scarecrow.

"Tori. Good to see you. Please sit down." He politely pulled out a chair that looked like something the Goodwill had rejected.

"Soda?"

"No thanks, Luscious. I've got a lot to do," I fibbed, "so I can't stay long. I'll just take the pictures of the stolen trumpet collection and be on my way."

Luscious opened a manila envelope and let some photos spill onto the desk's plastic laminate top. I picked out two that showed the most detail.

"Are these things really worth money?" I asked him.

"Chief Yoder says there's collectors of fire department memorabilia who'd pay lots of money for them."

"Some of them actually are attractive," I admitted. "This one's really quite ornate."

"Chief Yoder says the bigger the chief, the fancier his horn."

I stifled a giggle when I realized Luscious had spoken seriously.

I put the pictures inside my notebook and dropped it into my purse. "Okay, Luscious, I'll see that at least one of these gets into the paper. Maybe some pawnbroker will recognize them."

"More likely an antique dealer," Luscious said. "I guess you know there's been a lot of old stuff stolen in this area lately."

"I haven't paid much attention."

"Over to Gettysburg, the park people found big holes where robbers been digging up shallow graves on the battlefield. And last year some things went missing from the museum."

"Would they be valuable?"

"Good Lord, yes. The thief even took General Meade's sword."

"But that doesn't make sense. What antique dealer would buy something that recognizable?"

"No reputable antique dealer would. But there's private collectors who'll pay big bucks to own a piece of history."

"Thanks for the information. I'll check it out. Maybe there's a story in it somewhere. By the way, Luscious, I have the names of some people who work at the Penn National race track." I opened my purse and pulled out my notebook. "Mrs. Macmillan says they can verify that she was there all night Friday and most of the day on Saturday. You might want to check them out, just to be on the safe side."

"I already did, Tori. They all said the same thing: She spent the night at the stable with a friend whose horse was running on Saturday."

"Good for you, Luscious." I was surprised he'd thought of doing that.

Luscious opened the top drawer of the gray-metal army surplus desk, pulled out a folder, and handed it to me. "Here's the coroner's report on Mack Macmillan's death." As his face reddened even more, something I hadn't thought possible, he said, "Henry has declared it an accident."

I nearly flew out of my seat. "An accident? That's the most idiotic thing I've ever heard. Does Henry Hoopengartner think the bullets crawled into the guns by themselves?"

"Must have been a mistake on the part of that big guy who loaded them. He don't look none too bright to me."

I had to agree with him on that point, but when it came to guns and bullets, I was sure Woody Woodruff knew exactly what he was doing.

"I gotta go with Henry's report, Tori. As far as him and me is concerned, the investigation is over." He didn't look me in the eye. "It's not like I got people to put on this. With Garnet gone, there's just me and one part-timer."

"That's what you get for electing a gas station owner as coroner," I said unkindly. "Accident, my foot." I opened the folder and skimmed the report. The only thing I learned that I hadn't known before was that the medical examiner had determined Macmillan had prostate cancer.

On my way back to the office, I dragged myself into the drugstore on the square, which still had an old-fashioned orange-and-blue Rexall sign out front, and picked up the prescription Dr. Washabaugh had called in for me. My shirt was drenched, my feet were aching, and I hoped I'd never have to wear or even see my ghastly gold blazer again.

CHAPTER 9

As I wrote the article about Mack Macmillan's death, I thought how anticlimactic it was to write a news article like this for a weekly newspaper. By the time the paper came out on Saturday, the Lickin Creek Grapevine would have spread every detail. I was still surprised at how little interest there had been in his death. A gaggle of TV reporters and wire service people had showed up for a day and a half, then moved on. As far as most of the world was concerned, it was as if he'd never existed. I finished the story with a line saying the coroner had ruled it an "accidental death."

"Why do you suppose there hasn't been more fuss made about Macmillan?" I asked Cassie as I handed her the finished product. "I know he retired from Congress a while ago, but still . . ."

She shrugged. "It's probably because he wasn't really considered local. Mack lived in Gettysburg, and as far as Lickin Creekers are concerned, Gettysburg might just as well be on the other side of the world, not the other side of the mountain."

"I didn't know he lived in Gettysburg. Guess I

assumed he lived here, since he and his wife were so involved with the college."

"They have a horse farm on the edge of the battle-field, called Shoestring Hill Farm. A name in keeping with the good-old-boy image Macmillan liked to project." She added, "You look tired, Tori, Can you go home and take a nap? You should rest up for your surgery tomorrow."

"It's not surgery, Cassie. It's just a minor procedure. And no, I can't take a nap. I have to run over to the college and ask some more questions."

Jennifer was at her usual post in the hall of the administration building, but her face told me something was wrong. "I'm leaving," she said. "They expect me to do the work of three people for half pay."

"I'm sorry," I said.

"Don't be. I'm now a free woman!"

Jennifer's last official duty was to direct me to Professor Nakamura's office, which was on the second floor of the building. I chose to climb the circular staircase rather than use the elevator. That was an error, I soon decided. The staircase swayed, and although I only had to climb one flight, it was a long way up. Halfway, at the landing, I made the mistake of looking down through the center of the staircase, past the iron bars that braced it, and as I realized how far down it was to the marble floor of the lobby, my acrophobia was triggered. I grabbed hold of the railing, which shook, adding to my panic. I leaned my shoulder against the solid outside wall and practically flew the rest of the way up the stairs. On the firm safety of the second floor, I vowed to use only the elevator from now on.

Although a light fixture hung from the ceiling, it was

not turned on, and the hallway was very dark. Professor Nakamura's office was at the end of it. I rapped on the door, and a female voice told me to enter.

I was in a small interior reception room, which was crowded by a desk and two visitors' chairs. The woman sitting at the desk introduced herself as Professor Nakamura's secretary.

"I need to speak to him," I told her. "President Godlove has asked me to look into Mr. Macmillan's death."

A small smile crossed her face. "I imagine he's also told you to lay the blame anywhere but on the college."

"Not in so many words. Is the professor in?"

She shook her head. "He doesn't have classes on Thursdays, so he takes the whole day off."

"Can you give me his phone number? I can talk to him at home."

"Not today. He's out of town."

"Conference?"

"No, he's either hugging trees or saving deer. I'm not sure which cause it is today." She shook her head. "The old fool thinks he should be right out there with the kids. Keeps telling me 'you're only as old as you feel.' " Although her words were edged with sarcasm, the tone of her voice and the concern on her face showed me she was genuinely fond of him.

"I've heard Professor Nakamura turned in his resignation when Macmillan became chairman of the board. Do you have any idea why?"

"If I did, I wouldn't tell you."

I respected her loyalty. "I'll try again tomorrow," I said. "By the way, do you know a woman named Moonbeam Nakamura in Gettysburg?"

Her smile faded. "The kook? Of course I know her.

She's Ken's daughter-in-law. Or I guess I should say *ex*-daughter-in-law."

"Bad feelings there?"

"Heavens no. He thinks she's fabulous."

This time I took the elevator down to the hall, where the receptionist's desk was deserted.

If I couldn't question the professor himself, perhaps I could learn something from his ex-daughter-in-law, Moonbeam Nakamura, the holistic healer of Gettysburg. I needed to drive over there anyway and look into the story Luscious had told me about antiques being stolen from the battlefield. Since he'd suggested there might be a tie-in with the robbery at the fire department, I thought it important to follow through. I could take care of two tasks in one trip.

In Gettysburg, I headed south on Baltimore Street, passing the Memorial Church of the Prince of Peace—a dark gray stone edifice with a red door and a round bell tower—many small two-story houses, some with shops on the ground floor levels, and the historic Dobbin House Tavern. The skyline was dominated by a huge gray tower topped by an alien spacecraft, which seemed to grow taller as I got closer. When I came to a confusing intersection where tourist Gettysburg collided head-on with history, I had no idea which road to take, but I've always heard when in doubt, go right. So that's what I did, and drove past several art galleries, a lot of T-shirt and souvenir shops, the National Civil War Wax Museum, and the Lincoln Train Museum.

At last, I saw a sign directing me to the National Park Service Visitor Center. I turned in, just missed being rear-ended by a house on wheels, and parked behind the building next to a huge overflowing trash container. The tower I'd seen driving in, loomed over the battlefield, dwarfing both the visitor center and the

Cyclorama building. I could see an elevator going up inside it, and figured it had to be a tourist attraction, albeit a strange-looking one.

Because the tourist season was over, the visitor center wasn't crowded at all. I glanced into the gift shop and was tempted by the large display of books, but my nonexistent bank account wouldn't allow me to go in. Standing behind a long counter were several park rangers in khaki uniforms, but they all looked busy, so I decided to look at the exhibits. On the main floor were lots of guns, which I didn't find particularly interesting. Downstairs, I found some more interesting displays. In light of what Luscious had told me about General Meade's sword having been stolen from the building, I carefully examined the display cases. They didn't look particularly secure. Most had glass fronts, held in place by exposed screws. Even the doors to the cases appeared to have locks that could easily be picked. There seemed to be quite a few exit doors for a burglar to escape through, but I did notice they all were wired to sound an alarm if opened.

Back upstairs, I approached a ranger, who looked up from the map spread on the counter before her and smiled a greeting. I whipped out my notebook, told her I was a reporter from the Lickin Creek *Chronicle*, and said I was working on a story about the theft of General Meade's sword.

The professional smile was still there, but a shadow came down over the rest of her face. "I don't know what you're talking about," she said.

Suddenly, my arms were seized from behind. I screamed, and several tourists turned to stare at me, then ran from the building. Obviously, they'd taken me for a terrorist.

"Please be quiet, ma'am. We just want to ask you a few questions."

I was hustled into an office by two burly rangers. "Just what do you think you're doing?" I said indignantly

"You were acting suspicious, miss. Snooping around the exhibit cases. We'd like to know why."

"May I please get my ID cards out of my purse?" I was afraid they'd shoot me or something if I moved without permission.

"Go ahead."

I produced enough identification to prove to them that I really was Tori Miracle and that I really worked for a newspaper. Then I had to explain why I was examining their cases so closely.

"Off the record, miss, we're trying to downplay the thefts. Some people around here already think we don't take proper care of the collection. The articles disappeared way back last spring, and the fuss has died down. We'd like to keep it that way."

"You said *articles*. What else was stolen?"

The two men glanced at each other. "Some battle flags, belt buckles, insignia, all things that could be easily carried out by one or two people."

"All from the display cases?"

One of them shook his head. "Ninety-two percent of the collection is stored in the basement, below the exhibit area."

"Everything that was taken was quite valuable, I suppose?"

"To the right person."

"Did they disappear during working hours?"

"No. We found them gone when we opened up in the morning. Why are you so interested?"

"Some valuable antiques were stolen this week from

a Lickin Creek collection. I thought there might be a tie-in."

"What was stolen?"

"Some trumpets from the volunteer fire company headquarters. Why are you laughing?"

"I hardly think the kind of petty thief who'd steal some old tin trumpets is in the same class as the cat burglar who stole General Meade's sword."

"So you're saying Lickin Creek has a lower class of thieves than Gettysburg? That's an odd kind of snobbery."

The two men quickly ushered me out of the building, as though afraid I might contaminate a tourist or two.

"I know when I'm not wanted," I said, shaking my arms free from their grip.

While trying to get my car started, I seethed with anger. However, the day wasn't wasted. I still had time to visit Moonbeam Nakamura. While waiting for the traffic to subside at the square, I recalled my brief encounter with her in the restaurant. Moonbeam was the only person I'd talked to who had referred to Mack's death as murder. And she seemed to be in a relationship with the repulsive reenactor Woody Woodruff. *I can help you,* she had said. Had she been trying to tell me in code that she knew what had happened? I had a lot more to ask her than why her father-in-law had disliked the retired congressman.

This time, the street was empty when I parked in front of Dreamgate. How anybody could make a living tucked away on this remote back street was beyond me. The sign on the door said CRYSTALS, CANDLES, ESSENTIAL OILS, COLOR THERAPEUTICS, AND CHANNELING: CLASSES AVAILABLE IN AROMATHERAPY, FENG SHUI, DRUMMING, AND REIKI. AURA READINGS BY APPOINTMENT. If there was anything she'd missed, it had probably been accidental. Moonbeam seemed to provide something for everybody, or at least everybody whose tastes were New Age.

The door swung open before I touched it. "Come in. Come in." Moonbeam stood before me in a long white dress with a crinkly pleated skirt. So many strings of agate beads hung from her neck, I wondered how she could stand up straight. Around her shoulders was draped a purple rayon shawl embroidered with roses, decorated with sequins, and edged with fringe. She wore Birkenstocks as big as Volkswagens on her feet. I thought she looked like a refugee from a German fairy tale. Garnet's sister would have found her outfit attractive. I didn't.

"I knew you'd come today."

"Oh yes, I nearly forgot—you're psychic."

"I am. But that's not why. When I learned you are having surgery tomorrow for breast cancer, I thought . . ."

"Where did you hear that? It's not true. I can't believe the way rumors spread around here."

She stepped back as though affronted. "I don't remember where I heard it. Guess it's just one of those things that float in the air."

Great! Now my personal health issues were "floating in the air." The Lickin Creek Grapevine obviously had longer tendrils than I suspected for it to reach all the way to Gettysburg.

The air inside the shop smelled of patchouli incense, and the only light came from dozens of burning candles set about the room. My eyes smarted from the heavy smoke and odors.

". . . and I thought you'd be in for some help," she continued as if I hadn't interrupted her. "Come sit down and let me think about what you need." She led me to a cozy corner in the back of the room, where two chairs faced each other across a low table. I sat on the chair she pointed to and watched as she lit a purple candle and placed it on the table.

"Look, Moonbeam. I didn't come for a health consultation. I only want to ask you a few questions about your father-in-law and your . . ." I grasped for the right words and finally came up with "your friend, Woody."

"Close your eyes and relax, Tori."

"How long have you known Woody?"

"Take a deep breath and hold it." From somewhere came the sound of a choir of angels.

"Is he trustworthy?"

"Let's try that again, Tori. Take a deep breath, hold it . . . good . . . now, exhale slowly."

"Can you think of any reason he'd want Representative Macmillan dead?"

"Picture a place where you have been truly happy. Now imagine you are there."

"Could he have been mistaken about the ammunition he took to the college?"

"You are walking in that special place. Take a deep breath. Exhale and let the tension flow away from you. You are happy in your special place."

A tropical beach. Palm trees. Turquoise waters. Sand scrunching beneath my feet. Salt spray tingling my nose. Sun burning my skin, but in a good way. Gentle waves caressing my ankles, rolling away, coming back.

From far away, someone called my name. I smiled and looked around for the person. "Tori . . . Tori . . ."

I saw no one. Was she hidden by the dunes?

". . . when you wake up you will be totally refreshed. Whenever you are feeling down, your special place will always be there for you. Now open your eyes."

My eyes popped open. "You hypnotized me!"

She smiled. "Don't you feel better?"

"I do. But . . . that's not what I came for."

"I know what you came for. And I can also tell you what you want to know about Woody. And maybe even my father-in-law, although I can't imagine why you're interested in him. Why don't you come home with me and have dinner? We can talk there."

"I'm not sure . . ."

"There's no need to be nervous, Tori. I'm not as weird as I look; I dress this way because my customers expect it. I'm a member of the Chamber of Commerce, volunteer at the hospital once a month, drive an SUV, and have a teenage daughter who's at the age where she gives me weekly migraines. How much more normal can a person be? The only really odd thing about me is I'm a registered Democrat—a rarity in south-central Pennsylvania."

She called out to someone in the back. "Phoebe, I'm going now. Please be sure the door is locked when you leave. I don't want another call from the police telling me the door's open."

A young woman dressed all in black including her lipstick, and heavily hung with silver crosses, stuck her head through the bamboo curtain. "Like it was my fault . . ."

Moonbeam sighed. "It was your fault, Phoebe. You didn't lock the door." She picked up her purse, an antique mesh bag, and said to me, "Let's go."

Maybe I was still hypnotized, but I went with her.

"You can follow me," Moonbeam said. "My car's right in front of yours."

It only took five minutes to reach Moonbeam's Victorian house on the edge of town. It sat far back on a large lot. On either side were smaller, modern ranch houses.

"Used to be my parents' farmhouse," she told me as I joined her on the sidewalk. "Now I've only got a few acres left."

"It's lovely," I said, admiring the turret, the stained-glass windows, and the big front porch that circled around one side of the building. As we climbed the steps, I heard dogs barking inside.

"After my divorce, I took in a boarder," Moonbeam explained. "It's awfully expensive keeping up an old house like this. She's an animal cruelty prevention officer, so I never know what I'm going to find when I come home."

When she opened the door, an animal the size of a wolf leaped at me. In the resulting commotion, while more than one person tried to pull it away, I realized it hadn't ripped my throat out. In fact, the beast was doing its best to drown me with its huge pink tongue.

"I'm so sorry," a woman said, pulling him off me. She had him under control now, his black collar tightly gripped in her hand. "He's half coyote, but he's really lovable."

"Tori, this is my housemate, Gloria Zimmerman."

Gloria was a beautiful woman with short light brown hair, who stood only a little taller than me. And probably weighed a lot less. Even though she was wearing a tan unisex uniform, she struck me as looking far too glamorous to be an animal cruelty prevention officer.

After I had shaken her hand, the one that wasn't restraining the coyote, Moonbeam took me into the living room.

"This is my daughter, Tamsin," she said.

The girl sprawled on the sofa in front of the TV didn't look up. "What's for dinner?" she asked. The first thing I noticed was her hair, for it hung to her waist, straight and shiny like her mother's, but whereas Moonbeam's hair was silvery blond, Tamsin's could be described as black as a raven's wing. "Can we have pizza?"

Moonbeam looked at me. "What do you think?"

"I'm a pizza addict."

"Good. I'll call." She went out of the room, leaving me with the teenager, who had never turned her eyes away from the television set.

"What an unusual name," I said, thinking it my duty to make conversation.

"I hate it. My grandfather picked it." She pointed the remote at the TV and changed channels. "I hate watching news. Who cares about all that dumb stuff."

She wasn't paying any attention to me, so I sat down across from her and studied her. With her flawless ivory skin, dark almond-shaped eyes, and high cheekbones, she could have been beautiful. But the permanent sulk on her face ruined the effect. I could understand how she gave her mother migraines.

While she watched cartoons, I looked around the living room, noticing the many knickknacks and family photos that made it feel quite homey. An oaken cabinet with glass doors displayed small ceramic figures, and one in particular caught my eye—a tiny carousel horse mounted on a wooden base. It reminded me of Darious's carousel, and I was walking over to take a closer look at the figurine when Gloria came in with her arms full of adorable kittens. She handed two to me, and I sat down to pet them. One was orange and white, just like Fred, and he purred as I scratched his little chin. The mother cat, a large black-and-white tabby, jumped onto the arm of my chair to make sure I wasn't hurting her babies.

"Would you like to have one?" Gloria asked. "I rescued them this morning from a trailer. Their owner died a couple of days ago and nobody thought about the cats. They probably wouldn't have survived another day without food or water."

I reluctantly passed the kittens back to her. "I already have two cats."

"How about a homeless llama?"

I laughed. "I'm kind of homeless myself."

"An emu, then?"

"No thank you. My cats are quite enough."

The door bell chimed, and Moonbeam called from the back, "Can you get that, Tamsin?"

Tamsin made no move to get anything, and Gloria's arms were full of cats, so I went to the front door. A delivery man stood on the porch, and I was glad to see he held two large boxes. I'd be able to eat all I wanted instead of pretending one slice of medium pizza was all I ever had. Moonbeam paid him, refusing to take any contribution from me.

The four of us—Moonbeam, Tamsin, Gloria, and I— were soon sitting in the dining room at an enormous mahogany table, dividing the first pizza. Tamsin complained about the pepperoni, claiming to be a vegetarian, but I noticed she only picked off a few pieces before gobbling down several slices.

"Now," Moonbeam said, after we had eased our hunger, "what is it you wanted to know about my father-in-law?"

"I heard a rumor that he had some sort of grudge against Macmillan. More than a grudge really, because it was enough to make him resign rather than work with the man. Do you know anything about it?"

"Not much," Moonbeam said. "I remember when he wrote his letter resigning effective the end of this semester, I tried to talk him out of it. But he said he had no respect for the man and didn't want to work with him. When I asked him why, he seemed reluctant to talk. Finally, he said it had something to do with Macmillan's war record. He said it happened a long time ago, and it was something he didn't want to talk about. When Ken talks about the war, Tori, he means World War II."

"Was he in the service?"

"Oh yes. He's very proud of having served in the 442nd Regiment in Italy and France."

"I've heard of it—the Go for Broke regiment—all Japanese Americans."

"Right. But after the war, he became a Quaker. So now he's a pacifist. Since the Korean War, he's been actively involved in antiwar protests."

"And other good causes, too, I gather." I didn't mention his secretary had called him a tree-hugger.

"Gramps is a do-gooder," Tamsin said. "I think he's dumb."

"Has anyone seen my Tylenol?" Moonbeam asked. "Tamsin, why don't you get started on your homework?"

The girl grabbed a wedge of pizza and slammed out of the room.

"Teenagers." Moonbeam sighed plaintively. "I don't understand why I have so much trouble . . . Well, never mind. I haven't been much help to you so far, Tori. I know you're trying to find out why Macmillan was killed, but I am sure my sweet father-in-law had nothing to do with it."

"You seem very close to your father-in-law even though you're divorced," I remarked. "That's kind of unusual."

"Dad's a wonderful man," Moonbeam said, spearing a piece of pepperoni from the pizza. "I don't know how he raised such a dumb-ass son."

"Where is your ex living?" I asked.

"About six blocks from here. He teaches math and coaches football at Gettysburg High School. Had a midlife crisis which only a former, much younger, student could help him through."

"Oooh. Nasty stuff. Sorry to have brought it up."

"Don't feel bad. I'm better off without him. And he does make a point of seeing Tamsin regularly."

"I'm not sorry to see him gone," Gloria said. It was the first comment she'd made since we sat down to eat, and it caught me by surprise.

"Who? Moonbeam's husband?"

"No, Mack Macmillan."

"Did you know Mack?" I asked.

"Unfortunately, yes. After his retirement, he became a lobbyist for the Pennsylvania dog breeding industry."

"For years I've tried to get a law passed in Harrisburg outlawing puppy mills. I've testified at the state capitol a dozen times, but it never got anywhere because of him."

"What's wrong with selling dogs?" I asked. "Isn't dog breeding a legitimate business?"

She shuddered. "Sure, if it's done humanely. But many farms here in Pennsylvania, especially ones in rural areas, are puppy mills where hundreds of dogs are penned up under the worst conditions imaginable. The bitches are bred immediately after having a litter, so they never get a chance to get their strength back. The puppies are shipped off to pet stores before they should leave their mothers. They're often sick or have congenital defects and need to be destroyed. It's just awful. The poor things live their whole lives packed together like . . . like animals."

"They *are* animals," Moonbeam pointed out.

"No creature of God should live that kind of life."

"You're telling me Macmillan supported this?"

"He certainly did. No big surprise, considering he raised puppies at his own farm. Dogs can bring in big bucks, if you've got enough of them to exploit."

"I thought he owned a horse farm," I said.

"True. But that's his wife's pet project. I think the puppy sales support the horses."

This conversation reminded me of the sad little white dogs I'd seen at the Amish farm. "Do you have any authority over the area west of Lickin Creek?"

"I do. Why do you ask?"

"There's a farm out there. The Hostettler place. They've got some dogs penned up there under disgusting conditions. You probably should take a look."

Gloria helped herself to another slice of pizza. "I'll check it out," she said.

"As long as we're speaking ill of the dead," Moonbeam said, "I might as well tell you I didn't like him much either. He started coming into the shop last summer, and was always rude to us, especially to Phoebe."

"Can't say I blame him for that," Gloria said. "She asks for it. But you never said anything about him being a customer. How come?"

"Because, even though there are no formal rules about patient–healer privilege in holistic medicine, I didn't think I should mention it."

"Are you saying that Macmillan was a client of yours?" I had trouble picturing the dignified congressman in her shop.

"Since last summer. He came in for the first time about a month after his wife's accident. She was still in the hospital." Moonbeam paused for emphasis. "He bought powdered rhinoceros horn!"

"Moonbeam! You don't sell that stuff, do you? You know rhinos are an endangered species!" Gloria was so indignant, she spluttered a piece of pepperoni halfway across the table.

"Don't look at me that way, Gloria. It's synthetic. I get it from China."

"How can you be sure . . . ?"

I broke into their argument, hoping to get us back on the subject. "Isn't rhino horn supposed to be an aphrodisiac?"

Moonbeam looked as pleased as a teacher whose students had finally grasped long division. "Exactly, and his wife was still in the hospital."

"Maybe he was looking forward to her return," I suggested.

"Not on your life, Tori," Moonbeam said. "While she was in the medical center, he was running around with a topless dancer from the Brick Shed House. My guess is she wanted more from him than companionship. That's why he came to see me."

"What's the Brick Shed House?" I asked.

"An adult toy store. I'm surprised you haven't noticed it on the road between here and Lickin Creek. It's set back from the road behind a stockade fence."

Gloria snickered. "The guys think nobody can see them go in if they park behind the fence."

"Do you know the name of the dancer he was seeing?"

"Lillie White." Moonbeam giggled. "Isn't that a hoot of a name for a topless dancer?" She changed the subject. "At Dreamgate you asked me some questions about Woody. I guess I should tell you we're very close. *Very* close, if you understand what I mean."

I didn't want to tell her he'd made a pass at me, and I didn't have to because Gloria broke in. "He's an S.O.B., Moonbeam, and you know it. He'll go after anything that wears a skirt. If I've told you once, I've told you a thousand times, he's using you—for you know what."

Moonbeam turned to her boarder with fury in her eyes. "And I've told you a thousand times I don't want to hear any more negative comments about Woody. You don't know him the way I do."

"I hear he took Leslie Schmalberger to the dance at the high school last week. Rumor has it they did a very sexy tango."

Moonbeam's lower lip quivered, but she still stood up to her housemate. "Woody and I had a few problems to work out. We decided to date other people for a while. But we're going to get back together. I'm sure of it."

"So . . . who have you dated?"

"That's mean-spirited, Gloria. You know I haven't gone out with anybody."

The silent air over the table was charged with electricity.

How could someone like Moonbeam, who was obviously well educated and even attractive in an oddball sort of way, be so blind when it came to her choice in men? My best friend, Alice-Ann, was the same way. For once, I was proud of being sensible, even felt a little virtuous, for having picked someone as steady as Garnet.

From the living room, Tamsin called, "Mom! I forgot chorus practice is tonight. You've got to take me. Right now."

As Moonbeam grimaced, I shoved a kitten off my lap and reached for my bag. "I have to go too. Thanks for dinner, Moonbeam. And for all the information."

"I'm sorry I couldn't tell you more about my father-in-law. He teaches on Friday mornings, so you can catch him at the college."

On my way across the mountain, I noticed the Brick Shed House for the first time. It was a large concrete building, not brick, I noted with amusement. On top was a large sign, red letters on a yellow background, that said ADULT BOOKS, TOYS, AND VIDEOS. Smaller signs, nailed to the stockade fence, said OPEN 24 HOURS, LIVE NUDE DANCERS, and TRUCK PARKING IN BACK.

Since I was here, it seemed like a good idea to go in and ask Lillie White about her relationship with the former congressman, but when I pulled into the gravel parking lot I saw half a dozen cars parked with their backs to the fence to hide their license plates from view, and lost my nerve. I'd come another day when there were no customers to see me.

For a few hours, while I'd been with Moonbeam, I hadn't given any thought to tomorrow's surgical procedure. But now, in the car, driving back to Lickin Creek, worry and fear of the unknown overwhelmed me. With my head swimming and my eyes brimming with tears of self-pity, I barely noticed I'd passed the turnoff to the borough. I kept driving, past one farm after another, until I came to a boarded-up peach stand. There, I turned right and continued on until I saw the black mailbox with the name Hostettler in white letters.

I parked as close to the barn as I could, and walked slowly, as though in a trance, toward the Mail Pouch tobacco sign. When I came to the door in the foundation wall, I knocked, rather gently, almost as if I didn't want anyone to know I was there. Just as I was about to give up, the door opened and there stood Darious, wearing only a pair of jeans. His golden curls were tousled, as if he'd just awakened from a nap.

He blinked a couple of times, then smiled. "Tori! I was just dreaming about you. What are you doing here?"

"I need to ride your carousel again."

He stood back while I slipped inside. And suddenly I was in his arms, and his lips were pressed against mine.

CHAPTER 10

 "TORI, TIME TO GET UP." ETHELIND'S VOICE entered my dreams like fingernails raking a blackboard.

I yawned and tried to bury my face back in the pillow, but my outstretched hand found Fred's soft fur, and while I rubbed his belly I thought about what had happened last night. I'd done nothing to be ashamed of, really, so why did I feel like Scarlett O'Hara in the famous "morning after" scene?

After that first kiss, I'd convinced Darious that wanting to ride his carousel was not a sexual metaphor, and after that he'd been a perfect gentleman. He took me into his workshop, offered me a soda, and showed me he had my picture, cut from the *Chronicle,* in a frame on his workbench. After that, I rode the carousel until I felt all tension and fear leave my body. Then I sat with him in the chariot and poured my heart out. I explained my worry about the upcoming biopsy, shared some of the abandonment issues I'd been going through because of Garnet's leaving, and lastly, told him of my hostess, Ethelind, and my fear that she would never leave. He didn't say much, but somehow I felt a lot better when I was through. Unburdened, I came home and slept dreamlessly. That was all there was to it.

So why did I feel so guilty about one little kiss? Well, two actually, if you count the one he gave me as I was leaving.

"Tori! Are you up?"

"Sure am, Ethelind." I reached for the brown plastic prescription bottle beside my bed and peered at the label. "Take one or two tablets if needed for anxiety." Dr. Washabaugh had reluctantly called in a prescription for two pills. I was feeling very anxious, so I took both. As I showered and dressed, I decided to put last night's escapade behind me. It had been a momentary digression. Simply an incident triggered by my vulnerable emotional state. Nothing like that would ever happen again.

Despite my anxiety, I must have fallen asleep in Ethelind's car on the way to the hospital. When I opened my eyes, I was staring at a brick wall.

"We're here."

I swung my legs to the side and let myself drop down to the ground. Unfortunately, my knees buckled, and I tumbled to the pavement.

Ethelind screamed, and a security guard came out and hoisted me to my feet. "What's wrong with you?" he asked.

"Nothing. I'm still sleepy. This is the middle of the night for me."

After that, everything else seemed to happen in a fog. I vaguely remember being led into a room, where I removed my clothes from the waist up and put on a paper gown that opened in the front. I was told to lie down on a narrow bed, where a woman opened up my gown and painted my right breast brown. "Just relax," someone said. "Dr. Washabaugh will be right in."

I closed my eyes. When I opened them, Dr. Washabaugh was standing next to me. "Are you going to do it now?" I asked.

"It's all done, Tori. I think you might have taken more tranquilizers than you really needed this morning."

"I only took two."

She sighed. "I would have bet on it. Okay, Tori. Go home and sleep it off. I'll call you when I get the results."

"Do I need to rest?"

She laughed at me. "Only until the tranquilizer wears off. After that you can do anything you want."

"So when will you call me with the results?"

"In a few days. Try to keep busy. And don't worry."

A nurse helped me get back into my clothes, and wheeled me out to the car. After that I don't recall much of anything until I woke up, once again, in my own bed with a cat pressed tightly against either hip. They considered it their job to stay with me on the rare occasions when I was sick.

"That's enough," I told them, shoving them away. "You've raised my body heat to near boiling." I felt a little hungover, but was surprised I had no pain. I lifted my shirt and studied the offending area. There was nothing to see but a small Band-Aid.

I followed the trail of noise and nicotine downstairs to the library, which served Ethelind as a TV room, where she was absorbed in a talk show. She didn't notice me, so I continued on to the kitchen and dialed Dr. Washabaugh's number. I was hoping that maybe, just maybe, she already had the results of my biopsy. The phone rang a number of times, but there was no answer. Even if the office was closed, it seemed to me at the very least she ought to have an answering machine. I rechecked the number and tried again. Still no answer.

According to the kitchen wall clock, it was only a little past four. Someone should be there. Then I remembered I'd promised Cassie I would be in at ten to proof the paper. Somehow I'd managed to sleep all day. I tried calling the *Chronicle* to apologize but only got the answering machine referring me to my own number.

I returned to the library, where Ethelind jumped to her feet and gently led me to the sofa. There, she covered me with a wooly afghan, put a pillow behind my head, and poured me a cup of tea from her favorite Staffordshire pot.

"I could get used to this," I sighed. Fred, who had assumed his favorite position on my stomach, seemed to agree.

"I was worried about you, Tori." Concern showed in Ethelind's eyes.

"No need," I said. "Dr. Washabaugh said I could do anything I wanted to do."

"I was talking about the handful of pills you took this morning. All day long, I've been checking on you every fifteen minutes to make sure you were still breathing."

"It wasn't a handful, Ethelind. The instructions said to take one or two as needed. I needed two."

"I'll get dinner," Ethelind said. "I didn't think you'd be feeling very chipper, so I fixed something easy to digest. Boiled eggs, kippers, scones, and floating island pudding."

"Yummm. My favorites!" I said.

Ethelind left the room and reappeared with a tray, which she placed in front of me on the coffee table. She served us each a large helping, then settled down to noisily enjoy her kippers. I pushed the food around on my plate.

"You're not eating much," Ethelind noted.

"Must be the aftereffects of my surgery," I murmured, trying to sound weak.

Ethelind transferred my kippers to her plate. "No point in letting them go to waste. I have to order them in."

The grandfather clock in the hall chimed four-thirty. "Let's catch the early-bird news." Ethelind pointed the remote at the TV and switched channels.

". . . and in a surprise move today, Lickin Creek police have made an arrest in the slaying death of retired Representative Edward Macmillan. Charged is Woody Woodruff, a Gettysburg entrepreneur, well known for his . . ."

I struggled to sit upright. In the process Fred tumbled to the floor.

"Do you have a phone in here?"

"I only have two extensions. One in my bedroom, and the other in the kitchen."

I struggled off the sofa, ignoring her tirade about the phone company monopoly and its conspiracy to bankrupt the college professors of the world.

"Well?" she asked when I returned.

"It's true. Luscious arrested him this afternoon. He said he was under tremendous pressure from the old boys' network to make an arrest."

"You mean the informal group of wealthy businessmen who are direct descendants of the town's founders?"

I nodded. "They pretty much run Lickin Creek, don't they? You can see them almost any day having lunch in the back of the drugstore. The local equivalent of the smoke-filled room." I thought for a minute about exactly who it was I'd seen there. "President Godlove is one of them, isn't he."

From the look on Ethelind's face, I knew I'd hit the nail on the head.

I groaned. "I know he wants to resolve this, and especially make sure nobody blames the college, but I do wish he'd talked it over with me first."

"You don't think it was Woody's fault?" Ethelind looked incredulous. "He'd be my first choice. He was the one who loaded the guns."

"That's just the point. If Woody were going to murder someone, why would he do it in such an obvious way?"

"He's not exactly a rocket scientist, Tori."

The phone rang again, and Ethelind went to answer it.

She came back carrying the portable telephone, which she handed to me.

"Tori? Tori, is that you?" I recognized Moonbeam's voice, despite the panic that pitched it an octave higher than usual. A flood of screeches and sobs came through the phone as soon as I answered.

"Ohmygodohmygodohmygod! WhatamIgoingtodo? WhatamIgoingtodo?"

"Calm down, Moonbeam." I couldn't resist adding, "Take a deep breath. You need to visit *your* special place."

"Oh shut up," she snapped, but at least she was speaking in a normal register. "Did you have something to do with this?"

"Me? Of course not. How can you even think such a thing?"

"Because the police chief said you put the idea in his head. You said the bullets didn't crawl in the guns by themselves. Ohmygodohmygod. WhatamIgoingtodo?"

"I had nothing to do with this, Moonbeam. What is he charged with? Murder?"

"Manslaughter. Will they keep him in jail?"

"You can post bail."

"Bail?" she wailed. "I don't have any money. WhatamIgoingtodo?"

I did my best to calm her down, but could offer no other suggestions. After a few more sobs, Moonbeam hung up.

"Poor thing," I muttered. "She's one of those women who's born to be victimized by men."

Ethelind refreshed the teapot and poured another round. "Nothing like a cuppa to settle the nerves," she said, turning up the volume on the television.

". . . and in late-breaking news, a local physician has been found murdered in her office today." As I watched with growing horror a camera zeroed in on a familiar doorway. "The body was discovered at noon today by her assistant, Vesta Pennsinger, who said she came late because the doctor had surgery scheduled."

The camera swung to where a shocked and bewildered Vesta Pennsinger, Dr. Washabaugh's chatty receptionist, leaned against the wall. "I came late today because the doctor had surgery scheduled," she said.

"Why do they always tell you what you're going to hear . . . ?" The doorbell rang, and Ethelind rose to her feet. "Tori, are you all right? Oh my God, Dr. Washabaugh is your doctor, isn't she?" The bell rang again. "Who could that be? I'll be right back."

On TV, Vesta was still speaking. "I smelled smoke soon as I opened the door. That's when I saw the flames and called the fire department." Vesta started to cry and the camera zoomed in for a close-up.

"The body of Dr. Washabaugh, who apparently had been shot several times, was found by firemen after the fire was extinguished. The fire chief speculates that she had interrupted a burglary in process. The fire then was most likely set to cover up the crime."

A man in a fire chief's uniform appeared on screen and said, "The fire was most likely set to cover up the crime."

Ethelind came back in, carrying a small box. "Funny, there was nobody there. Just this pretty box with your name on it, Tori."

In a daze and still shocked from what I'd just heard, I took it from her, untied the ribbon, pulled off the wrapping paper, and lifted the lid. There was an unsigned card on top that said *Get well soon*. The item inside was covered with bubble wrap. I took it out, removed the wrap, and gasped. A beautiful, delicate china carousel horse sat on top of a walnut box. When I placed it on the coffee table, the tiny horse danced and twirled as the music box played "In the Good Old Summertime."

CHAPTER 11

"IT LOOKS VERY EXPENSIVE." WITH BOTH HANDS, Ethelind carefully held the music box. "Funny whoever sent it didn't sign the card. You sure you don't know who it's from?"

"I'll probably get a call today," I said, thinking I'd avoided blatantly lying about who might have sent it.

She looked at me with concern in her eyes. "Are you going to be all right?"

"About waiting for the biopsy results? I'm okay. Dr. Washabaugh told me that more than eight hundred thousand women have breast biopsies each year, and only about a hundred and eighty thousand of them are actually diagnosed with cancer. The rest are benign lumps, so the odds are definitely in my favor."

I sat down at the kitchen table and picked up the *Chronicle*, glad to see our paperboy had actually delivered it on time.

I glanced over the front page. My article about Mack Macmillan looked good. There were no glaring errors. Of course there was no mention of Woody's arrest. That's the problem with a weekly! The news is never current. Neither was there any mention of Halloween, which was coming up soon. When I questioned Cassie about that, she said that it was a long-standing policy not to mention the holiday in the paper. Too many locals thought it smacked of Satanism.

Surprise! There was a brief mention of Dr. Washabaugh's murder on the bottom of the front page. Cassie must have heard the news on TV and called the printer with a last-minute change. Good for her! When Cassie heard the news, she thought of the paper. When I heard the news, I'm ashamed to say my first thought had been, "Now how am I going to get my test results?" I decided to call the office receptionist on Monday and ask if they had come in. Surely she would be there. Or I would call her at home.

Ethelind, her feet enormous in fuzzy gray slippers, shuffled over to the counter where she poured Tasty Tabby Treats in the cat bowls before starting to make coffee. They ate as if they hadn't been fed in weeks.

"I've been thinking," Ethelind said, peering at me over the rim of her coffee mug, "that I might postpone my departure for little while longer. I don't like to think of you being sick and alone."

Oh no. "Please don't," I exclaimed, so abruptly that she stared at me in astonishment. "I mean, please don't do that on my account. I am just fine." I swung my right arm in a circle to show her how fine I was. It hurt, not because of the biopsy but because it was still healing from having been broken last month.

"I'd be glad to stay . . ."

"I won't hear of it."

"At least let me take care of you today, Tori. You pop upstairs and get back in bed. I'll bring you some breakfast."

"Thanks very much, but I have somewhere I have to go today."

Ethelind waited, head cocked, while I struggled to

think of someplace I could go. Then I remembered Charlotte Macmillan had invited me to go riding today. I hadn't thought about it since Luscious had confirmed her alibi, but now it seemed like a perfect excuse.

"Riding!" Ethelind looked incredulous. I didn't blame her. "You?"

"I love to ride," I said. "I even took lessons in college." I really didn't love to ride. In fact, I didn't even like to ride. But it was true I'd taken lessons. Everybody who goes to school in the southwestern United States does.

Murray Rosenbaum, my next-door neighbor and best friend in New York, had sent most of my belongings to me when I sublet my apartment. The boxes had been placed in one of Ethelind's thirty or forty spare bedrooms, and I dug through a few until I found my riding clothes. Saying a little prayer to the Goddess of Yo-Yo Dieting that they'd still fit, I carried them back to my room.

At the edge of Gettysburg, I stopped at a Sheetz convenience store for directions to Shoestring Hill Farm. The middle-aged woman behind the counter appeared impressed. "Biggest spread around. You can't miss it. Take a right, hang a left, go about six-tenths of a mile, backs up on the battlefield. You lookin' to buy the place?" She took in my riding clothes. "You'uns ain't going riding there, are ya?"

"Why, yes, I am," I said, wondering why her lips were twitching. I paid for a Diet Coke and left. Probably she was just jealous of my opportunity to hobnob with the rich and famous.

I found the farm, just as the Sheetz clerk had described. I stopped at the top of the hill and looked down a long, tree-lined private drive to a grove of trees, where I saw a beautiful two-story gray stone home built in the traditional Pennsylvania style, door in the center, two windows on either side, and a row of five windows on the second floor. I counted at least four chimneys. To the right of the main building was a glassed-in sun-room, overlooking the pond. Nearby, partly concealed by more trees, were a large horse barn, a riding ring, several smaller houses, and some long block buildings. The property, divided in many places by rail fences, extended forever, covering at least one hundred acres, I'd heard, but since it shared a border with the battle-field, there seemed to be no end to it. Even I, an out-sider, knew Mack Macmillan's campaign slogan had been "Mack—a man like you," meant to convince his constituents he was really just a good old boy. He may have called his home Shoestring Hill Farm, but it reeked of money. Lots of it.

I pulled into a gravel area, where at least ten trucks and horse trailers were already parked, and followed the sound of voices to the barn. As I walked in, conver-sation stopped and about twenty pairs of eyes turned to stare at me. Everyone there wore riding breeches, high leather boots, hunting coats, and black helmets. I sud-denly realized that while my high-heeled cowboy boots, fringed leather jacket, and jeans were the proper riding costume for New Mexico, they were all wrong for south-central Pennsylvania. Most definitely wrong! No wonder the woman at Sheetz had laughed at me. I was glad I'd at least left my cowboy hat in the car.

Eyes were politely averted and conversations re-sumed as I brazened my way through the crowd to find Charlotte Macmillan.

"She's outside, by the pool," a woman told me.

Charlotte was standing by a long table, on which

were several coffee urns and boxes of baked goods. She, too, wore the establishment riding garb. She looked just like everybody else there, except for the tan elastic mask hiding her face. Her lips smiled when she saw me, and she greeted me with as much warmth as if I'd been a member of the royal family come to play polo.

"I was positive you'd take me up on my offer to interview my friends," she said.

I shook my head. "There's no need for me to do that, Mrs. Macmillan. The police have already verified your—"

"Alibi. You can say it." Again, I admired her forthrightness. "And please call me Charlotte. It makes me feel ancient when you call me Mrs. Macmillan."

That was something I could understand.

"Won't you have some breakfast, Tori?" She pointed to the spread on the table. "The sticky buns are from the new bakery here in town and are just wonderful. I swear a day doesn't go by that I don't buy some."

Since I'd had to lie down to zip my jeans up that morning, I regretfully turned down the sticky buns but did accept a cup of coffee. It was surprisingly good, putting an end to my theory that nobody in south-central Pennsylvania could make decent coffee.

"Let's pick a horse for you to ride," she said, linking her arm in mine. "You look like an experienced rider."

"Don't judge me by my Roy Rogers cowboy suit, please. I've ridden, but I'm no expert." As we walked toward the horse barn, I heard dogs barking in the distance. "Pets?" I asked.

"No, I breed dogs."

Moonbeam's roommate, Gloria, had told me that Mack Macmillan lobbied for the puppy-mill people. Had he run one also? "I love dogs. May I see them?"

"I'm afraid not." She led me into the barn, where

there were rows of box stalls on either side. "The bitches get nervous when strangers come around the puppies, Tori." Three or four horses whinnied a greeting. "How about Maizie here? She's very good-natured."

I looked up, way up, at the most enormous creature I'd ever seen. Maizie bared her teeth at me. *The better to eat you with, my dear.* "I think I'll need a stepladder," I said.

Charlotte chuckled. "I'll have her saddled up. You two will get along just fine." She waved to a young man, who put down his pitchfork and came over. With her fingers moving at lightning speed, she signed to him, and he opened the gate to the stall and led Maizie out into the center of the barn.

Charlotte noticed me watching. "I hire hearing-impaired students from the Learning Center," she said. "It's a good opportunity for them and saves me a little money."

"Where did you learn to sign?"

"My dear mother taught me. It was my first language. You certainly are full of questions"

"It's my nature as a journalist, I guess."

"Did your asking questions have anything to do with the arrest of that terrible man yesterday?"

"Woody? No, that came as a surprise to me."

"You do believe he caused my husband's death, don't you?"

And she thought I asked questions! "Actually, Charlotte, I don't understand how an accident of this nature could have occurred. He's staged dozens of executions and should know how to do it right by now."

"Maybe it wasn't an accident. That man was known to hold a grudge against Mack."

"What about?"

She shrugged. "I've always tried to keep my nose out of my husband's business affairs, but there was a time about a year ago when he was trying to buy some farmland east of the battlefield to put up a one-stop shopping mall. The downtown merchants felt it would take business away from them and formed a committee to put a stop to it. Woody was their spokesman. He and my husband had a number of public battles."

"What happened? Is the mall going to be built?"

"No, while half the people in town were fighting my husband, another developer came in and quietly put up a mall south of the battlefield. Mack blamed Woody and his damn committee for making him miss the opportunity to get rich."

The horse was ready then. After an embarrassing moment when I couldn't get on Maizie's back and had to be boosted up by two young grooms, Charlotte and I joined the rest of the party, already mounted and eager to ride.

"Perhaps you'll want to take Maizie around the ring a few times to get used to her," Charlotte said. She appeared to be doubtful of my riding abilities. That made two of us. I'd only used a western-style saddle before. On this, there wasn't even a pommel to grasp. I probably should have been grateful she didn't have me riding sidesaddle.

"Giddyup," I ordered. Nothing happened. I clicked my tongue against my teeth and nudged old Maizie with my heels. She shot forward, nearly toppling me from my perch.

She galloped right past the entrance to the ring, and I began to fear we'd be in Hanover before she slowed down, but after a minute or two she began to walk more sedately. I managed to pick up the reins and get the horse turned around. The stone farmhouse looked like a dollhouse from where we were.

"Nice and slow, girl. Nice and slow." Maizie cooperated. I sat high in my saddle wishing Garnet could see me now. The horse seemed to know the way back to the barn without any assistance from me. Shortly, she brought me up to the back of one of the long block buildings I'd noticed earlier. There was a row of metal cages, and inside the cages were dozens of barking dogs. The breeding kennel! As Maizie carried me past, I saw these dogs were living in doggie paradise. Well-groomed dogs in clean cages. So different from what I'd seen at the Amish farm. There were Labs, some adorable beagles and golden retrievers, all the different kinds of outdoorsy dogs one would expect to find at an elegant farm like this.

Maizie took me back to the barn, where the other guests were already mounted and ready to go.

"Where did Maizie take you?" Charlotte asked.

"Just around that building," I said, pointing to the kennel and not mentioning Maize had taken me on a fifty-mile detour. "Your dogs look very well cared for."

"I told you not to go back there."

"I didn't have any choice." I patted Maizie between her ears.

"Let's go, we're holding up the others."

I followed her quietly. I think I'd expected the hunting scene from the Albert Finney version of *Tom Jones*, with dogs chasing foxes and horns blaring, but this was not that kind of day. The horses set off across the fields, some galloping, some trotting, and some, like mine, walking sedately. Charlotte stayed next to me, as if she feared I'd fall off, which was a distinct possibility.

"Now we're crossing into the national park," she pointed out as we came to a low wall built of heaped gray stones. "We're supposed to stay on the marked trails." She pointed to a small brown-and-white picture of a horseback rider. "Don't go off alone. People frequently get lost here."

She led the way, talking to me over her shoulder, pointing out things I never would have noticed if I'd been alone. "The stone walls were here before the battle, built with rocks the farmers cleared from their fields. Just imagine what it must have looked like here, with thousands of young men crouched behind these walls, firing at other young men just a few hundred yards away. We're in Pitzer's Wood, where General Longstreet had his troops on July second. There's an observation tower up ahead if you'd like to climb up and take a look at the area."

"I'll skip it. I don't like heights," I told her. "You are certainly knowledgeable about the battle."

"It's hard not to be when you live here. And my husband was such a historian that he made it all quite real for me."

"You must hate the idea of moving," I said.

"I'm not going anywhere. Why did you think I'm about to move?"

"It was something someone said. The checkout clerk at Sheetz asked if I were going to buy the place. I assumed it was for sale."

"Mack and I had talked about moving to Arizona for his health. Obviously there's no need for me to move now. Let's hurry. The others are already out of sight."

"Don't you want to be up front with your friends?" I asked as we rode up a steep hill.

"Not really. They all know their way around the battlefield. You don't."

We were now on a narrow trail, which wound

through dense woods. "You can see how easy it would be to get lost," she pointed out.

Despite the closely set trees, I saw a man walking slowly, holding something in front of him. He noticed us at about the same time, and ducked out of sight behind a tree.

"What do you suppose he's doing?" I asked.

"Poaching. That's a metal detector. He's looking for shallow graves to dig up and rob."

"Isn't that illegal?"

"Of course it is, but people do it all the time. There's a lot of money to be made in selling things from the battlefield. In the old days, you didn't even have to dig. The stuff was lying all over the ground." We were on a ridge, now, overlooking woods, fields, and rocky plains.

"That's Little Round Top," she said, pointing to a hill. That rocky area beneath it is Devil's Den. And just to the side of it is the Wheatfield. There were more than four thousand dead and dying down there on the second day of the battle."

I wanted to show I knew something about the Battle of Gettysburg, so I asked, "Where did Pickett's Charge take place?"

"Near the visitor center. That's where the High Water Mark is, the place where the South lost the war. After that, on July Fourth, Lee's army began to retreat."

We rode downhill, through another heavily wooded area. This time, when we came out of the trees, we were not alone. There were two groups of about a dozen people each, gathered around picnic tables, but they didn't look like ordinary picnickers. Many in the first group carried American flags, others signs that said SPARE THE DEER and NO MORE KILLING AT GETTYSBURG. The picketers in the second group carried signs that said HUNTERS DO IT WITH CLASS and HUNTERS HAVE RIGHTS TOO. A man with silver hair in the first group looked up at us in surprise. He was no more surprised than I when I recognized Ken Nakamura.

Charlotte dismounted. "Let's stretch our legs a minute. I take it you two have met."

Professor Nakamura walked over to us and bowed low to me. I did the best I could, bowing from the saddle on top of my horse. He inclined his head just slightly when he turned to Charlotte, a sign of disrespect that she didn't seem to recognize.

Before I dismounted, I took a look around to see if there was a wall or something nearby that I could stand on to get back on Maizie. I spotted a stone wall, about three feet high, and figured that would do.

"What are you doing here?" I asked Ken.

"Protesting the deer hunt. Every year, the park service sends out sharpshooters to thin the deer herd. We want to stop the heartless slaughter of these innocent animals. We try to post a presence every Saturday, at least until we're chased away."

"And that other group?"

"Hunters who think they, and not the park's official gunmen, should be allowed in to shoot the deer."

"Can we sit down, please?" Charlotte was fanning her face mask. "This thing is so damn hot. I feel like I've been sweating in a sauna."

She perched on a boulder near the edge of the woods and patted a spot next to her. "Come sit down, Ken. We haven't talked since Christmas."

He didn't move.

As if he forgot he was holding a flag, his fingers opened, and he dropped it. "I'll get it," I said, stepping forward and bending over. I heard a cracking sound and something rushed past my left ear with a whistle. "What the—?"

Another crack off in the distance, caused me to turn back around. Ken Nakamura was on his knees, clutching at his chest. As I stared in disbelief, blood oozed between his fingers. He toppled sideways, and I dropped to the ground beside him.

"Get help," I cried. The men and women from his group rushed over to us. "Someone's shot him." I ripped off my jacket and was using it to stanch the flow of blood from his wound.

Even the pro-hunting group had gathered around us by now. With them there, I felt safer, for they protected us from more flying bullets.

"I called 911," a woman said, showing me her cell phone. "So did I," said half a dozen other people.

Ken was still conscious but was losing blood rapidly, and I feared for the worst. I kept pressure on the wound and hoped for a miracle. After what seemed like hours, but was in reality only a few minutes, a park ranger car pulled up, followed by an ambulance.

The emergency medical team from the ambulance made us all move back, put an IV in Ken's arm, did their best to stabilize him, then carefully placed him on a stretcher that they then carried to the ambulance.

"Can I go with him?" I asked. "I'm a friend of the family." That wasn't exactly a fib; after all, I'd had dinner with his daughter-in-law only a few days ago.

"I guess," one of the EMTs said, and I climbed into the back of the ambulance before he could change his mind.

I leaned out of the door. "My horse!"

"I'll take care of Maizie," Charlotte called. "Please call and let me know how he's doing."

As the emergency vehicle bounced across the field, the EMT asked me, "What happened?"

"Somebody was shooting in our direction. I heard at least two bullets. I was right next to Professor Nakamura, talking to him, when he was hit."

"Lots of boulders in Devil's Den. The shooter could have been hiding out there. I'd better call the park service and have them search the area."

"He's had plenty of time to get away. We were all so busy tending to Ken that we wouldn't have seen him."

"I wonder why this happened," the technician said. "Was it some nut protesting the protest? Or a hunter taking advantage of the confusion to bag himself a deer? . . . Does Professor Nakamura have any enemies that you know of?"

"I don't really know him all that well," I admitted. The medic looked sharply at me. "I'm more of a friend of a relative."

At the hospital, I hung around outside the emergency room until Moonbeam arrived. "My ex is on the road with the high school football team, so I can't even let him know." We hugged, then she went inside to see how Ken was doing. I promised to wait for her.

Soon I was approached by two policemen who said they wanted to ask me some questions. One of them whipped open a notebook and asked my name.

When I said, "Tori Miracle," the two men exchanged glances I didn't understand. I proceeded to tell them everything I had seen and heard just prior to the shooting, which wasn't much. "I didn't even realize what was happening, until I saw Ken Nakamura bleeding from the chest." I couldn't even tell them what direction the shots had come from.

The man with the notebook wrote down everything I

said. When I was finished, he said, "Are you Tori Miracle from Lickin Creek?"

"Why, yes, I am. How did you know that?"

"I have a report on my desk from the park service. There was a Tori Miracle caught acting in a suspicious manner around the exhibit cases at the visitor center yesterday. Was that you?"

I acknowledged that it was indeed me. "But I wasn't doing anything wrong. I was only trying to see how difficult it would be to steal something." They exchanged those glances again, and I realized that had not been a smart thing to say.

"And you don't think that's odd behavior?"

"I wasn't charged with anything."

"I know that," the policeman said, snapping shut his notebook. "But you'd better be aware we'll be keeping a close eye on you from now on."

Moonbeam came out of the ER, looking terribly downhearted, and answered a few questions about why her father-in-law had been on the battlefield. "I understand you have a close relationship with Woody Woodruff," one said.

"I do." Moonbeam looked defensive. I couldn't blame her.

"He's in jail, isn't he? For another shooting?"

"No, he isn't. I bailed him out last night."

After a few more questions, the police seemed satisfied that they'd gotten all there was to get from us, and left.

As soon as we were alone, I asked, "How could you afford to post bail, Moonbeam? You said you had no money."

"I used my house as collateral. It's all I had. Don't look at me that way, Tori. He'll pay me back." She appeared so dejected, I didn't tell her what I thought of her boyfriend. "You don't think they're going to blame this on him, too, do you?"

"Just because he had the opportunity doesn't mean he had a motive. I don't think there's any reason to worry."

"Please don't leave me," Moonbeam said. "I don't want to wait alone."

Ken was transferred to the Cardiac Care Unit, and Moonbeam was allowed to visit him for five minutes every hour. Once, while she was in there, I took a chance on going down to the lab to see if I could get my biopsy results. "Sorry," the woman behind the desk said. "We send those reports to your doctor. You'll have to get them from him."

"My doctor is a she. And she's dead. Can't you please—"

"It will be sent to his, I mean her, office, and that office will forward them to the doctor who takes over the practice. You'll probably hear something in a week or two."

I grumbled and snarled all the way back to the CCU, but there was absolutely nothing I could do. Moonbeam thought I was upset about Ken, and took my hand and tried to console me by saying, "He's going to be fine, Tori. I know he is."

Finally, a doctor came out and told us Ken was stabilized. "Why don't you go home and get some rest," he said to Moonbeam. "We'll call you if anything changes."

She nodded, and we walked slowly to the door. "Can I ride with you to Lickin Creek?" she asked. "I need to feed Dad's pets, and I don't think I'm up to driving alone."

For either of us to get to Lickin Creek meant I had to go back to Shoestring Hill Farm to retrieve my car.

Moonbeam drove, and Charlotte met us in the parking lot.

"How is he?" she asked. "I've been so worried."

"Stable," Moonbeam told her. And she added optimistically, "He's going to be all right."

We transferred to my car for the trip back to Lickin Creek. Moonbeam sat quietly next to me, sniffing occasionally into a Kleenex. Once we were in the borough, she directed me to Ken's house, which was in the historic district near the college.

She had a key to the back door. We walked through a small vestibule into the large, sunny kitchen, which was swarming with small dogs and cats. "Gloria knows what a softy Dad is," Moonbeam said as she began to open cans of cat food. "If she rescues a small animal that nobody wants, she knows she can always count on him to take it in."

A small white dog with fluffy hair, black-rimmed eyes, and a curly tail put his paws on my knees and begged to be loved. I picked him up and was surprised to find he weighed a lot less than my Fred. "I saw some dogs like this at an Amish farm recently. Only not groomed. In fact they were a disgusting mess. I told Gloria about it. I hope she follows through. What is he?"

"He's a bichon frise. I think they're distant relatives of the poodle family. Very popular and expensive, right now. The farmer's probably making a lot of money supplying pet stores with bichon puppies."

I reluctantly put the sweet little ball of fur down and helped Moonbeam by scooping dog food into a row of bowls along one wall of the kitchen, while she tended to the ferrets in the next room. There were birds and guinea pigs upstairs, a black-and-white gibbon in the living room, and a snake in a terrarium in the dining room.

"Having to look at that every mealtime would be enough to make even me give up eating. Come to think of it, maybe I should get one, I might actually stick to my diet."

"I understand they eat snakes in China," Moonbeam said.

"They do. There's a place in Taipei called Snake Alley where you can pick out a live snake, and they'll skin it and cook it for you right there. I think of it every time I go to a restaurant that has live lobsters on display for customers to choose from. That makes me sick, too."

Finished with the feeding, we went back into the kitchen. The cats and dogs were chewing with relish. Each animal had its own dish, and I was glad to see there was no fighting.

On the kitchen table were several scrapbooks and a notebook. "I wonder what Dad's working on," Moonbeam said. "He didn't mention any research project to me." She opened the top scrapbook and looked at the first few pages. "This is wonderful. I've never seen these before. It's family stuff," she said. "Maybe he's going to write a family memoir. Just look here, these are Ken's grandparents. See how distinguished they look. I'm so glad somebody took the time to write names under the pictures, otherwise I wouldn't know who they were if . . ."

"He's going to be all right," I reassured her.

She smiled bravely and stared for a long time at the stiff portrait of a solemn-looking young woman in a formal kimono and a distinguished gentleman in a morning suit. She turned the page, revealing a family group, mother, father, and two children. "Ken's mother and father. The baby is Ken. The older boy's name is Masao. I wonder who he was?"

"A brother?"

"I don't think so. Dad's never mentioned a brother."

"Maybe a cousin, then. Or a friend. You can ask him when he's feeling better." Please let there be the opportunity, I prayed.

She picked up the notebook and opened it. "It's all in Japanese. Dad said you speak the language. Can you read it?"

"I never learned how," I admitted. Learning to read Japanese had been on my list of things to do longer than starting a diet.

She put the notebook down and picked up another scrapbook. The black pages were covered with the kind of black-and-white snapshots found in almost any family scrapbook, children playing on a lawn, a fishing boat at a dock with its small crew waving from the deck, school photos, backyard barbecues, unnamed adults smiling at the unseen photographer. Then she turned a page to reveal a yellowed piece of folded newspaper. She unfolded it carefully and laid it on the table. It was page 1 of a Long Beach, California, newspaper, dated December 7, 1941. The headline read JAPANESE ATTACK PEARL HARBOR.

I turned the next page of the scrapbook and found another clipping, this one dated December 9, 1941, which reported that President Roosevelt had declared the attack on Pearl Harbor a "day of infamy." The headline simply said WAR.

Glued to the following pages were more articles about the early days of the war in the Pacific, all from Los Angeles area newspapers. I read through them with some interest, remembering that my grandfather had served with the navy in the Pacific during WWII. I stopped when I came to a folded piece of paper, which had been inserted between two pages but was not glued in. I carefully unfolded it, noticing that it was already torn in several places and had holes in it as if it had been thumbtacked to something. It was a poster, I realized, carrying the notice ALL PERSONS OF JAPANESE ANCESTRY, BOTH ALIEN AND NONALIEN, WILL BE EVACUATED FROM THE ABOVE DESIGNATED AREA BY 12:00 NOON. Penciled on the bottom was a date: 04/07/42. I had a funny feeling I knew what was coming. There were no more family photos, no more fishing boats, no more happy faces. There was nothing more in the album.

"Did your father-in-law ever tell you he was interned during the war?" I asked.

"What do you mean by *interned*?" Moonbeam stared blankly at the poster, uncomprehending. "I don't understand. What does this mean?"

"It means all Japanese Americans on the West Coast were put into camps for the duration of World War II."

She gasped. "Dad's never said anything about it. I never heard of such a thing."

"It's a shameful part of American history that isn't taught in schools, Moonbeam. "It's not something the 'land of the free' acknowledges with pride."

"How come you know about it, then?"

"I didn't go to American schools."

"Tell me what happened," she begged.

"I don't know the details, Moonbeam. You should ask your father-in-law about it. I do know that more than a hundred thousand people were imprisoned, including small children, even babies."

"But not if they were American citizens, right?"

"It didn't matter if they were American citizens or not. If they had even one drop of Japanese blood, the government looked at them as security risks."

"I am shocked. I wish he'd talked to me about this. It's part of my daughter's heritage."

I patted her hand gently. "I'm sure he was going to, Moonbeam. That's probably why the books are on the table."

I stayed with Moonbeam until Gloria and Tamsin arrived. They were prepared to console her by holding a drumming session, so I quickly said good-bye and left.

CHAPTER 12

SATURDAY EVENING, AS I WAS WATCHING A FINE performance by Vincent Price in *The Masque of the Red Death* on television, Doctor Godlove called to thank me for my work in looking into Mack Macmillan's death. "I'm quite satisfied with the results of the investigation. Luscious Miller told me you persuaded him to press manslaughter charges against Woody Woodruff. I'm very glad that nobody connected with the college or from Lickin Creek was associated with the unfortunate incident."

I sputtered a couple of times before I got my voice under control. "But I never suggested Woody was responsible. I merely reminded Luscious that the guns didn't load themselves. He assumed I meant . . ."

Godlove interrupted me. "Of course, the college would like to express its appreciation for your efforts. We'll be sending a small check as a thank-you."

"I don't want your check. And I'm not satisfied that Woody was to blame. I'm going to keep asking questions."

There was a long pause. Then the college president said, "Please don't do any more investigating. That's an order."

I hung up and counted to ten twice to let myself cool off. He had no business giving me orders. And in my mind and in my heart I was sure Woody would not have made such a terrible mistake. Not at something he took such pride in. Somehow, someone had gotten hold of the keys to that storeroom. And I was determined to find out who that someone was.

Every TV cop show and every movie I'd seen recently had a scene set in a strip joint. I'd always thought the scenes were superfluous, added only for viewer titillation, and yet that's exactly where my investigation was taking me—a porno shop called the Brick Shed House, which advertised nude dancers.

The sign over the door said OPEN 24 HOURS. There were no cars in the parking lot behind the stockade fence, only a disreputable pickup truck parked by the side door marked STAFF ONLY. That was good. There would be nobody here to recognize me. Even better, there would be nobody there for me to recognize. I knew I'd have a difficult time facing a man at a church social if I'd once come face-to-face with him in a porno shop.

To disguise myself, I'd stopped by Garnet's house on the way out of town and borrowed some of his old clothes from Greta. In them, I looked the way I thought most Lickin Creek men looked—country macho. A pair of Garnet's khakis were rolled up at the bottom, a very large red-plaid shirt concealed my too ample bosom, and a John Deere tractor hat covered my unruly curls. I'd even padded my feet with two pairs of wool socks and I wore his oldest hunting boots. With a pair of sunglasses on, I thought I could fool almost anybody into thinking I was a man, especially if the place was dark.

The sign on the door said CUM IN. I overcame my disgust, pulled the sleeve of my shirt down over my hand so my bare skin wouldn't come in contact with the door, and gingerly pushed it open. The interior of the Brick Shed House was lit by only one small red light bulb, hanging from the ceiling, and an EXIT sign over the side door. I blinked, and the room I was in slowly began to reveal itself. A glass counter to my right, shelves of videos straight ahead, magazine racks on my left, and a few plastic chairs were all I saw. An unfamiliar, unpleasant odor made me feel terribly unclean.

Remembering the way a lot of young Lickin Creek men walked, I tried to swagger slightly as I crossed over to the shelves. There, I pretended to browse for a minute, pulled a magazine out, and sat on one of the plastic chairs. While I feigned an interest in the well-worn magazine, I looked around for any sign of the person I'd come to see, Lillie White, Mack Macmillan's former girlfriend.

While I was so occupied, I didn't notice a man approaching, and I nearly fell off my seat when he said, "Do you want a booth?"

With my head down, I shook my head.

"Hot tub? Massage?"

"Nope."

"Lap dance?"

I made my voice as low as it would go and said, "Lillie White here?" I knew she was because I'd called and asked only half an hour ago.

"Let's see your ID, son."

Oh Lord, I hadn't thought of that. To him I must

look like an underage teenager. "Don't have it with me," I growled.

The man grabbed my chin and jerked my head up. He stared at me for a minute, then began to laugh.

"What's so funny?" I muttered as I pulled away from him.

"So you're one of them . . ."

"One of what?" Too late, I realized he knew I was a female and misunderstood my reason for being there.

"You people always try to dress like men," he said.

I let my voice return to its normal register. Might as well go with it, I thought. "I'm here to talk to Lillie White."

"Sure you are, honey. Well, you ain't gonna like it. Lillie don't swing your way."

"I said I want to *talk* to her."

His scornful smile showed what he thought of that statement. "Twenty-five bucks and she's all ears—for fifteen minutes."

I dug in my pocket for my money. After counting the crumpled bills, I said, "All I've got is twelve dollars."

He took it from my hand. "Close 'nuff. She's through that door in the back." He walked over to the counter and pressed a button, which triggered a buzzing noise. "Go ahead. Can't keep my finger on this damn thing all day."

The walls of the back room were covered with dark vinyl panels that some optimistic person must have thought looked like wood. Like the front room, its only light came from a dim red bulb. There were four Formica-covered tables with about half a dozen chairs squeezed around each one. All the way in the back was a small wooden platform, which couldn't have been more than four feet square, and behind that hung a red curtain.

I sat down at the table closest to the platform and waited. Nothing happened, so I called out, "Yoo-hoo. Anybody here?"

The curtain was pushed to one side and through the open doorway behind it came a young woman. She wore a shiny purplish-blue polyester kimono, too much makeup, and shoes with ankle straps and the highest heels I'd ever seen. Her hair was long, permed to the breaking point, and the color of the hay bundles in the fields of local farms.

She walked over to a portable CD player on the edge of her small stage and pushed a button. A Bee Gees tune that had probably been popular around the time she was born blared out at top volume. I covered my ears and yelled, "No music. Turn it off, please."

Lillie White looked surprised, but cut off the music. Before I had quite realized what she was doing, she untied her robe and let it drop to the floor. She stood before me wearing nothing but a G-string and pasties, and began to gyrate to an unheard beat.

"Please," I said with averted eyes. "Put your robe back on. I only want to talk."

"Whatever." She picked up the robe and put it on.

"Sit down, please." I pointed to an empty chair at my table.

"You only got twelve minutes left," she announced.

"Then I'll talk fast. You are Lillie White, aren't you?"

She nodded.

"I want to ask you a few questions about your relationship with Mr. Macmillan."

"You a cop?" she asked, narrowing her eyes.

"No. Just a concerned citizen."

She giggled. "Never heard that one before."

"I've been asked by the college to make some inquiries about his death." I didn't think it necessary to mention that last night President Godlove had called and told me to stop my investigation since he was satisfied that Woody was to blame. I wasn't about to stop, because in my mind and in my heart I was sure Woody was not involved.

"You sure talk fancy, sort of like a teacher I had once. She wasn't from around here."

I sighed. This was getting me nowhere. I decided to be blunt. "Lillie, did you have an affair with Mack Macmillan? Answer yes or no."

"Sorta."

"What does *sorta* mean?"

"I mean we went out for a while, and he sorta fell in love with me. It don't count as an affair if you're going to get married, does it?"

"The man was already married, Lillie."

"Yeah, but he was going to divorce her."

It occurred to me that if Lillie truly believed that, she was even dumber than she looked. "How did you meet him?"

Her eyes opened wide as if *she* thought *I* was dumber than I looked. "Here, of course."

"You mean Mack Macmillan was a customer of . . ." I struggled for a descriptive word and came up with "this establishment?"

"Not a customer, silly. He owns it." Tears began to streak her pancake makeup. "I mean, he done owned it." She covered her face with her hands, and I noticed her nails were bitten to the quick. "Nobody was supposed to know, but I guess it don't make no difference now."

While I waited for her sobs to stop, I thought about Mack Macmillan. He was hardly the kind of person he'd appeared to be. Not exactly "a man like you," as his political campaign ads proclaimed, unless *you* happened to own a porno shop and cheat on your wife with a stripper.

I felt really sorry for her. Only about twenty years old, stripping in the seediest place this side of Atlantic City, and deluded by an older, wealthy man into thinking he was going to marry her.

"Lillie, you seem like a nice girl. Why are you working in a place like this?"

"The only other choice is fast food. I got a four-year-old daughter to support."

"You don't look old enough to have a four-year-old." Now I *really* felt sorry for her.

"Got pregnant in high school. My first time." She shrugged. "Shit happens."

"What is she going to think of you when she gets older?"

Lillie unsuccessfully tried to toss her stiff blond hair. Under the makeup, she was actually pretty. "Kayla ain't gonna know. I'll quit when she starts school. I'm working on my general equivalency diploma so's I can get a good job."

"Does her father help support her?"

"Said she ain't his kid."

"There's DNA testing, you know."

"Can't test a guy's DNA when you don't even know where he is." Lillie crossed her arms over her chest. "Time's up," she announced.

CHAPTER 13

I ARRIVED AT THE OFFICE SHORTLY AFTER NINE. To get there that early was a triumph, since I'd spent most of the previous night awake, missing Garnet and feeling sorry for myself. Only when the sky began to lighten had I fallen asleep.

"You look awful," Cassie said.

"You're not exactly brightening my day with remarks like that."

"Sorry, Tori, but your eyes are puffy, your cheeks are pillow-grooved, and your hair is standing straight up in back. Why don't you go home and go back to sleep. I can handle everything that's scheduled for today."

"I'm fine." I smoothed my hair down as best I could, knowing it would snap back as soon as I removed my hand, and took a look at the calendar lying open on my desk. "What's this, Cassie?" I asked. "There's something down for six-thirty tonight, and all it says is Foster's Elevator."

"I told you about that. It's the shower for Janet Margolies's new baby."

"It's being held in an elevator? Small, select group, I guess."

Cassie laughed. "Don't be silly, Tori. Foster's Elevator is a grain elevator and feed store in Mountain View. Everybody knows that."

"Even though I've had plenty of opportunities to discover that Lickin Creek is very different from Manhattan, I think holding a baby shower in a feed store is just a little peculiar. Don't you?"

She shook her head. "Not if the feed store happens to be owned by your father, and it's got a large meeting room upstairs."

"I give up." I picked up a story sent in by one of our freelancers and pretended to read it, but I was seriously thinking about going home for a nap.

Cassie answered the phone a couple of times and handled whatever crises loomed on the horizon. The fourth time, though, she covered the receiver and spoke to me. "I think you ought to take this one, Tori. It's Maggie at the library, and she sounds awfully upset."

"Maggie, what's the matter?" I asked. She was crying so hard I couldn't understand what she was trying to say. "Has something happened to Bill?"

"No," she wailed. "It's the"—sob . . . sniffle . . . sob—"the gutta-percha. It's gone. Stolen."

Cassie, still listening on her extension, looked at me quizzically. "Gutted perch?" she mouthed.

"Tell you later. No, not you, Maggie. I was talking to Cassie. Do you want me to come over?"

"Please." Sniff . . . sob . . . sniff.

As I hunted for the camera and some film, Cassie said, "Sounded like she was talking about a fish. What's the big deal about a gutted perch?"

"Gutta-percha, Cassie. It's a rubberlike material. Maggie has a display at the library of objects made of it. I think it was on loan from the town historian."

"And it was stolen? Poor Maggie! I wouldn't want to be on the receiving end of Gerald Manley's temper."

"Ah, here it is." The camera was on top of the file cabinet behind a potted snake plant, the only plant that hadn't died since I'd taken over the office.

I ran down Main Street toward the library. From a block away, I could see the Lickin Creek police cruiser parked in the tow-away zone out front.

Maggie fell into my arms the instant I entered the building. She was sobbing harder than before. "What am I going to do?" she moaned.

"Tell me what happened?"

She pointed at the empty display case. Shattered glass lay on the floor and on the table where the neat display of Civil War books still stood.

"Hi, Tori," Luscious said, coming to stand beside me. I smelled brandy, not necessarily on his breath, but surrounding him as if it were oozing through his pores. Evidently, last night, while I'd cried myself to sleep in bed, Luscious had quieted his loneliness in a different way.

The door burst open and Gerald Manley rushed in. His silver hair looked worse than mine, and he obviously had pajamas on under his coat. "You'd better have a good explanation for this, young lady," he barked at Maggie.

I could see her shaking, but she regained her composure for long enough to say, "I'm so sorry, Mr. Manley. In all the years I've had displays in the library, nothing like this has ever happened."

"How did the thief get in?" I asked Luscious.

"Through a window in the rear of the building," Maggie moaned. "Nobody would see him. There's nothing back there but the parking lot and the playground of the Third Street Elementary School. Both are empty at night."

Manley turned a furious face to Maggie. "Don't you check the windows and doors before you lock up at night?"

"I usually . . . I think I did . . . I don't remember . . ."

"Does the library have insurance to cover losses like this?" I asked her.

She nodded, but Manley jumped in before she could answer. "Those daguerreotype cases are priceless. One of a kind. Collected over a period of forty years. There's no way I can replace them."

Maggie collapsed into a maple chair, put her head down on the table, and cried so hard I feared she'd shake something loose. I patted her shoulder in an awkward attempt to comfort her.

"Do you have any photos of the display?" Luscious asked.

"Yes," Maggie gurgled. "Top desk drawer."

In Maggie's office, where three distressed-looking staff members were huddled, I found the pictures and brought them back. While Gerald Manley explained to Luscious exactly why his gutta-percha daguerreotypes were so valuable, I took a few pictures of the empty, shattered display case.

"May I take one of the pictures of the collection with me for the paper?" I asked Luscious. He handed me the stack, and I selected one that showed a close-up view of a southern soldier in his gray uniform.

"Daguerreotypes of uniformed soldiers are the rarest," Manley said. "Especially one that shows a Reb."

"I'll run these pictures around to some pawnshops," Luscious said.

"They'll never turn up in a pawnshop," Manley told

him. "Whoever took them already had a buyer lined up."

Luscious accompanied me out the front door. "I didn't want to say anything in there," he said, "but I had a call this morning about another robbery."

"My God," I exclaimed. "What's happening to this town? We might as well be in New York. What else was stolen?"

"Some things from the Lickin Creek Archeological Society's collection."

"I didn't even know Lickin Creek had an archeological society. Does it have a museum?"

"Not yet, but they're working on it. Right now, they got all their discoveries on the second floor of a barn out at Snider's farm. A team of amateur archeologists went there yesterday afternoon to put away some things they'd just dug out of a privy at the Coffman farm, and that's when they discovered some of the boxes were gone."

"What was missing?"

"They don't exactly know. Seems they got an inventory, but nobody kept a list of what was in what box."

"Let me guess. They also don't know when the boxes were taken. Am I right?"

Luscious nodded. "Sometime in the last two weeks is the best they can say."

Gerald Manley stuck his head out the door and yelled something unpleasant at Luscious. "Gotta go," Luscious said, and reentered the building.

I paused for a moment on the library steps and looked down at the quaint, peaceful square, where the little mermaid poured water into the fountain. The old cannon, aimed at the cars coming down Main Street, had recently been polished and looked better than new. And the Garden Society had decorated the small lawn area around the base of the fountain with pumpkins and alternating pots of rust-colored and gold chrysanthemums. Only a few vehicles passed by as I stood there. Once rush hour was over and all the Lickin Creekers had driven through the borough to get to their destinations, there was not much reason for people to come downtown anymore. Where once there had been thriving department stores, dime stores, drugstores, and dress shops, there were now only dark, empty windows. Lickin Creek was peaceful, that was true, but it was a peace gained from the flight of local businesses to the mall or their closures last year after a huge discount store had arisen overnight on the edge of town.

Under Lickin Creek's placid public face, something sinister was happening. First, Mack Macmillan's bizarre shooting death, followed by Dr. Washabaugh's murder. And now this series of strange thefts: the fire department's antique trumpet collection, Manley's gutta-percha collection, and the robbery of the barn where the Archeological Society kept its collection. Putting these calamities together with the robbery from the Gettysburg park service's collection, it looked like someone who was very knowledgeable about the value of certain types of Civil War relics was methodically targeting local antique collectors.

I went back to the *Chronicle*, where I began to write an article about the two recent burglaries. I was nearly finished when the phone rang.

"More cancellations?" I asked Cassie as she gestured for me to pick up my extension.

"Nope. It's that strange lady from Gettysburg."

"Moonbeam," I said into the receiver. "Is anything wrong?"

"Not at all. In fact the news is great. Dad's doing so

well, he may be out of the hospital by the end of this week."

"Super! I'm delighted."

"Tori, I told him you saved his life, and he's anxious to thank you. Can you come today? He's allowed to have visitors between two and four."

"I'll be there," I promised. To keep myself awake until then, I threw myself into the task of changing the farmers' advice column from Lickin Creek lingo to English.

"Is *you'uns* singular or plural?" I asked.

"Usually plural, but it is often incorrectly applied to a single person." That rasping voice certainly didn't come from Cassie. I looked up, startled, to find Helga Van Brackle standing in the doorway, holding a small cardboard box.

"Come in," I said. *Where the heck was Cassie?* My unspoken question was answered when the rest room door opened.

"Please sit down." I moved a pile of books from the guest chair.

Helga frowned and sat on the edge as if she feared something would rub off on her tailored black suit. She placed the box on my desk. "Home-made sticky buns," she said. "My thanks for your part in finding Mack's killer." She opened her purse and pulled out an envelope. "This check is from the college—a small thank-you."

"I already told Doctor Godlove I wouldn't accept a check. If you insist, I'll donate it to the Salvation Army in the name of the *Chronicle*."

She dropped it on top of the box of sticky buns. "I really don't care what you do with it, Tori. I'm only the messenger. I'm afraid we've had a few more difficulties, and I'm here on behalf of the college to ask for your participation in another event."

I sat back as if confronted by a cobra. "The last time I participated in an event at the college, it turned out to be a disaster, Helga, as you well know. I don't want to get involved with anything there, again, ever."

She waited without saying anything, and after a minute my curiosity got the better of me. "What kind of difficulties?"

"As I'm sure you know, this is the week we hold our annual fund-raising tour. It begins on Tuesday night and runs through Saturday."

"I didn't know."

"Silly me, I forgot you're not local." She gave a little deprecating laugh, which made me want to slug her.

Cassie piped in with an explanation. "People pay five dollars to have students dressed in costume take them through the oldest buildings on campus and tell them ghost stories. It's all done by candlelight and very spooky. It's an 'old' tradition that started about ten years ago. I think the college is trying to capitalize on the popular ghost tours of Gettysburg."

Helga took exception to that last statement. "Our campus has been haunted as long as the battlefield. We just haven't made a big deal out of it."

"I was mistaken for the ghost of a nun once," I said.

"I can't imagine why." Helga stared pointedly at my jaunty red, white, and blue outfit with the nautical theme that had looked really cute in a Provincetown secondhand store window two summers ago.

"So you're telling me that the college does a Halloween ghost tour to raise money, and . . ."

Helga gasped. "Not Halloween! Lickin Creek does not, I repeat, does not celebrate that Satanic ritual.

And, of course, we at the college respect that. We call it the Harvest Time Legend Tour."

Impatiently, I asked again, "What kind of difficulties?"

"Lizzie Borden quit last Friday."

"You mean you now have no PR department?"

"Not until Janet returns from maternity leave. And she says she's not coming back one day early! President Godlove suggested you might take over Lizzie's duties during the tour."

"Isn't it a little late to be organizing something that's taking place this week?"

"Everything is ready to go. But we need someone in the administration building to supervise the students, make sure the ticket taker is on the job, keep things moving smoothly."

"So get a faculty member to do it," I said, turning back to my desk.

"We're spread as thin as butter on hot toast right now. There are no faculty members available." She paused. "That does give me an idea. We like to have someone well known play a ghost every year. I suppose we could switch the head of the music department over to supervisor, and you could take her part. She wasn't keen on being in costume, anyway."

"Now you're talking. I was once the lead in *Blithe Spirit* in high school."

Helga stood up and brushed more imaginary dust from her skirt. "Then that's settled. I'll see you there Tuesday evening at six."

She'd outwitted me, I realized, and had gotten exactly what she'd come for. Flattery gets me every time, and I liked the idea of being "well known."

"I'll send a student over to your house with your costume. You'll probably have to shorten it." She strode to the door, then paused and said, By the way, have you turned up anything new about Mack's death?"

"No. President Godlove told me the investigation was over and I should stop looking into it."

"He doesn't *really* believe it was an accident, does he?"

"I don't know what he really believes. All I know is what he told me, and that was he was satisfied with the coroner's report and Woody Woodruff's arrest."

"He's an idiot."

Cassie started to laugh, then covered her mouth.

"He certainly is. I should have been named president. I'm far better at fund-raising than he will ever be. Besides, I'm a woman, and it's a women's college. The position should have been mine. Everybody knows that. I was next in line, and I was better qualified to run the college than the outsider they brought in."

"What happened?"

"The trustees didn't show good judgment. That's what happened. I'll see you on Tuesday."

A few minutes after she left, I turned to Cassie and asked, "What's the *real* story?"

"According to the Grapevine, Helga and Mack had a longtime relationship that ended abruptly when he went off to learn sign language and came back married to his teacher, Charlotte. In anger, Helga said some nasty things about his new wife, and they got back to him."

"Like what?"

"She called Charlotte a gold digger. Said the only reason a young, attractive woman would marry an 'old fart like him,' her words, was to get her hands on his money."

"If Helga thought Mack was an old fart, why did she want him?"

Cassie grinned. "Who knows? Besides, time has definitely proved her wrong. Charlotte has always been a devoted wife to Mack, even after he lost most of his money in that shopping center deal gone wrong last year. To me, that proves she married for love.

"Anyway, when Helga's name came up as the perfect candidate for college president, Mack persuaded the board of trustees to look elsewhere. He said a lot of things about her that later proved not to be true, but it was too late. Godlove was already on the job."

"Do you think Helga was angry enough to want him dead?" I mused.

"It happened a while back. I doubt she'd hold a grudge that long."

"From the way she talked, it sounded like more than a grudge, Cassie. I wonder what Helga knows about firearms."

"Really, Tori. You're beginning to sound obsessed. The college has moved on, Mack's family has moved on. Don't you think you should too?"

I pushed my way through a jungle of helium-filled balloons and potted plants to find Ken Nakamura, pale and drawn, propped up in his hospital bed. Moonbeam was spoon-feeding him a creamy yellow substance.

"You look wonderful," I lied as I cleared some magazines off the only vacant chair. Why do I always feel it's necessary to say that to someone in the hospital? Usually they look like they're on their last legs. Ken wasn't quite that bad, but he didn't exactly look "wonderful," either.

His right arm was in a sling, his chest was wrapped up like a mummy.

"I wish I could give you a hug," he said, "but that'll have to wait. Moonbeam told me you saved my life."

"I didn't do anything," I said truthfully.

"No need to be modest, young lady. If you hadn't thrown me to the ground, the next shot could have been fatal."

Although I had no recollection of doing that, I decided to relax and enjoy the glory. There would be time later to tell him what really happened, that I'd bent over to pick something up, didn't recognize the sounds I heard as shots until I saw him drop to the ground covered with blood, and that someone else had called 911.

A nurse bustled in, took his vital signs, told him he was "looking good," but should not allow his visitors to wear him out. "You're the heroine who saved him, aren't you?" she said to me.

I started to shake my head, but stopped when she continued, "The EMTs told us he'd have bled to death if you hadn't kept pressure on that chest wound. That was quick thinking on your part."

How about that? Maybe I *did* deserve some of that praise, after all.

After Moonbeam had finished feeding him his tapioca, she turned the crank to lower the head of the bed, then said to Ken, "Dad, at your house I saw your family scrapbooks and a notebook with Japanese writing in it. Tori said you might have been interned during the Second World War. Is that true?"

Ken sighed. "Yes, dear, it's true."

"Why didn't you ever tell me?"

He closed his eyes, and I saw how frail he was. "For a long time I tried to forget. Now, I realize I am old, and Tamsin needs to know. That's why I got the books down from the attic—I plan to translate Masao's journal after I retire."

"Who is Masao?" Moonbeam asked.

"My brother."

"I didn't know you had a—"

Ken interrupted her. "Masao died in 1943. Time has blurred the details, but his journal brought back my memories of the most shameful chapter in our country's history."

He leaned back, eyes closed, and for a moment I thought he'd fallen asleep. Moonbeam looked questioningly at me. I put my finger to my lips. "Wait," I mouthed.

With his eyes still closed, Ken began to speak. "My father came to America more than one hundred years ago after the Meiji government took his family's land. I'll tell you his story someday. After a series of adventures, he ended up in Long Beach, California, where there was an established *nikkei* community."

Moonbeam looked at me for translation. "People of Japanese ancestry," I explained.

"We had a good life there. My father owned several fishing boats. We were very comfortable. My mother never had to work in the canneries. There was even enough money to send Masao to Japan for his education. A child of ten when he left us, he returned a man of twenty, shortly before the Japanese bombed Pearl Harbor. He was an American, but thought as a Japanese; he told me he felt like a stranger in his own land."

"I can understand that feeling," I said.

"Yes, I think you can. May I have a sip of water, please?"

Moonbeam held the straw to his lips for a moment. He continued, "President Roosevelt signed an order in 1942, which gave the government the right to confine potentially dangerous people from military areas. That 'military area' ended up being the entire West Coast. Anyone of Japanese descent was considered to be a security risk and was ordered to report to a camp."

Moonbeam's voice was pitched high with indignation. "But you were American citizens."

"Masao and I were citizens because we were *nisei*, born in America, but our parents were *issei*, Japanese-born, and excluded by law from becoming citizens. Besides, citizenship made no difference. The order included anybody with even a drop of Japanese blood. More than a hundred and ten thousand of us on the West Coast were considered to be security risks, even the small babies. Some of them were actually *sansei*, the second generation of Americans, but we all were sent to relocation centers."

"How many camps were there?" I asked.

"Ten, I think, not including some prisons. My family was sent to Topaz in Utah, a place that we called the 'jewel of the desert.' "

"Why didn't the Japanese Americans rise up in protest? Contact the media? Do something to stop it?" Moonbeam asked indignantly.

Ken smiled. "We were loyal to our government, no matter how badly it treated us. It's a trait called *on* in Japanese. And there is also the Japanese belief that difficult situations must be endured, represented by the phrase *shikata ga nai*."

"It must have been awful for you, Dad." Moonbeam stroked his good hand. "How long were you there?"

"Myself—less than a month. The American Friends Service Committee arranged for some of us to go to eastern colleges, and I was one of the lucky ones. My brother couldn't go, because he was a *kibei*, a Japan-educated *nisei,* and considered to be a greater security risk. I joined the army in 1943.

"I have felt great guilt over the years for leaving my family when I did—wondered if I'd stayed with them would things would have ended differently? You see, they were moved to Tule Lake in California when Masao became a 'no-no man.'"

"What was a no-no man?" I asked.

"There was a questionnaire that all internees had to fill out, and everyone was expected to answer yes to two ambiguous questions at the end of it. The questions were ridiculous. They called upon the *issei* to swear allegiance to America, which had refused to give them citizenship. The *kibei,* like my brother, thought they were trick questions; if they answered yes, they would be acknowledging a prior allegiance to the Japanese emperor. If they said no, it would be considered an admission of disloyalty to America. My brother, like many of his Japanese-educated friends, and my father answered 'no-no' to the two questions to show their outrage at what America had done."

"How dreadful," Moonbeam groaned. "I had no idea . . ."

"Over eighteen thousand people were jammed into the Tule Lake camp. Soldiers with machines guns stood guard in turrets, and tanks patrolled the perimeter to prevent people from escaping.

"The camp was overcrowded, the sanitation deplorable, the food insufficient, and the living conditions impossible. My mother tried hard to keep family customs alive. She even taught Japanese dancing to the little girls there. But my father lost the will to live. Masao's journal said he sat and smoked all day and wouldn't talk to anyone.

"Finally, *kibei* youths rioted, and the army moved in

to squelch them and took over the entire camp. The young rebels were locked up in the 'stockade.' They were cut off from their families by a twelve-foot-high wall and denied medical care. Masao died there, of pneumonia, after being beaten by the guard in charge of his barracks. Not long after, my father died of a broken heart."

"And your mother?" Moonbeam asked.

"She stayed at Tule Lake until 1946, because she had nowhere else to go."

It was Ken who was now stroking Moonbeam's hand, trying to still her tears. "Don't cry, my dear. They are at peace. And you, my dear daughter, will share everything I tell you about them with your daughter, who will tell her children, and our ancestors will never be forgotten."

I grabbed a couple of tissues and walked over to the window looking out over the parking lot and blew my nose. After I'd regained my composure, I said, without turning around, "I'm very touched you shared this with me."

Ken answered in a tone of voice that chilled me to the bone. "I really don't want to see you. Please leave."

I spun around, thinking he was talking to me and wondering why he'd had such a sudden change of attitude. I quickly realized he wasn't speaking to me, but to Charlotte Macmillan, half hidden by balloons near the doorway, her mouth open in a little "oh" of surprise.

"I wanted to see how you're feeling," she said, without coming into the room.

"Please leave," Ken repeated in a firm voice. She stepped backward and was gone.

"What was that about?" Moonbeam asked.

"I think I know," I said.

"Do you?" Ken asked, staring intently at my face.

"The guard responsible for your brother's death was Mack Macmillan, wasn't it?"

"What makes you think that?"

"It just now came together. First, your refusal to work with Macmillan when he was made chairman of the college's board of trustees. And his wife's telling me a few days ago he'd been in the army during World War II, stationed out west somewhere. And third, the way you reacted to her presence."

"I don't think Macmillan was directly responsible. But he was mentioned in Masao's diary as being one of the cruelest and most sadistic guards in the camp. I learned that only a few months ago while skimming over the journal."

"And that's when you submitted your resignation to the college?"

Ken yawned. "I could not work with a man for whom I had no respect."

I was able to ask no more questions. The old man, exhausted from telling his story, was fast asleep.

CHAPTER 14

I PURCHASED AN ADORABLE LITTLE TERRY CLOTH jump suit for Janet Margolies's baby and some wrapping supplies in the hospital gift shop just as the volunteer was closing up, then wrapped the present while sitting in the front seat of my car. That's when I noticed the pink and blue paper I'd selected had small gold writing all over it that said *Get well soon.* Too late to do anything about it now, I thought, and secured the paper with Scotch tape. If I didn't get to the elevator in Mountain View soon, I'd miss the event. I'd forgotten a card, so I tore a sheet of paper from my notebook and wrote, *To Baby Margolies, with love from Tori,* because I couldn't remember whether Janet's baby was a girl or a boy. I attached the note to the package top with a sticky-backed silver bow. A clumsy five-year-old could have done a better job, but I hoped Janet would be so thrilled with the gift that she'd overlook the messy covering.

To find Mountain View, I followed the map Cassie had drawn for me, which had me driving on mountain roads so twisty and narrow, I felt sure I would plunge to my death at any moment. Every now and then I'd come to a wide spot in the road where there would be a small outpost of civilization, usually a couple of trailers, a barn or two, a general store with an antique gas pump, and a hand-painted sign offering deer processing. And there was always a church, with a bulletin board out front. Although twilight was rapidly changing to nightfall, I could still see they carried homey messages like THE HARVEST IS RIPE, ARE YOU READY FOR THE PICKIN'? and ARE YOU READY FOR HEAVEN OR FOR HELL? My favorite was IF YOU GIVE THE DEVIL A RIDE, HE'LL SOON BE DRIVING. The many dire warnings about eternal damnation led me to believe that truly cheerless people must live in these desolate hamlets.

Shortly after I passed a log cabin decorated with a banner that read GET US OUT OF THE U.N. NOW, I came to a sign that announced I was in the Village of Mountain View. The village was a metropolis compared to the places I'd just passed through. Large, well-maintained homes with wide porches faced each other across the road. The post office was in a lean-to attached to one of the houses, and I noticed a FOR SALE sign out front. Was the position of postmaster for sale along with the building?

A large steel building at the crossroads in the center of the village housed the recreation center and municipal offices. Directly across from it was Foster's Elevator, Inc., a complex of buildings that was nearly a town in itself. Most of them were white and of the Victorian era. Behind these were huge towers, silos, I guessed, and ladders that seemed to reach to the sky. Some buildings were obviously barns and garages. The paved parking lot was large enough for a hundred cars and trucks. Tonight, it was nearly full.

I parked on the edge of the lot in front of a sign that informed me that Nutro pet foods and lottery tickets were available here. Foster's Elevator, Inc., certainly looked like a prosperous, going concern, so I wondered why the bulletin board facing the road announced a going-out-of-business sale. I approached the front door of what appeared to be the main office building. Two porch lights on either side illuminated the front steps, which led to a wide veranda. The front door was slightly ajar, and a tattered poster advertising Vacation Bible School, apparently left over from last summer, flapped loosely in the evening breeze as I pushed open the door and entered the office. Inside, the office was deserted, except for some old oaken furniture, but I heard a lot of noise coming from the stairwell in the back of the room, indicating the party was being held upstairs.

The dark wood banister felt as smooth as satin beneath my fingers as I climbed the wide steps to the second floor of the building. I could almost imagine myself coming down that staircase in an elegant ball gown while Rhett Butler waited eagerly at the bottom for me. That's when I realized the building must have once been someone's lovely home.

The entire second floor was one large room, and it was filled with more women than I'd ever seen in one place. I paused for a minute at the top of the stairs and looked around trying to see if I could recognize anyone.

"Tori," someone cried. "Come in, come in." Janet Margolies was at my side, propelling me into the mob. "Hey, everybody. Look who's here. Tori Miracle, the writer."

"Please, don't make me out to be something special," I said demurely.

"But you are special, Tori." We'd reached the refreshment table, where Janet introduced me to a middle-aged woman who was ladling punch into little plastic cups. "Mom, this is Tori Miracle. Tori, my mother, Mrs. Foster."

"Welcome," Mrs. Foster said with a warm smile. "Have some punch?" Without waiting for my answer, she handed me a cup of red liquid. "Cookie?"

"Chocolate chip, please." I accepted two cookies wrapped in a paper napkin.

"I've heard lots about you," Mrs. Foster said while I shuffled my feet and tried to blush. "You'uns must be mighty relieved to have that cancer scare over."

The punch I'd just sipped went down the wrong way, half choking me to death. When I'd finished coughing it up, I spluttered out, "What . . . what are you talking about?" But it was too late for an answer, for she and Janet were heading toward a table covered with presents.

As Janet began to open her gifts the women pressed forward, overwhelming me with the combined odor of their perfumes, hairs sprays, bath powders, and makeup. My eyes began to water, and I finally had to push my way through the happy throng to the back of the room, where I found a row of metal folding chairs and sank into one next to Lizzie Borden. She had a napkin spread over her lap with a selection on it of every kind of cookie I'd seen on the table.

"I understand you left the college," I said.

Lizzie grinned. "For what they paid me, they could only push me so far." She raised her hands and held them about six inches apart. "I was expected to do my work, Janet's work, and anything else that nobody wanted to handle. Like I told President Godlove, they'd have me in the classroom teaching if they thought they could get away with it."

I nibbled at my cookie. While I didn't care for a lot

of Pennsylvania cooking, I'd never found fault with the baked goods. "Who's taking over?"

Lizzie shrugged. "Who knows. Who cares. I emptied my briefcase on Janet's desk and walked." She giggled. "I hear you're going to take over my job at the ghost tour."

"Word does get around quickly. But I'm not going to do your job, I'm going to be a ghost."

"Well, don't let them stick you in the attic. It gets hot as hell up there at night. Spooky, too."

A tiny gray-haired lady was perched on the edge of the chair next to me, balancing herself with a collapsible cane. "Congratulations, young lady." she whispered. "I done heard you been cured of the big C."

"Where on earth did you hear that?" I blurted out.

"Shhh . . ." Several women stared at me with disapproval.

"Sorry." When I turned back to the woman, she was hobbling toward the unattended refreshment table.

"What do you suppose she meant?" I asked Lizzie. "She's the second person this evening to congratulate me on my 'cure.'"

"And she probably won't be the last," Lizzie assured me.

"But I haven't even heard my test results yet. Dr. Washabaugh's office has been closed since her death."

"Someone's seen the report. And since the Grapevine's never wrong, let me be the third to congratulate you."

A roar of laughter up front caught our attention. Naturally, there were some mandatory gag gifts: a baby bottle that looked empty until turned on its side, a DO NOT DISTURB sign for the parents' bedroom door, and a little pair of blue booties for the "next" baby.

After the last of the offerings was opened, Baby Margolies made her grand appearance in the arms of her doting grandmother. Her name, I learned, was Parker, which I was sure would lead to confusion in the future. After we had all dutifully oohed and aahed, she was carried off to bed.

Janet sat down on the empty chair beside me With one hand, she held out a plate. "How about a sticky bun, hot from the oven?"

I accepted one and quickly put it down on my napkin so the syrup wouldn't burn my fingers.

"Seems like everywhere I go, someone's insisting I eat one of these. And of course, I can't say no."

"I'll come teach you how to make them if you like. My secret is I use a packaged hot roll mix, so they're fast and easy."

"And good." I licked a piece of nut off my sticky finger.

"Tori, I love the little suit. Parker will look really cute in it next summer."

"Is it too big? It looked really small to me."

"That's okay. They outgrow those newborn sizes really fast."

"Sorry about the wrapping paper."

"I didn't even notice that it said 'Get Well Soon.' " She laughed heartily, and I joined in.

"This is the first elevator I've ever seen," I told her. "The buildings look quite old. Has it been in your family for a long time?"

Janet nodded. "Since before The War." Like most local people, she referred to the War Between the States as "The War." "My dad's the fifth-generation Foster to run it."

"I noticed the going-out-of-business sign out front. Does that mean you don't want to take over?"

Her face grew grim. "I'd love to, but I don't have any choice. The elevator's being torn down next year."

"Why?"

"To make room for the new highway."

I laughed. A highway here in the mountains? She couldn't be serious. "Highway to where?"

"From nowhere to nowhere. It was dear old Mack Macmillan's last bit of pork barreling before he retired. His lasting memorial to himself. We call it the Mack Macmillan Highway to Hell. Darn it, I'm letting my emotions ruin my party. Sorry about that. Speaking of the devil, has President Godlove still got you looking into Mack's death?"

I shook my head. "He's satisfied with pinning it on Woody Woodruff's incompetent handling of the guns."

"The reenactor?" She sounded incredulous. "He's the best in the business. He'd never make a mistake like that."

"That's what I thought. But no one else had access to the guns after they were locked up, except . . ." *Except you.* Just how affected was she by Macmillan's plans for the Highway to Hell? "Those keys *were* in your possession all night, weren't they?"

Janet looked wary, as if she could read my mind. "Yes, Tori, they were. There's absolutely no way . . . wait a minute . . . I just remembered something . . . no, it's too silly."

"What?"

"After we were finished, I went upstairs to get my briefcase. Woody, Darious, and Lizzie got out of the elevator on the first floor, but Mack rode all the way up with me."

"Did he come into your office with you?"

"No. He said he had to pick some things up from his office. I'd no sooner got inside than I had the urge to go to the bathroom. That's the worst part of being pregnant—you have to go all the time."

"What does this have to do with the keys?" I asked.

"You asked me if they were in my possession all night, Tori. I'm trying to tell you they were, except for about five minutes when I was in the john. My purse and my keys were on the desk in my office where I dropped them when nature called."

"But the only person on the floor with you was Macmillan. Are you suggesting he switched keys with you? Why would he do that?"

Janet got to her feet and threw her hands up in the air. "I'm not suggesting anything, Tori. I'm only telling you what happened. I know what you're thinking, and I did not, I repeat, I did not reload those guns. Excuse me. I think my mother needs help."

She stomped off through the throng of guests. From where I sat, it looked to me like her mother had everything under control at the refreshment table.

⌒

The clock was chiming half past nine when I got home. The cats were waiting for me in the kitchen, and by the furious swishing of their tails they let me know they were all alone and not happy about it. On the table I found a note from Ethelind saying she'd gone to the Shepherdstown Opera House with some friends and would be home late. I hadn't had an evening to myself since I'd moved in, so I decided to use the time alone to curl up with a good mystery and a cup of tea and try to forget that Garnet was in Washington, D.C., probably having a great time without me.

I was transferring boiling water from the kettle to Ethelind's Blue Italian Spode teapot when the telephone rang. I finished pouring, dropped in two Darjeeling teabags, then answered.

"Hi." It was a man's voice. A very husky-sounding man's voice.

"Who is this?" It wasn't Garnet. I'd recognize his voice anywhere.

"Darious."

"Oh!"

"You didn't tell me you're a reporter."

"If you don't know that, you're the only person in Lickin Creek who doesn't."

"What are you doing tonight?"

"Getting ready to have a cup of tea. Why?"

"Just wondered if you wanted to take a ride tonight. I put the jumper on the carousel."

I sighed. This wasn't right. I couldn't let myself fall into a relationship I didn't need or want. "Sorry. I'm not up for it tonight."

"The hippocampus misses his sea nymph."

"Darious, please stop. I'm not coming over."

"You and that college professor got something planned?"

"She's not even here. I'm reveling in the solitude. I've fixed a pot of tea, and I'm going to read for a while, then go to bed early and catch up on my sleep."

"Heard your guy left. Thought you might be lonely."

He was beginning to annoy me. "Look, Darious. I'm afraid I've given you the wrong impression."

"I don't think so." His voice was low and intimate.

"Good night," I said firmly, then hung up the phone. Had I misinterpreted? I thought not. He knew Garnet was gone, and he was ready to move in. I didn't want to get into that kind of messy situation, and I knew I'd have to straighten him out before much more time went by.

Before I was finished placing the teapot, milk pitcher, and a cup and saucer on a tray, the telephone rang again.

"Hello," I snapped, knowing I sounded impatient.

"Hi, Tori. This is Woody."

All I could think of saying was, "Oh no!"

If he thought that was an odd greeting, he didn't say so. "I wondered if you were busy this coming weekend?"

Another man trying to make a move on me, and Garnet barely out of town! "Busy? Yes, this weekend and every weekend for the rest of my life. And don't ever call me again." I banged the receiver down hard enough to rupture his eardrum. The nerve of these men! Garnet had only been gone one day, and already two guys were trying to pick me up.

Ethelind was a confirmed Anglophile, and her library contained all the great English female authors of the Golden Age of Mystery, the period between the two world wars. I selected an old favorite, Dorothy L Say-ers's *Gaudy Night*, and settled down in the front parlor under a crocheted afghan to lose myself in Oxford. Outside, an autumn wind was howling through the trees, a sure sign that our beautiful but hot Indian summer was near an end. But inside, I was warm and cozy, with my cats, my tea, and my book.

My peace was shattered abruptly when I heard a ringing noise coming from the upper reaches of the house. Fred and Noel heard it at about the same time. Fred reacted by crawling beneath the afghan to hide, while Noel stared intently at the ceiling as if she could see through it.

"It sounds almost like my alarm clock," I told them. "Could I have accidentally set the alarm for ten at night when I was trying to turn it off this morning? I'll be right back."

After marking my place in my book, I ascended the grand front staircase to the second floor and my bedroom at the end of the hall. Sure enough, my alarm clock was cheerfully ringing next to the bed. I pushed the button to quiet it, then reset it to ring at eight tomorrow morning.

The cats were pacing nervously in the front parlor when I came back. I apologized for leaving them, and they settled down after I'd stroked them for a little while. I poured myself another cup of tea, opened my book to the marked page, and returned to the world of Lord Peter Wimsey and Harriet Vane. After a short while the pages began to blur. I yawned and tried to keep reading, but it was all I could do to hold the book upright, much less turn the pages.

I gave up and let the book drop to my chest. With my eyes closed, my thoughts drifted back to the investigation I'd been trying to put out of my mind for the evening. I gave in and decided to think about who might have had a reason to kill Mack Macmillan. His wife? Because the spouse is always number one on suspect lists. But Charlotte was away the weekend he was executed, and everyone who'd known the Macmillans as a couple spoke of her devotion to him.

Woody Woodruff? He and Macmillan had had some sort of row about property development. But would he be stupid enough to kill an enemy in a way that made him the obvious suspect? I didn't think so.

Janet Margolies? Her family's business was being torn down to make way for the Macmillan Highway to Hell. The execution was her idea, and she had invited Mack to play the role of the victim. She had the keys to the storeroom where the guns were kept in her possession. Janet Margolies could be a suspect.

Darious DeShong? Involved, like Woody, with loading the guns. But other than that, there was no reason to suspect him. I could see no connection between him and Macmillan.

Ken Nakamura? Had he held Mack responsible for his brother's death and his family's disintegration? The old professor claimed to be a pacifist, but was he really?

Gloria Zimmerman? She'd said she was glad he was gone. Had a grudge against him because of his lobbying support for puppy mills. Not really a motive for murder, unless there was something I had missed.

Lillie White? Mack hadn't spent as much time with her after Charlotte had gotten out of the hospital. Did Lillie, a woman scorned, seek revenge?

Helga Van Brackle? Still furious with Mack for dumping her for Charlotte. Being at the college, she might have had the opportunity to get hold of the storeroom key.

Was there anybody in the Caven–Adams County area who didn't have a motive for killing the man? Maybe Cassie was right about me being obsessed. Maybe I should move on as she had suggested. I wasn't concentrating. I yawned and stretched, feeling very sleepy.

Someplace very far away, the wind whistled through the treetops. Almost as if it were a living creature, it sniffed at the windows, looking for a way to force itself into the old house. I pulled the afghan up to my chin as protection against the drafts and drifted off to sleep.

A man stood in the room, his back to me. "Garnet?" I tried to sit up but couldn't. I was paralyzed, unable to move a muscle. The man turned, ever so slowly. I smiled and started to reach out to him, but his face was a blank void, as if he were wearing Charlotte Macmillan's elastic mask. A gaping hole appeared where his mouth should be, only it was larger and blacker than any mouth I'd ever seen. Cold permeated my body. I wanted to scream, but no sound came out. The mouth hole grew larger. I thought of a wide-mouth bass, coming closer as if it wanted to swallow me whole. And as it drew near, I could smell evil. The mouth laughed, and it was not a man any longer, but a dragon. The foul smoke rushing from his mouth nearly choked me.

Gagging from the stench, I mustered all my strength and turned my face away from the beast, and something soft touched my cheek. A tear? Not paralyzed anymore, I brought my hand up slowly to wipe it away. Something sharp raked across my nose. I flung my arms out, connected with a cat, and was scolded by a sharp cry, followed by another, and another.

I sat up, choking, trying to figure out where I was, why everything was so dark. The disgusting smell from the stranger's mouth was still there, making me cough, choke, wheeze.

Softness pressed against me. "Fred?" I muttered into the darkness.

Reeeow!

The stranger with no face and a huge black mouth—he had to have been a dream. I was awake now, wasn't I? Why was I having so much trouble seeing? Why was the terrible odor still there? I must still be dreaming, I decided, and lay back on the couch.

Meeeow!

This was no dream. Fred was head-butting me and yelling at me in cat talk to get up. This time I flung the afghan off and got to my feet. And I realized that the room was not dream-darkened but was instead filled with a thick, acrid smoke. An orange glow on the small Persian carpet under the tea table was actually a smoldering fire, and little tongues of flame were already creeping up the afghan.

Wide awake at last, I grabbed the smoking afghan and rushed out of the room with it, wrestled open the front door, and heaved the thing onto the front lawn. Then I ran back into the room and with superhuman strength, born from desperation and need, dragged first the rug then the couch out of the house, onto the grass, and as far away from the building as I possibly could.

Back inside, I threw open the parlor windows and let the air circulate. The fire seemed to have been confined to the rug and couch, but I called the volunteer fire department and stood by the door, ready to flee if anything flared up again.

Fred and Noel stayed close to me as the firemen charged in wielding a ton of fire-fighting equipment. The men checked the ceiling and walls, pulled down the drapes, and chopped a big hole in the floor to make sure the fire hadn't spread to the floor joists. After about an hour they seemed convinced that there was no further danger. By the time Ethelind walked in the worst of the smoke and smells had dissipated.

Most of the trucks departed, leaving the fire chief and a few men to try to determine what had started the blaze. I tried to watch them, but my eyes kept blurring, and I grew so dizzy, I had to sit down. I hadn't felt this peculiar since the morning of my biopsy when I'd overdone the anti-anxiety medicine. I saw Chief Yoder bend over and pick up an ashtray that must have overturned during the commotion, perhaps as I'd knocked the tea table over trying to get the rug out from under it.

"Looks like you were a lucky young lady," he said,

scooping a few cigarette butts off the floor. "Don't imagine you'll be doing much smoking when you're sleepy from now on."

"Look, Chief, I don't smoke."

He cocked his head and looked skeptically at me. "Your voice sounds kind of slurred. Were you drinking?"

"I was not drinking. Except for some tea." Ethelind's beautiful teapot and teacup lay on the floor, but by some miracle they didn't seem to be broken. "And I wasn't smoking. Why should I lie about it? Everybody who knows me will tell you I detest the smell of cigarettes." Ethelind nodded her confirmation. "In fact, if that ashtray full of butts had been on the coffee table, I couldn't have sat down in here to read without emptying it and washing it out first." I blinked, trying to bring the offending container into focus.

"Are you trying to tell me that someone came in here and planted a dirty ashtray in the room while you were sleeping?" He laughed. I couldn't blame him. It did sound ridiculous.

"Hey, Chief." One of the firemen who'd been outside entered the room. "Take a look at this." He held out a bag for Chief Yoder to inspect.

"What is it?" I asked, after the chief had looked, smelled, and even tasted the contents of the bag.

"Stuff I found on the rug you dragged outside," the firefighter said. "Looks like a pile of dirty clothes that near burned up."

Chief Yoder looked thoughtful and nodded. "Did you leave some of your underwear on the floor?" he asked me.

"Of course not. Wait a minute, do you think someone deliberately set this fire?"

"I'm beginning to think so, miss. Did you hear anything? See anything?"

"No, of course not." Then I remembered something *had* happened. "My alarm went off upstairs at about ten o'clock. I thought I'd set it wrong. Now I wonder if it wasn't a trick to get me out of the room." I looked at the empty teacup on the floor and began to shake. "My God, someone must have put something in my tea while I was upstairs. I got really sleepy a little while after I came back down. No wonder I feel so groggy."

Chief Yoder and one of the men got down on their knees and inspected the teapot and cup. "There's a little tea left in the pot," the chief said. The assistant carefully carried the teacup and pot out of the room. "We'll check the contents," the chief said. "Do you have any idea how somebody might have gotten in?"

I started to say no, then realized I really had not checked to make sure anything was locked before I'd settled down to read. I'd been in Lickin Creek long enough to almost think like the natives that a locked door was "unneighborly." Certainly locking up wasn't a major concern the way it had been in my Manhattan apartment.

"You need to be more careful," the chief warned.

"I will."

"Can you think of anybody who'd want to hurt you?"

"Nobody. I mind my own business and expect everybody to mind theirs. Why are you laughing like that?"

"Because I've heard you're the biggest buttinsky to hit town since the Secret Service organized a fishing trip here for President Carter back in the seventies."

"But I haven't done anything to warrant this." I gestured to the ruined parlor. "Oh my God!"

"What?"

"I just thought of something. Did you know that Professor Nakamura, from the college, was shot over in Gettysburg?"

"Yeah. I heard about that. Damn shame. Nice guy like that. Probably some poacher out on the battlefield shooting at deer and hit him by accident."

"That's what I thought. But what if it wasn't an accident?"

"You think he was shot deliberately?"

"No, but I was standing right next to him when he was hit. Now that this has happened, I wonder if someone was aiming at *me*."

CHAPTER 15

CASSIE WAS PREPARED FOR MY MORNING-AFTER headache. "Smoke inhalation," she said. "It'll be days before you cough it all up. I didn't expect you to come in today."

I gratefully accepted the two Extra-Strength Tylenol she pressed upon me and washed them down with a glass of tepid tap water. I knew my nauseous condition came partly from the smoke, but I also blamed the unknown drug someone had slipped into my tea. "I needed to get out of the house. The cleaning crew sent by the insurance company is ripping the place apart."

"Are your cats all right?"

"They feel a lot better than I do. Smoke rises, I guess, so they didn't get as much as I did. Thank God for Fred. He woke me up by scratching my face. If it hadn't been for him, we'd all be dead."

"He's a real hero," Cassie said, agreeing with me. "How did Ethelind react when she got home?"

I shuddered at the memory. "You'd think I had personally taken an ax to her floor. It took nearly a half hour and many dozens of apologies before she settled down. She even suggested she might not go to England after all because she was afraid of leaving her house in such incompetent hands."

"But it was an accident. You couldn't help it."

"You're right about one thing. I couldn't help it. But, Cassie, I don't believe it was an accident. That fire was deliberately set. I'm sure of that and Chief Yoder thinks so too."

Cassie gasped. "How could someone start a fire right next to you? Surely you would have woken up."

"I was drugged, Cassie. Someone slipped something into the teapot while I was upstairs. The chief took what was left to a lab today to determine what was in it."

Wondering why someone would want to kill me made my headache worse. And the physical discomfort reminded me I still hadn't heard anything about the results of my biopsy, except from the gossipy women at the baby shower who all seemed to know I was okay. "Cassie, can you please call Dr. Washabaugh's office for me?"

"Sure. Do you think someone's going to be there?"

"I don't know. Maybe there's another doctor filling in."

She dialed and listened to the receiver. "Someone's answering. Oh, shoot, it's an answering machine." She listened a moment or two longer before hanging up. "Patients can come in any afternoon this week to have their records transferred to other doctors' offices. No appointment needed."

"I'll be there. What's happening this morning?"

After returning a few phone calls, I started on my rounds. First, a local farm where a giant pumpkin was on display. Second stop, the Caven County Prison to photograph the new caterer serving lunch. Back in the heart of town, I took pictures of some children from the

Catholic school painting giant pictures of spooks, spirits, and shadowy shapes on windows of deserted stores. I was glad to see that some people could still have fun celebrating Halloween.

The fourth and final photo opportunity was a picture of three ladies from the Lickin Creek Garden Society placing fresh potted chrysanthemums around the base of the fountain in the square.

I glanced at the clock tower on the old Market building, now used for the borough offices, and saw it was getting late. I'd have to hurry if I wanted to get to Dr. Washabaugh's office before it closed. For a minute I even thought I might postpone going, put off getting the bad news for one more day, but I knew I'd have to face it sooner or later. I got in the car and headed out of town.

Because there was only one car parked in front of Dr. Washabaugh's former office building, I feared, then hoped, I was too late. The door, when I tried it, was locked. Feeling relieved because I wouldn't have to face my worst fears today, I turned to leave. At that moment the door flew open, and I heard Vesta Pennsinger's cheery voice. "Now, don't you go away, Tori. I was just getting the place redd up. What a busy day. You wouldn't believe how many people showed up." She ushered me into the waiting room, chatting all the while. "Now, don't tell me. Let me guess why you'uns is here."

"No games please, Vesta. You know damn well I came for the results of my biopsy."

"I can't give it to you directly, Tori. I'm supposed to forward it to your new doctor, and then you can . . ."

That was the last straw! Summoning up the image of John Travolta in *Pulp Fiction*, I grabbed Vesta by the front of her white smock and pulled her close to me.

Right in her face, I muttered, "Give me my test results, Vesta. Or I'll . . ." I left it to her imagination to guess, since I really had no idea of what I'd do if she wouldn't give me what I wanted.

She fell back against the divider wall when I released her and smoothed her clothes. "Okay, already. I'll get it. Hang on."

She darted through the door, and I followed close behind, watching as she went through the papers in the top section of an in-box on the counter.

After a few minutes she waved a piece of paper at me. "Here. You can read it for yourself."

My hand shook as I took the report from her. I focused on the page of medical terminology, wondering what it all meant. One word leaped off the page. *Negative.* "That's good, isn't it?" I asked. *Please let it be good!*

Vesta took it from me and read quickly through it. "You're okay, Tori. It was a cyst. Nothing to be concerned about. Be sure and get a mammogram every year."

To my great surprise, I burst into tears. "I'll get you something to drink," Vesta said, hurrying from the room. She returned in a few seconds with a paper cup full of ice water, which I swallowed in one gulp.

Vesta pulled a couple of Kleenexes from a box on the countertop and handed them to me. I wiped my cheeks with one and blew my nose in the other. "Thanks," I said. "I am so relieved! Don't know why I cried. Feel like an idiot." I looked at her crumpled smock front where I'd grabbed her. "I'm sorry about that."

"It's okay, Tori. Everybody reacts differently. One woman who came in earlier got bad news about her Pap smear. After I told her, she actually started laughing."

"That *is* strange."

"And two men and one woman threatened to sue me because of all their records being burned up. Like we set that fire on purpose. Poor Dr. Washabaugh . . . it was just awful. I walked in and found her lying right there with papers from our files piled up around her . . . and burning . . . and the smell . . ." She covered her face, and her shoulders shook as she sobbed.

I walked over to the counter to get a Kleenex for her, and noticed a report lying on the top of the stack in the in-box. It appeared to be test results. Edward Macmillan's name jumped out at me as if it were in neon letters. I read through it, feeling no qualms about invading his privacy; after all, he wasn't alive.

It was snatched away from me by Vesta. "You can't read that," she snapped. "It's confidential information."

"Look, Vesta, don't tell me about confidentiality. Not when you've spread rumors about my medical condition all around Adams and Caven counties."

Indignantly, she said, "I don't know what you're talking about."

"Of course you do. Nobody knew about my biopsy except Dr. Washabaugh, my landlady, and you. And obviously you were the only one who knew it came back negative. Last night, I was congratulated by people I didn't even know. It had to be you who told them."

She hung her head. "I didn't mean no harm, Tori. My mother always said my big mouth'd get me in trouble."

I couldn't help feeling sorry for her. She didn't appear to be malicious, only a woman who enjoyed being in a position where she had confidential information that nobody else knew.

I retrieved Mack Macmillan's test results from her. It was from the Gettysburg hospital, and just as the coroner's report had said, Mack Macmillan had prostate cancer.

"I guess he didn't know he had cancer, if this has come in since his death," I said.

"He knew. This was a follow-up test. The results came in the same day as yours."

"Was he going to have surgery?"

Vesta blew her nose as she shook her head. "The urologist Dr. Washabaugh sent him to doesn't recommend surgery for men over seventy. He said it was a slow-growing type of cancer and Mack could live ten years or more if something else didn't kill him first."

"I imagine he was glad to hear there was no immediate danger," I said, thinking of my own relief.

"Not really. He didn't handle it real good. Even cried. Practically had to be carried out of here. Kept saying there had to be a mistake. That's why Dr. Washabaugh ordered the second set of tests."

CHAPTER 16

IT HAS BEEN SAID REPEATEDLY BY TOURISTS DRIVING past Lickin Creek on the Interstate that one can smell the grease from Lickin Creek's dozens of fast-food restaurants for miles before the town is visible. To celebrate my good news, I stopped at one of the eateries that Lickin Creek is so well known for and purchased dinner: two hamburgers, a double order of fries, a fried apple pie, and a Diet Coke, which I ate in the car while watching the ducks from the Lickin Creek comb the parking lot for crumbs.

Back in Moon Lake, the cleaning crew had finished its work. Ethelind wasn't happy with the lingering smell of smoke, but they had assured her it would dissipate if she left all the windows open. Neither was she happy with the repairs made to her parlor floor, since the carpenters had used a wood that didn't exactly match the existing hundred-year-old planks, and she wasn't happy with me, either, on general principles. The cats took refuge under the bed in my room while I changed clothes. Although I wasn't exactly thrilled with what I had to do tonight, it was a lot better than staying home with my infuriated landlady.

When I entered the kitchen, Ethelind turned her

scowl on me, stared for a moment, then burst into gales of laughter. She clutched at her chest and collapsed into a chair, straining to catch her breath. "Oh, my, Tori. I've seen you wear some god-awful outfits, but that one takes the cake!"

I stared down at the voluminous blue skirt that lay in ripples on the floor around my feet. "I didn't have time to shorten it."

Ethelind stopped laughing long enough to say, "Please tell me that isn't the latest thing in cocktail gowns from Barney's." Impressed with her own wit, she blew her nose into a paper napkin and laughed some more.

"I'm a nun," I explained.

"A bloody Flying Nun, I'd say."

I adjusted the enormous wings of my starched white cornette. "A Sister of Charity," I said with great dignity. "You can call me Sister Camilla O'Neil. I died of blood poisoning while tending the wounded at the Lickin Creek College for Women during the Civil War." A brief biographical sketch had been enclosed with the costume, with a note telling me how to act and what I should say whenever someone entered the attic.

With yards of navy blue cotton bunched up on my lap, I drove to the college, thinking that it was all worthwhile if my costume had brought the smile back to Ethelind's face. At the college, I was directed to a parking place behind the administration building. Thankful I wouldn't have to hike up the hill from the visitors' lot, I got out, shook the wrinkles out of my habit, and entered the building through the back door. A group consisting of nuns, Union and Confederate soldiers, and college girls in long gowns was gathered at the foot of the stairs, listening to Helga Van Brackle give directions.

"You're late," she said to me.

"Only a little," I said with a smile, determined to show everyone she didn't intimidate me one bit.

"I'll get to you in a minute, Tori. Please be patient while I tell the girls what to do." Even though she spoke to me as if I were a freshman, I kept smiling. One of the gowned students winked and handed me a program, and I read *The Lickin Creek College for Women presents the Annual Harvest Time Legends Tour featuring Tori Miracle as the Nun in the Attic*.

"Excuse me," I said. "What's this 'featuring Tori Miracle' business?"

Helga simpered as the girls giggled. "You're our Celebrity Ghost this year. I thought you knew that."

"I didn't expect this," I said gruffly, but way down under my habit I was tickled with the attention. Maybe I wasn't a big name in the literary world, but at least I was recognized in south-central Pennsylvania.

The girls were to be the guides and ticket takers, I learned. They represented the six original students who had been brave enough to seek out higher education equal to that offered to men. A man in a black suit played the part of the Presbyterian minister who had founded the college in 1860. Another man in black, with a stovepipe hat and a beard, was obviously portraying Abraham Lincoln. Keeping a low voice, I asked one of the guides, "What's he doing here? I never heard anything about President Lincoln coming to Lickin Creek."

Unfortunately the acoustics in the hall were very good, and Helga threw me a dirty look. "If he hadn't died at such an inopportune time, I'm sure he would have visited our town when the war was over."

Helga handed each of us a flashlight, a supply of candles and matches, and a small lantern. "Make sure all the lights are off in your area, then assume your assigned positions. The first guests should be coming through in about ten minutes, so please have your lantern lit with the chimney on. And keep your eye on them. We don't want a repeat of last year's near-tragic accident. Repairs to the second-floor carpet took all our profits. And don't use your flashlights unless it's absolutely necessary."

The other nuns flocked to the staircase, and I started to follow them, but Helga put her arm on mine and stopped me. "You're the attic nun, Tori. You can take the elevator up."

"Why do I have to sit all alone in the attic?" I grumbled to the pretty girl in a powder blue silk gown who pushed the elevator button.

"That's where they always put the Celebrity Ghost. Guess they figure nobody would climb all the way up there unless there was someone worth seeing." She chewed a fingernail for a second or two and looked nervously at me a couple of times. Finally, she asked, "Just what are you famous for, anyway?"

"I wrote a book."

"Oh. Why haven't I ever heard of it?"

I wanted to shout, *because you're an ill-educated slob with no literary taste whatsoever*, but deep down inside I knew it would have been unusual if she *had* read my poor little novel. Last I heard, it had been spotted on a remainder table at Barnes & Noble; maybe somebody would pick it up there.

She pulled the grate open. "I'll get off here," she said. "I'm going to be on the third floor. I'm the beautiful virgin who committed suicide when my lover deserted me. According to legend, I still wait for him at my bedroom window."

"During the war?"

"No. It happened before that, when this building was still a private home. Better go up and find your spot," she said. "We've only got four minutes till lights out." She waved as I closed the elevator door.

I went up to the floor where the PR department had its offices. There were a few other offices there too, mostly empty, since no one wanted to be stuck in the unpleasant attic. But there was one, I recalled, that had been given to Mack Macmillan when he became chairman of the board of trustees. It had not yet been reassigned, and I wondered if it had been thoroughly searched. As I passed by, I tried the door and found it locked.

The hallway was hot and airless. Now I remembered Lizzie saying to me, "Whatever you do, don't let them stick you in the attic." I wished I'd listened. *Spooky,* she'd called it. It sure was. I found the chair where I was supposed to sit in a shadowy alcove near the back of the main hallway, facing the stairs. I switched off the overhead light, followed my flashlight beam back to the chair, lit my candle, and pulled out my information packet to read through it once more. A cool breeze ruffled the pages of my job description and caused the candle flame to flicker, reminding me to put the chimney on. Lizzie Borden once told me nobody in their right mind stayed in this building after dark. I really wished I hadn't agreed to sit in this creepy attic alone.

After a short while I heard footsteps on the stairs below, and the voice of the girl from the elevator telling her story of unrequited love. She demonstrated real dramatic talent and even had me looking over my shoulder for etheric figures. The footsteps grew louder as the group climbed the staircase, and I blew out the candle in my lantern as my directions said I should, then waited quietly until they were all in the hallway. There were about fifteen people in the first group of visitors, and I could see them quite well because they were all carrying small illuminated lanterns, but I knew they couldn't see me lurking in the alcove. Several were small enough to be children, but I couldn't really tell since everyone wore costumes and masks. The guide hushed them, saying she thought she heard something, and that was my cue to turn on my flashlight beneath my chin to illuminate the white wings of my cornette. There were several screams, and I figured I must look pretty darn scary.

Using my best *woo-woo* voice, I said, "I am Sister Camilla O'Neil of the Sisters of Charity. I nursed soldiers at Gettysburg, then came across the mountain to assist after the Battle of Lickin Creek." *Was there really a Battle of Lickin Creek? I couldn't recall ever hearing about it.* "I cared for the rich, the poor, the officers and the privates, the white man and the Negro. One poor soul said my cornette made him think of angels' wings." I paused here and shook my head to make the elaborate white headdress jiggle. "I emptied bedpans, fed those who could not feed themselves, changed dressings, and combed the lice from their heads and beards. And then one day, while cutting the dressing away from an infected wound, I accidentally sliced my finger. By nightfall, red streaks had rushed up my arm and taken over my brain. I was carried here, to this very attic, where I lay upon a bare cot and with feverish eyes looked out through a dormer at the heaven I was soon to visit. Within my—"

"Mama, I have to go to the potty."

I stopped short. *Where was I? Oh yes, the cot.* "Within my brain was one thought only, to—"

"Now! Mama. I can't wait."

The guide turned on her flashlight. "I'll take her."

The mood I'd strived to create was all but gone, and I decided to expurgate my death scene. "And there I died, grateful for having suffered in the service of my Redeem—"

"Sorry to interrupt you, Miss Miracle," the guide said. "But we're going to have to leave." To the assembled people, she said, "The bathroom door's locked. We'll have to go downstairs at once."

The little girl clutching her hand was sobbing miserably and hopping from one foot to the other. She ran to a masked woman in a gypsy costume I assumed was her mother and buried her face in the woman's skirts.

The people turned around and disappeared down the stairs. The guide trailing behind said to me, "That happens all the time. Someone turns the button to lock it, then forgets to turn it back when they leave. There's supposed to be a key in the PR office. Could you take care of opening the door before the next group gets here?"

"Sure. We Sisters of Charity are up for any kind of job, no matter how menial it may seem."

I knew where the keys hung, on the wall just inside the doorway to Janet's office. When I entered the room, the first thing I saw was the mess on Janet's desk. The jumbled contents of Lizzie's briefcase lay where she had dumped it out after resigning. It gave me an idea, and I dug through piles until I found the keys for the basement storeroom. I took them with me when I went to unlock the bathroom door.

With the door open and the bathroom ready for the next emergency, I returned to the top of the staircase and listened for a moment. There were no voices coming from the floor below me, and I knew I had plenty of time left because the maiden in the window took at least ten minutes to tell her story.

I tried the first key in the door of Mack's office and nothing happened. But when I inserted the second key into the lock, the door swung open easily, as I thought it might. I closed the door behind me and pressed the light switch next to the door. An overhead light came on, illuminating the small room.

Janet had told me that after the guns were loaded she'd kept the storeroom keys in her possession all night. But there had been one short interval where they hadn't been with her. That was when she'd had to run down the hall to the rest room. If a key switch had been made, it had to have been done then. And Mack Macmillan was the only person around who could have done it. Macmillan must have taken one of the storeroom keys while Janet was in the rest room and substituted one of his office keys so she wouldn't know it was gone.

But why? Why would Representative Macmillan have wanted access to the loaded guns? Was the answer here in his office? I knew it was quite possible that Luscious, short of time and help, might well have overlooked something when he searched the office. I stepped inside and closed the door.

The room had a few pieces of nice furniture in it, a carved mahogany desk, a comfortable chair behind it, a brown leather couch against one wall, and a bookcase, on which were a few sets of leather-bound books that looked as if they'd been chosen more for their looks than their contents. On the wall hung a large gold-framed photograph of Mack Macmillan in the uniform of a Union Army general. One hand rested on a table, the other on the hilt of his sword. He looked very official. Very real. Other than that, there was nothing very personal in the office. It was obviously not a place where Mack Macmillan spent much time.

I opened the door to listen for approaching visitors, but there was still no sign or sound indicating that anyone was coming. I turned off the light and left the door ajar in order to hear the next group coming, then followed my flashlight beam to the desk. Not knowing what I was looking for, I pulled open the top drawer. A ring with two keys on it practically jumped into my hand. It was identical to Janet's key ring, which I held in my hand. I tried both in Mack's door, but only one fit. Before I left the building, I decided, I would try to unlock the storeroom door with the other. When I went back to shut the desk drawer, I noticed a plastic Baggie jammed in the back left corner.

Using two pencils as chopsticks, so as not to leave fingerprints, I pulled the Baggie out of the drawer and dropped it on the desktop. Through the clear plastic, I could see what looked like twists of paper and foam rubber earplugs. Wonder Wads, Woody had called them, the foam gizmos reenactors used to hold the black powder in their gun barrels. I dropped the bag into one of the many pockets of Sister Camilla's voluminous skirt and left the office, carefully closing the door behind me. I was dying to take the Baggie to Luscious at the police department and would have left right then, except I knew he wouldn't be at the office and there was really no point in upsetting the college's Harvest Time Legend Tour. The bag of gun powder and Wonder Wads could wait until tomorrow.

I was about to take my seat when I heard a faint rustle behind me. Probably another breeze, but what I thought was *rats*! I pulled my chair closer to the stairs. I would be much too close to the audience there to be really scary, but on the other hand *rats*!

"Tori." A voice as soft as an angel's was calling my name.

Spinning around, I demanded, "Who's there?" There was no answer. Had I imagined it?

Then again, it came. "Tori."

Was it the ghost of the maiden on the lower floor? Of course it was she, I realized. She'd ridden up with me on the elevator and knew my name. She must have tried to call me earlier when I was in Macmillan's office, and become worried when I didn't answer. I leaned over the low banister and called out softly, "I'm here. What do you want?"

The girl's voice floated up the stairwell. "I didn't call you."

As I started to straighten up, a sound behind me caused me to look over my shoulder, and I caught a glimpse of a nun, standing in the shadows. "Hi," I said. "Please tell me you're here to take my place. This attic is freaking me out."

Instead of answering my greeting, she moved forward as though propelled by a demon. Before I could turn all the way around, I saw the quivering of white angel wings as something hit me hard in the middle of my back. My stomach hit the railing, and I grabbed hold of it with both hands to keep myself from tumbling over. The cracking noise the banister made as it broke away from the floor was the loudest and most terrifying thing I'd ever heard.

Still clutching the part of the railing that had separated from the rest of the staircase, I fell forward. Directly in front of me were two crossed iron bracing rods that spanned the stairwell, and added support to the circular staircase. I landed on top of them with a painful thud that threatened to dislodge my internal organs, felt myself start to slip, let go of the broken railing, and grabbed hold of one of the two braces. I lay there, face down, spread-eagled on the iron bars, looking down at the floor four storys below me. Afraid to move, I called out, "Help me." But only a squeak came out of my mouth.

"Holy jeez!" The maiden from the third floor leaned out over the railing and looked up at me. "Don't let go!"

"I'll try not to." The nun's habit I wore weighed about fifty pounds. How long before its weight dragged me down?

The staircase shook as she ran down the stairs, and I tightened my grip on the iron rod and shut my eyes.

After what seemed like a couple of hours, I heard and felt her running back up the stairs followed by a thundering herd of would-be rescuers.

"Try to look at us," a woman said, "and not down."

I lifted my head an inch, opened my eyes, and saw a row of Halloween masks staring down at me. "Help," I whimpered.

"The fire department's coming," a man said.

"What are they going to do?"

"Get her down with a ladder? How the hell do I know?"

"I'm slipping," I cried. "I can't hold on much longer."

"Someone get a net." I recognized Helga's authoritative voice.

"Like where?"

There was no answer.

A man dropped down on the floor so his face was almost level with mine. All I could see through the balusters was a red clown nose and one eye.

"Tori, listen carefully. You are going to have to work your way back to the other side of the stairwell where the railing is broken. When you get there, I'll be able to pull you to safety."

"I don't know how . . ."

"Start by turning around. I'll tell you exactly what to do. Keep holding on with your right hand and with your left hand, reach out and grab the bar on your left."

"I don't think . . ."

"Good. Don't think. Just do as I say. It's not far. You can do it."

I groped with my left arm, trying not to look down and afraid to move my head to look for the bar. And at last, my fingers touched the cold metal bar and closed around it.

"Now, reach out with your right leg till you feel it lying on the next bar."

I did as he directed. The incongruous thought popped into my mind that I must look like someone playing Twister.

Calmly, he directed my movements, until I had completely turned my body around.

I heard footsteps, and the masks appeared on the side of the staircase where the bannister had broken away.

"Now, all you have to do is hold tight and try to wiggle your body slowly toward me," the man said. "Straddle the bar. That's good. Move one hand, hold tight with it, then move the other."

I said a quick prayer and tried to do what he had told me, but before I could work up the courage to loosen one hand's grip, the weight of my heavy skirt pulled me off balance. I was suspended beneath the bar then, hanging on with both hands and feet. Someone screamed. It might have been me.

"You're okay," the man called. "Try sliding one hand, just an inch, then the other. Good! Do it again. One inch at a time."

The arm I'd broken last month throbbed with pain. "Hurts . . . don't think I can . . ." I felt my fingers slip about a millimeter.

Then an angel's voice called out softly, "Tori. Think of your special place. Go there now, Tori. Go to your special place, and you'll be safe."

I was on a beach, overlooking the turquoise and lavender waters of the China Sea.

"Close your eyes and turn your face to the sun, Tori. It will give you strength."

I looked up, seeing nothing, feeling the warmth seep through my skin, my shoulders, my hands, my fingers.

"Now slide. One hand. Slide. The other. You are strong, Tori. Slide. Slide. You are getting close to your special place. Slide. Slide. Good. Slide. Slide. Good."

Encouraged by the voice, I concentrated on my movements. Slide one hand, then the other. Slide one hand, then the other. Over and over, an inch at a time, until someone firmly grasped my left wrist.

"I've got you," the man said, "but don't let go of the bar."

"Don't worry," I gasped. I'd returned to reality from my special place, and I knew I could still fall, that the danger was still there, but the touch of the stranger's hand was reassuring. Two strong hands firmly gripped my other wrist.

"We've got you," the man said. "On the count of three, let go and we'll pull you up."

Before I could protest, I heard him count, "One, two, three . . . and up."

I was roughly jerked upward, and my chest hit the floor, causing pain to bounce through to my spine. I felt hands reaching for me, tugging on my arms, my waist, my skirt, my legs, and then they dragged me to safety.

Then my ordeal was over, and I lay facedown on the carpet, in a jumbled, quaking heap.

Someone stroked my back, and I whimpered.

"You're safe now," said the voice of the man who had rescued me.

"Tori, it's me, Moonbeam. Can you sit up?"

Now I knew whose soft voice had sent me to the security of my special place. And still my fingers clutched at the carpet pile. "No. Can't. Don't want to."

Strong hands helped me to a sitting position. I knew somehow that they were the same strong hands that had kept me from falling, and I clung to them as if I still depended on them for my life. "Thank you," I murmured. "I can't say it enough. Thank you, thank you, thank . . ."

The man laughed, and I suddenly realized the circus clown who had saved me was Woody Woodruff, the man who, up till now, I'd thought was the most disgusting scumbag I'd ever met.

Moonbeam, in a pink ballerina costume, touched my face. "You're all right," she said, and her hypnotic voice calmed me.

"How did this happen?" Helga Van Brackle, quite a sight in a low-cut Scarlett O'Hara gown, stood with arms akimbo glaring down at me.

"I was pushed."

Murmurs of surprise and disbelief whirled across the landing.

"It's true. I heard someone call my name. I thought it was the girl on the floor below me, so I leaned over to see what she wanted. And that's when I was pushed."

"Did you see who did it?"

I shook my head. "Not really. But I think I saw something fluttery and white, like a bird . . . or angel wings."

Gasps of astonishment. Moans of sympathy. I looked up to see where they came from and felt as if I were surrounded by seagulls. More than half a dozen horrified Sisters of Charity, wearing huge, fluttering cornettes, stared first at me, then at each other. "But we were all in the basement," one protested. "At least, I think we were."

CHAPTER 17

DESPITE MY HORRIFYING EXPERIENCE, OR PERHAPS because of it, I slept hard and long. My waking dream was of flying over the ocean with a flock of gulls, no land in sight. My wings grew weary, and I tumbled head over heels into the black water, where I awoke with a start, covered with sweat. My arms throbbed with pain; no wonder my wings hadn't kept up with the other birds. Fred nuzzled my neck as if he'd shared my dream.

Maybe it had all been a dream. Falling dreams are common. So are dreams of flying. Flying made me think of wings, which reminded me of angel wings, and I sat up abruptly. It had not been a dream. Of that I was sure! The crumpled heap of blue and white clothing on the rug beside my bed brought it all back to me in vivid detail. Moonbeam and Woody driving me home. Ethelind making a big fuss over me. Moonbeam helping me out of my shredded habit and into a T-shirt. Ethelind bringing me a glass of sherry once Moonbeam had gotten me into bed. Woody wishing me happy dreams. Had he really said, "Don't let the bedbugs bite"? The sherry glass, untouched, sat on the bedside table.

In a few days' time I'd been shot at, nearly burned to

death in my sleep, and been pushed off a balcony. I was Calamity Jane. Hardluck Hannah. Woeful Wanda. Typhoid Tori—no that one didn't apply—at least people hadn't been dying around me, I was the one who was encountering one calamity after another. I knew I could go on forever wallowing in self-pity and browbeating myself with alliteration, or I could get up, get dressed, and go to work. I chose to get up.

The aroma of fresh coffee attracted me like a magnet. I shoved my feet into my sneakers and, without bothering to tie them, shuffled down the back stairs into the kitchen.

Every flat surface was covered with dishes, baskets, and boxes full of food.

"What's happened?" I asked Ethelind.

"The neighbors heard about your accidents. This is the way Lickin Creekers handle disasters, with loads of food." She poured coffee into a mug and placed it on the table. "Here you go. Like the Brits, I prefer tea, but I know how you like your coffee."

Without tobacco, I thought, but accepted the offering.

"There's a pretty nice ham from the Hubers, across the lake, and a frozen lasagna from the Younkers. Margaret Umpleby sent a cake. Let's see what else is here. Timmons, pie. Starlipper, spaghetti with beans. Rosenberry, homemade elderberry jam—now, wasn't that nice. It's so hard to make, everything it touches turns slimy. Charlotte Macmillan brought sticky buns on her way to work." She opened the box from Daywalt's Bakery and put a couple of the buns in the microwave oven. "Nice and fresh—it's today's date on the box. Oretta Clopper, scalloped oysters—I'd better put this in the refrigerator."

"Here you go," she said, placing a piping-hot gooey sticky bun in front of me. "Top off your coffee?"

"Yes, please." It didn't taste as dreadful as I'd expected. "How did all these people know about my accident?"

"Guess they saw it on the evening news last night."

I groaned. You mean I was on the news?

Ethelind smiled. "Tori, you *were* the news. They devoted the whole show, except for sports and weather, of course, to a video of you hanging from that bar."

I choked as a bit of sticky bun went down the wrong tube. When I recovered, I said, "Video? But there wasn't time for a TV crew to come in."

"That's the blessing, or maybe the curse, of affordable video recorders. Everybody and his uncle's got one. There must have been three or four there last night, videoing you from different angles."

"Oh my God!"

"At least the TV station covered your bottom with a fuzzy spot whenever they showed a shot of you from below. So nobody could see your underwear."

"Oh no!"

"Mayor Somping was interviewed, and he said if Woody wasn't waiting to go to trial, he'd give him a medal or something. He said the judge at Woody's sentencing would probably take it into consideration as evidence of Woody's good character."

"So he's skipped right over the trial to the sentencing. Sounds as if everybody's mind is made up that Woody's going to be found guilty."

"He's the perfect person to take the blame," Ethelind said. "He's not a Lickin Creek native, and he's not associated with the college. And he doesn't have any money to hire a lawyer."

"Poor guy." I picked up my sticky bun and nibbled

on it, savoring every bite. The thought of my ordeal being broadcast made me want to cry. "It's bad enough to be pushed over a railing," I said. "But I think it's nearly as bad having pictures of me in that situation broadcast all over the Tri-State area."

"Did you say you were pushed? Are you sure?"

"Of course I'm sure. Somebody hit me so hard in the middle of my back that I lost my balance."

"Were you already leaning over the railing?"

I nodded. "I thought I'd heard the girl downstairs call me. I was trying to answer without making a lot of noise and ruining the ghostly atmosphere.

"It could have been an accident. Maybe you just lost your balance, Tori."

"Sure, Ethelind. Just like the fire the other night was an accident." Her face hardened, and I realized it would have been better not to have reminded her of the damage done to her front parlor.

"That could have been an accident, too, Tori. You took a sleeping pill. Fell asleep sooner than you expected to. Dropped your cigarette. Happened to me that way a couple of times."

"Ethelind, I don't smoke. You know that."

"Nonsense, everybody smokes." She lit a cigarette to emphasize her statement, and I left the kitchen. She might be smoking, but I was the one who was fuming. The very idea—her insinuating I'd imagined myself in danger, that I'd caused my near-death twice in two days by carelessness. By the time I reached my bedroom, self-doubt had set in. Could she be right? Had I imagined the voice? Leaned over too far? Explained my clumsiness by inventing the story about a blow to my back? And the fire—maybe the tea hadn't been drugged. Maybe I just fell asleep. Maybe Ethelind had dropped a smoldering cigarette on the rug earlier, and it had taken all that time to start the fire.

What about being shot at? I asked myself. My inner voice reminded me I hadn't actually been shot, and I had no proof that someone had been aiming at me. Besides, what reason would anyone have for wanting me out of the way?

While I was musing over my situation, I showered and dressed. In slimming black slacks and a red sweater, I stood at the bathroom mirror and jerked a brush through my hair, noting I'd either have to get a haircut soon or let it grow long. Outside, the wind howled, and I knew I'd better throw a jacket on. I grabbed my purse from where it lay on the dresser, and as I walked around the double bed to leave I noticed the blue and white pile of nun's clothing on the floor. I'd take it with me and drop it off at the college. I bent over to pick up the costume, and as I stood, some items dropped to the rug. I gathered them, the key ring and the plastic Baggie full of Wonder Wads I'd found in Mack's desk last night, and put them in my pocket.

At the office, Cassie, as usual, was solicitous. But this time, she seemed to be holding back on her expressions of sympathy. I'd been through a lot lately. Certainly enough to wear anyone's patience thin.

I told her the whole story, starting with the ghostly voice calling my name, and ending with my dramatic rescue, which, of course, she had seen on the evening news.

"You really think someone's trying to kill you?" Cassie asked in an incredulous voice. "Don't you think you could be overreacting?"

"No, I don't." But I knew I didn't sound convincing. Ethelind had already planted seeds of doubt in my mind.

"P. J. often received death threats, Tori."

"She did? What for? Did a band of enraged gypsy moths threaten to get even with her for dissing them in the Farm News column?"

"Don't be silly. Anybody who writes for a newspaper is bound to make enemies. The point I'm trying to make here is that nobody ever followed through and actually tried to kill P. J."

My fingers touched the plastic bag in my pocket, and I had an idea that I didn't want to say out loud, not yet anyway. I crossed over to my desk and opened the folder of stories I'd been working on for this week's paper. All were more or less finished. I then looked over the material submitted by our freelance writers and found it all to be well written. A third folder held reports of club meetings, submitted by a dozen Lickin Creek organizations, from Elks to Rotarians. I worked for about an hour cutting and reorganizing these articles.

While I was scratching out and moving words around, Cassie went through the week's photos and selected about six she thought would reproduce well.

I called a few advertisers and reminded them we needed copy immediately if they didn't want to advertise last week's sales. Then Cassie called some subscribers and pleaded with them to come back to the fold. She even offered them a special rate for renewing.

By noon we were both looking exhausted, but happy. I still had Letters to the Editor to go through, and we had twenty of our disgruntled subscribers back.

I dropped my pencils into the cup and turned off the computer. "Think I'll take a long lunch break," I said. "Be back in a couple of hours."

Cassie nodded. "Have a good one," she said.

"I will," I told her, and my fingers once again touched the plastic Baggie in my pocket.

First I drove to the college. The central lawn looked as if nothing awful had ever happened there. More than a dozen girls, in jeans and LCCFW sweatshirts, crossed it on their way to the gothic-style library. There was a new receptionist at the desk busily sorting mail, so I walked right past her as if I had every right to be in the building and went down the stairs to the basement.

Even I, a smidgeon taller than five feet, had to duck to avoid some of the overhead pipes. Last night's adventure had left me feeling extremely anxious about being alone, and I paused for a minute to listen for footsteps. But all I heard was the clanking of pipes.

The corridor was lit by only one hanging bulb, and the door to the storeroom at the end of the hall was in almost total darkness. My neck bristled, as if someone was watching me. How I wished I hadn't listened to the ghost stories about the hospital in the college basement. But even if there were such things as ghosts, these were nuns, I told myself. It stands to reason that good people would turn into good spirits.

I tried the key that hadn't unlocked Mack's door last night, and it turned easily. When the door swung open, I didn't go in. There was no need to. I relocked the door, pocketed the key ring, and skedaddled out of there faster than a ghost could say "boo." I now knew how Mack Macmillan had died.

As I drove across the mountain, I noticed that while many trees were now in full autumn color, a great many others had already dropped their leaves. Even some of the evergreen trees had shed their needles, and their twisted brown branches stretched toward the sky above as if longing for the warmth of the sun. At one bend, the view was so spectacular, I pulled over and stopped for a minute to enjoy it. Below me the little river danced over gray, moss-covered rocks before disappearing into a copse of trees. Beyond were green and golden fields dotted with dollhouse-like farmhouses, barns, and silos. Then came orchards of peach and apple trees, their branches bare and stark against the sky. And off in the far distance were the hazy lavender-blue outlines of the next range of mountains. Once I'd thought of Pennsylvania only in terms of big cities like Philadelphia and Pittsburgh or small, dingy mining towns. Cities and mining communities were part of Pennsylvania, that was true, but they were far away from lush, mountainous rural south-central Pennsylvania. Here was proof that not all of America had been turned into Anytown, Anywhere, U.S.A. Here, at least, America was still a land of amber waves of grain and purple mountain majesty.

As I drove past Dr. Washabaugh's office, I saw a few cars and trucks in the parking lot. More people picking up their medical records and hearing the latest gossip from Vesta, I was sure. If they watched the evening news last night, I was probably the subject of conversation. I kept going until I came to the top of the hill that overlooked my destination, Shoestring Hill Farm.

The drive down to the stone house seemed to take forever, perhaps because I had no desire to tackle the task that would face me when I reached the house. On either side of me, horses played behind white board fences. The fences, the barns, even the wood trim around the windows of the house, looked freshly painted. The woodpile near the house was neatly stacked. Charlotte Macmillan had prepared her farm for whatever winter brought.

I knocked on the front door, waited, knocked again,

then noticed the small doorbell on the door frame. A moment later, the door opened inward and a Plain woman in a lavender dress, wearing a white net bonnet, looked out at me.

"Yes?" Her tone wasn't very inviting.

"I've come to see Mrs. Macmillan."

"Is she expecting you?"

"Yes," I fibbed. Anything to get in.

She stepped to one side, and I walked past her into a large center hall.

"Name?"

"Tori Miracle."

"Mrs. Mack's with her personal trainer. She should be finished in about fifteen minutes. You'uns can wait in the living room." She led me through a curtained archway into a large, expensively decorated room. The furniture was all mahogany and walnut from the Federal period, and although I'm no expert, it all looked genuine to me. No reproductions allowed at Shoestring Hill.

"Can I get you'uns a cup of tea?"

"No, thank you."

"Then I'll get back to my chores. Have a seat."

Instead of sitting down, I moved around the room admiring the furniture and the artwork. The painting over the fireplace was of a King Charles spaniel. The two behind the sofa were primitives of a man and woman. I wondered if they were the ancestors of either Charlotte or Mack Macmillan. An arrangement of autumn leaves on top of the Steinway grand piano repeated the soft gold of the silk wallpaper and the rust and moss green of the upholstered furniture.

French doors at one end of the room were closed, and velvet drapes, as green as an evergreen forest, hid from view what was behind them. They opened quietly when I pulled on them, and I stepped through the doors into a cool study, lit by diffused sunlight streaming through sheer curtains at the far end of the room. A great mahogany partners desk was centered on the Oriental carpet. The telephone on the desk had a light on it, and next to it was a small machine with a typewriter keyboard.

One wall, from floor to ceiling, was covered with books. I took one from the shelf and saw it was a treatise on the Civil War. Glancing quickly at its neighbors, I saw that the war was the subject of all the books. They ranged from modern fiction like *Killer Angels* to old leather-bound volumes dating from the late nineteenth century. At first glance, it looked like a collection any university library would be proud to own.

On the wall opposite the bookshelves hung a copy of the same sepia photograph I'd seen at the college, depicting Macmillan dressed as a Union Army general, with one hand resting on a table and the other on the hilt of his sword. Below the photo, a row of glass cases stretched from one wall to the other. The items on display were similar to what I'd seen at the visitor center at the Gettysburg National Park. Just about anything from the Civil War era was represented, from old canteens to lead bullets. One case was full of daguerreotypes. Another held musical instruments: drums, bugles, even harmonicas.

So involved was I with looking at the antiques that I jumped when Charlotte appeared by my side and said, "I'm glad to see you survived last night's ordeal."

"Did you watch it on TV?"

She shook her head. "I've been out of town for a few days, visiting a friend's horse farm in North Carolina. Lela, my housekeeper, told me about it when I returned this morning. It must have been a terrifying experience." She gestured graciously at the couch and urged me to have a seat. Almost immediately, Lela appeared with a tea tray. Charlotte filled two bone china teacups and asked me if I preferred milk or lemon.

"Milk, please. And two sugars."

With tiny silver sugar tongs, she dropped two cubes of sugar into one cup and passed it to me. It was a gracious ritual I had often watched my mother perform for her guests at the embassy. Charlotte sat back and looked at me over the brim of her cup. I wished I could see through the mask, for just a minute, to read on her face what must be running through her mind.

The telephone rang and flashed before we had a chance to talk. Charlotte excused herself and crossed over to the partners desk. After a few words about the sudden change in weather and assurances that she was just fine, she said, "I'm sorry. The stable will be closed Saturday. I'm going to a wedding."

When she returned to her seat, I asked, "That light on the phone. I presume that was for your husband?"

"Yes, of course."

"I heard he was deaf—I mean hearing impaired. How could he take phone calls when he couldn't hear?"

"There's a special operator who types the message as it's relayed to her. After it came up on the screen, Mack would type his response."

"Did you learn sign language to communicate with him?"

Charlotte laughed. "Tori, signing was my first language. My mother was hearing impaired, deaf as the proverbial post if you prefer. As an adult, when I wasn't working with horses, I taught signing. That's where I met my husband. He had lost his hearing suddenly from a viral infection, and he signed up for my class. We fell in love and were married shortly after. I interpreted for him in Congress until he retired. Still do, I mean I still did—"

"I can see how he depended on you, but how did he manage when you weren't around? I met him for the first time at the college and you weren't with him then."

"Mack could read lips if people spoke slowly and looked directly at him. And he often did things alone. I couldn't follow him around twenty-four hours a day."

"That explains why he thought my name was Dorie when we were introduced."

She nodded. "Right." Her eyes narrowed. "I'm delighted to see you, Tori, but I'm wondering why you're here."

My shaking hand sloshed tea into the saucer. I put the cup on the table in front of me and swallowed hard. "I have something to tell you about your husband's death."

"Yes?"

Damn that mask. I couldn't tell what her reaction was. "I have good reason to believe his death was not an accident."

"Do you mean you think Woody Woodruff murdered him?" Her voice was flat and unemotional, but I could imagine the turmoil going through her mind.

I shook my head. "No. I think your husband died by his own hand."

"I don't think I understand what you're getting at."

This was going to be difficult. I took a sip of my now-lukewarmtea. "Your husband committed suicide, Mrs. Macmillan."

"That's preposterous! How can you sit here in my living room and say such a dreadful thing?" I expected her to leap to her feet, call her housekeeper, and have me bodily thrown from the house, but instead she stayed in her chair and glared at me through her mask. "Tell me what gave you this crazy idea."

"I heard he took it very hard when he was told he had cancer."

"How do you know that?"

"I'm not free to say."

"Dr. Washabaugh's nurse, Vesta Pennsinger, told you, didn't she? That woman ought to mind her own damn business."

"I agree with you on that."

"Let me get this straight, Tori. You are telling me that my husband planned his own death because he was dying of cancer?"

"I also learned that this farm was up for sale until shortly after his death, when you took it off the market."

"That's true. Mack and I had decided to move to Florida for his arthritis. After he died, there was no need to move, so I—"

"It wasn't up for sale because you *wanted* to move. It was for sale because Mack made a lot of stupid investments using the equity he had in the farm for collateral. He had no choice but to sell it to pay off his creditors." Charlotte burst into tears, stopping my discourse.

"I'm right, aren't I?"

"Is this general knowledge?" she asked between sniffles.

I nodded. "I'm afraid so. You know how the Grapevine works."

"So what does anything you've said have to do with Mack's death?"

"I think what happened was your husband wanted to commit suicide instead of dying slowly and painfully from cancer. But he knew you'd be saddled with his debts if he did, so he looked for a way to make his death look accidental. The mock execution came up at just the right time."

"But a firing squad? No one would want to die in front of a firing squad."

"He would if he were a Civil War buff like your husband. When he learned of the execution plans, it must have seemed like the perfect opportunity to stage his own 'accidental' death. As I see it, he first browbeat Janet Margolies into letting him play the victim, even though he was much too old for the part. He made sure he was present when the guns were loaded. He switched keys with Janet while she was in the rest room. And later that night, he returned and replaced the foam blanks with lead bullets from his collection."

"You have no way of really knowing he did this . . . this dreadful thing to himself."

"But I do, Charlotte. In your husband's desk at the college, I found proof that he was the one who loaded the guns with live ammunition. In his top desk drawer, I found the ammunition he took from the guns and also the missing storeroom key. He'd probably planned to switch the keys back again but never found an opportunity to do so."

Charlotte wiped her eyes, and I saw that the mask she wore was dark with tears. I hated myself for what I was going to say next.

"Charlotte, I think you knew what he was planning to do. That's why you were out of town that weekend, wasn't it."

"No . . . no . . . no," she moaned.

"If you did know, then you'll be charged as an accessory." I wasn't sure what the crime was, but I think there must be one to cover insurance frauds. "I'm turning the Wonder Wads and the key over to the police. They'll be sure to ask questions. I hope you can answer them."

Charlotte stood, looming over me. I suddenly realized how muscular she looked, how strong she probably was from tending to her horses. She stood there a minute as if undecided about what to do, then sighed and said, "I have his suicide note, Tori. I'll get it for you."

She pressed a hidden button on the bookcase wall and one section of shelves opened like a door to reveal a six-foot-high safe door. She spun the combination lock several times and pushed down on the lever, and the door swung outward with a groan. I got up with the intention of peeking into the safe, but she blocked the entrance. "Nobody goes in here but me," she said, her voice as cold and brittle as ice cubes.

I stepped back a few inches to show her I had no intention of barging into her safe. She went inside, and as her back was to me, I stood on my tiptoes and tried to get a look inside. The safe was actually a room about the size of my apartment in New York, with rows of shelves, much like the bookcases, stacked high with boxes.

Charlotte emerged, closed the safe, and spun the lock. In one hand she held a thin brown manila envelope. "Take it," she said. "It's Mack's last message to me."

I opened the envelope, which was not sealed, and pulled out a piece of paper covered with handwriting.

"Go ahead and read it."

"*Dearest Charlotte,*" I read. "Are you sure you want me to continue?"

I took her silence to mean yes.

As you know, my financial situation has deteriorated badly. I trusted people who were not trustworthy, and I made some unwise investments. Unfortunately, I used our farm, the farm you love so much, as collateral, and the only way to settle my debts was to sell the farm and pay off my creditors. When I learned I had inoperable cancer and my days were limited, I worried about you, my dearest wife. You would lose first the home you have cherished, then have to face losing me from cancer.

When I heard about the plans for the mock execution, it came to me that I could leave this world on my own terms and you could still have the property. I cajoled Janet Margolies into letting me be the intended victim. Because I had watched Woody Woodruff's men put on other exhibitions, I knew he loaded the guns in advance, and I asked to be there when that was done. When we were finished, I followed Janet up to her office and switched one of my office keys for her storeroom key. If she hadn't gone upstairs on her own. I would have asked her to accompany me on some pretext. I knew she couldn't stay away from the bathroom for more than a few minutes, and that would give me time to exchange keys.

I loaded the guns with lead from my own collection. Before I locked the storeroom. I took one last look at the guns—it was my opportunity to change my mind—and I decided then to go on with my plan.

I stopped reading and said, "I wonder why he didn't get rid of the ammunition he took from the guns."

"He probably meant to, then ran out of time. Mack was always late."

"He *was* late the day of the shooting, I remember." I read on.

> *I want you to put this letter in our safe, my dear, and save it if there is ever any suspicion cast on you. If that is the case, bring this out, to prove you had no knowledge of my actions in advance. I'm afraid if that happens, you will lose the insurance money, but my Civil War collection is extremely valuable, and I have left it to you in my will to dispose of as you see fit.*

I looked up from the letter and asked, "Where is his will, Charlotte?"

"It's on file at Buchanan McCleary's office. He's our attorney."

I read the last line. *"God bless you and keep you safe, Your loving husband, Mack."*

"I had no idea he'd planned this awful thing," she said. "I'd never have left town for the weekend if I'd had any inkling of it. Mack was my whole life, Tori." She wiped her eyes with a Kleenex. "Now you know the whole sordid story, and Mack's carefully planned suicide was a wasted effort."

"I'm so sorry," I said.

"I guess you'll have to turn the letter over to the police, won't you?" Her blue eyes looked earnestly at me, and I sensed she hoped I'd be merciful and give the letter back.

"I'm so sorry," I repeated.

Her shoulders dropped. "I understand. It was wrong of me to have hidden it, but I always did exactly what Mack told me to do." She buried her face in her hands as her body shook.

I let myself out, taking the letter with me.

CHAPTER 18

BACK IN LICKIN CREEK, I DROVE IMMEDIATELY TO Hoopengartner's Garage, where I found Luscious in the tiny police office in the back of the station. He'd been drinking, I was sure. I smelled vodka, the daytime drink of choice for alcoholics who mistakenly believe it has no odor. But it did have an odor, one I was all too familiar with, having smelled it on my mother's breath for many years.

"What's up," he said, lurching to his feet. I feared he'd topple over if he tried standing for long, so I quickly sat down on the solitary guest chair and he followed suit with a relieved look on his face.

"This is what's up, Luscious." I positioned the letter on his desk so he could read it. He frowned, pulled back a little, squinted, then hunched forward. "I'll read it to you," I said, retrieving the letter. "It's Mack Macmillan's suicide note."

"Wow!" Luscious cocked his head, reminding me of a chicken. "Mack committed suicide?"

"Yes, Luscious." I read the letter to him.

"Wow, Tori. That sounds like he was trying to con his insurance company."

"Exactly, Luscious. And I have the foam wads and the keys he mentioned in the letter to back it up."

Luscious shook his head sorrowfully. "Mack Macmillan. I just can't believe it."

"He had cancer. Guess he didn't want to die that way."

"Mack Macmillan. Who would have thought it?"

I interrupted his head shaking and pondering to say, "Luscious, you'll have to call his insurance company, get someone started on this. They'll have to come to some agreement with Mrs. Macmillan to get the money back."

"My oh my oh my! Mack Macmillan. I can't believe it! He went to school with my pap-pap. Pap-pap's what we always called my grandfather," he explained. "Guess this lets Woody Woodruff off the hook. I'll tell the D.A. to drop charges against him."

I left the letter and other items with him, hoping he wouldn't lose them. I was depressed about Charlotte's plight. She'd gone from beloved wife to wealthy widow to impoverished widow in a very short time. She was extremely popular throughout the tri-county area, and I knew sympathy would be on her side. Once again, I would be Tori Miracle, the troublemaker from New York.

I drove back to Moon Lake with my brain spinning, coming up with all kinds of ridiculous ideas, like organizing a fund-raiser for Charlotte, having a bake sale, or whatever it is they do here in Lickin Creek to take care of their own.

Uriah's Heap, the only taxi in Lickin Creek, was parked in the driveway. There were two suitcases sitting by the back door. Could Ethelind really be leaving? It was too much to hope for, but when I opened the door, there she was, pacing the kitchen, purse in hand, fleece-lined raincoat draped over her shoulders. "Tori, am I glad to see you. I didn't want to leave without saying good-bye."

"You're actually leaving?"

"Yes, I just had a call. The *QE II* finally has an empty cabin. I'm flying to New York this afternoon and sailing in the morning."

"I'll miss you." And oddly enough, I realized I would.

She gave me a boozy kiss on the forehead. "You take good care of my house—and yourself, luv."

I waved until the Heap was out of sight, then went back inside and closed the door behind me. This time, I made sure it was locked. I'd never spent a night alone in a house as big as this, and I felt rather nervous, especially after the things that had happened to me in the past week.

I poured the contents of a can of chili into a bowl, heated it in the microwave, and sat down at the kitchen table. Fred and Noel sat quietly by their own dishes, not eating, as if they, too, suddenly felt deserted. I ate half the chili, washed it down with a Diet Coke, had a Snickers bar for dessert, then rinsed my dish. My meal, including preparation time, had taken only five minutes.

The ringing of the telephone echoed throughout the empty mansion. My former neighbor and good friend in New York, the almost-world-famous actor/Italian waiter, had warned me many times never pick up on the first ring—it makes you appear desperate. I ignored his advice and grabbed the receiver, cutting the second ring off before it had a chance to get up to speed.

"Tori, is that you?"

"Garnet!" Joy welled up inside me.

"Tori, are you all right? I've been so worried, ever since I heard about—"

"How did you hear?" I interrupted.

"Aunt Gladys called."

"I should have known. I'm really okay. My arms are a bit sore from all that hanging, but at least I'm not lying flat as a pancake in the LCCFW's marble halls."

"Hanging? What are you talking about?"

"I fell off the staircase at the college. Isn't that what you called about?"

He groaned. "Aunt Gladys told me you'd been in a fire. She never mentioned the other thing."

"Ooops!"

"Tori, don't try to be funny. I've only been gone a short while and you've had two disasters. Why can't you take better care of yourself?"

"There's no need to worry. Did your aunt Gladys tell you Professor Nakamura was shot?"

"No! Is he all right?"

"Last I heard, he was recovering nicely. Someone mistook him for a deer."

"Dare I ask what else is new?"

I told him the whole story about Mack's death being a suicide. He waited until I was finished, then said, "You did a good job getting to the bottom of it, Tori. I couldn't have done better myself."

I felt my cheeks flush with pleasure.

"But please, I repeat, please do not undertake any more investigations while I'm gone. No matter how incompetent you think Luscious is, he *is* the police chief. And I don't want anything to happen to you. You are much too precious to me. I've got to go now. Got tickets to see *Manon Lescault* tonight at the Kennedy Center. I'll call you on Sunday as we planned."

There was a click, followed by the buzz of an empty

phone line. I hadn't asked him how his Spanish lessons were going. Or if he had a comfortable bed, like the one he slept in at home, the bed he'd been born in. Or if he was eating properly. I hadn't told him about poor Dr. Washabaugh, or my biopsy either. I'd be better prepared on Sunday, even if it meant making a list of everything I wanted to talk about and keeping it by the telephone. While I was digging in Ethelind's junk drawer for a notepad, it occurred to me that I wasn't the only one who hadn't asked questions. Garnet hadn't asked me about the results of my biopsy.

I ate a Snickers bar for dessert, then realized I'd already done that. These long, quiet evenings were going to be perfect for finishing my book. I could set my laptop up on the kitchen table and work all night if I wanted to. This was going to be a great winter, I just knew it.

So why didn't I feel like setting it up now and getting started? There was something preying on my mind, and I decided I had to put it to rest before I could concentrate on my work.

"I'll see you guys later," I told the cats. They were still sitting by their bowls, side by side, as if waiting for something good to happen. "I'll bring you a special treat. Maybe a can of tuna." Their ears perked up. They always recognized the word *tuna*.

My little car protested, but eventually started, and I drove through the quiet streets of Lickin Creek. Although only a little past eight, the few stores that remained downtown were closed. The trees that lined the streets had already lost their leaves, and their stark branches sparkled with tiny white lights that looked like Christmas to me, but stayed up all year round. The fountain was illuminated by several spotlights, and I was glad to see someone had placed carved jack-o'-lanterns around its base between the pots of chrysanthemums. At night, downtown was as magical as the Emerald City of Oz. The mood was broken when a teenager in a souped-up car roared past, and a beer can flew out of the right rear window. I quickly passed through town and out of it, and was soon on one of the farm roads that wound its way through the peaceful countryside. The peaceful and dark countryside. I was alone in more ways than one.

Somehow, I missed the peach stand and drove nearly to West Mountain before I realized how far I'd come and had to turn around. I drove more slowly on the country lane until I found the mailbox that said Hostettler farm.

Flickering lights in the lower windows of the farmhouse indicated the oil lamps were lit. I couldn't imagine why people would chose to live in such a primitive way when there were so many modern conveniences available, but I had to admire the Amish for the way they held on to their beliefs in the face of the encroaching American culture.

The narrow road down the hill, which had been washed away the last time I was here, had been filled in with gravel, and I drove right down to the barn. I parked close to the building, then waited a moment to steel my nerves. Tonight I was going to tell Darious there was absolutely nothing between us, not now, and not in the future. Never ever. Hearing Garnet's voice on the telephone tonight had reinforced my feelings for him. I didn't need any other man in my life. Not now, not in the future. Not ever.

I was surprised to find the door to the barn slightly ajar. The other two times I'd been here, Darious had kept it locked, a precaution I could understand since I now knew how valuable carousel animals were. I pulled it open wider and listened to the carousel organ playing "In the Good Old Summertime." I smiled, as I could imagine Darious riding the newly repaired jumper on his carousel. Perhaps, after I talked to him, he'd let me take one last ride. There were no lights on in the little anteroom, so I crossed it slowly and carefully, until my foot bumped against a stone step.

After climbing the short flight of steps, I pushed open the door. The carousel music was much louder than it had been on my other two visits. Even though I called Darious's name, there was no way he'd hear me over the din. I slipped inside. The barn, as usual, was unlighted, except for the spinning carousel. Before me was a blur of lights, bouncing from the sparkling jewels on the animals and the gilt trim and mirrors of the carousel itself. I leaned against the wall for a moment to regain my equilibrium, for the sight and sound were overwhelming.

Regaining my balance, I walked slowly toward the merry-go-round, savoring the beauty of the moment, the lights, the colors, and the music. The golden chariot passed by me before it registered on me that someone was sitting in it. Darious, of course. Apollo the sun god riding his chosen chariot. I smiled and waited for it to come around again.

This time, I saw Darious was indeed in the chariot, but although I waved and tried to catch his attention, he paid me no attention as he spun past.

There was something about the way he looked that triggered a frisson of fear in me. The way he was slumped to one side, the way his head hung, the way he ignored me. Something was wrong.

"If there's one thing I hate, it's being ignored," I

muttered. "Here goes." I jumped onto the moving platform and caught hold of the head of a tiger to keep from falling off. "Steady, Tori," I admonished myself. After a moment I got my sea legs, or carousel legs, as I guessed they should be called, and started to work my way toward the chariot, walking against the counterclockwise direction of the machine.

I called his name but Darious didn't look up. There was a stain on his shirt. Like a salmon swimming upstream against the current, I moved slowly past the jumping horses that stood between me and the chariot, drawing closer and closer to Darious, who still seemed not to notice me. His eyes were open, yet not seeing. Not seeing, because . . . oh God . . . because his throat was slashed from side to side. Blood was everywhere. On the chariot, on his clothes, splattered on the horse in front of him.

I grasped the side rail of the chariot and found it sticky. Reluctantly, I touched his wrist with two fingers. It was still warm, but there was no pulse. Darious was dead. Beautiful, mysterious Darious. Apollo had returned home to Mount Parnassus.

Tears burned my eyes as bile rose in my throat, and the carousel continued to spin and the music continued to play. This had to be some sort of bizarre nightmare, I told myself. This is too surreal to actually be happening. I blinked and tried to will myself awake, but when I opened my eyes, Darious's body was a gruesome reminder that this moment was all too real.

I had to get away. I leaped free of the carousel and landed painfully on my knees. I rushed to the door with only one thing on my mind, getting away from the awful thing behind me.

I was terrified. What if the murderer was in here with me? Frightened half to death, I pushed on the door. It didn't move. I pushed, I pulled, I jiggled the latch, I even kicked it, but nothing budged. I was locked in. The windows were boarded up. There was no way out.

Darious's workshop. Maybe there was a way out through it. With my back to the barn wall, I cautiously worked my way toward that part of the barn. The carousel music was unbearably loud. The monster who'd cut Darious's throat could be right behind me, and I'd never hear it.

At last, I came to the workshop door. A frightened glance around convinced me that no one was close, and I took a deep breath and pulled on the door. It, too, was locked. I dropped to the floor, drew my knees to my chest, and covered my face with my arms. I wanted to cry but didn't dare. The monster lurking in the dark might hear me.

This was the moment when the cavalry should crest the hill or a knight in shining armor should ride in on a white horse to rescue me. But I knew I'd seen too many movies, read too many books, and there was no one coming to save me. No one even knew where I was. My life was in my hands and my hands only.

I had to find a way out. There must be another entrance. I tried to remember what the barn looked like from outside. Of course! There were huge double doors at one end, large enough to drive a tractor through. With any luck, they wouldn't be locked. Staying close to the wall, I inched my way across the barn until I reached the opposite end of the building. My fingers touched a metal hinge and I knew I'd reached the doors. Ignoring the danger that hid in the darkness, I turned around, found the latch, released it, and shoved. It, too, was locked. I collapsed on the floor, too terrified even to cry.

Windows. There were windows. All boarded up, but

maybe I could pry some boards loose. Not even thinking about the danger, I ran across the barn to where I
knew there was a window. Grabbing hold of a plank, I
tugged on it with all my might, but it was firmly fixed to
the window frame. If I had a crowbar or some kind of
tool, I might be able to pry it off, but everything was
locked away in Darious's workshop.

I closed my eyes and tried to envision the barn from
the outside, again. There were shuttered windows on
the levels above this floor. If I could find the stairs,
perhaps I could break through the shutters. By now, my
eyes were thoroughly accustomed to the dim barn interior lit by the flashing lights of the carousel. And I saw
no one. I remembered a ladder, next to the workshop
door, which led to a dark hole in the ceiling. Taking a
chance, I ran across the barn. And still, the monster
didn't come.

The ladder looked to be about one hundred feet
high, and the opening at the top of it was as black as a
moonless night. I clenched my teeth, took a deep
breath, and started to climb. It took forever, and I had
nearly reached the hole when I heard a sound coming
from above. A faint, rustling noise, as if someone who
was waiting there for me had changed position.

It took me two seconds to slide back down the ladder. I was attempting to pull the ladder out of the hole
when I heard *Meow*. I looked toward the sound and
saw two glowing cat's eyes looking back at me.

Not a monster. Just a cat. Now I realized the murderer must have slipped out and locked the door behind
him as I checked Darious for signs of life. I was still
trapped inside, but I was alone, and I was going to get
out if I had to tear the barn apart board by board.

Rather than do that, I moved the ladder back to the
opening, and when it was firmly in place, gritted my

teeth and climbed it. The cat was sitting on a cardboard box watching me when I pulled myself onto the floor. "Hi, kitty," I said, cheerfully. "Sorry to bother you."

With a twitch of its tail, it let me know it didn't mind. The shuttered windows at this level were firmly closed, but I recalled seeing a double set of doors right under the peaked roof of the barn. There would have been no need to lock something that high up. I found a rickety flight of stairs with no railing, and climbed it on my hands and knees.

My luck had returned. When I pushed on one of the doors, it swung open so easily, I had to grab the door-jamb to keep from tumbling out. My head reeled as I looked down. Even a person who didn't have acrophobia would get dizzy up here, and I'd had a fear of heights ever since I could remember.

I tried to concentrate on looking at the horizon. The barn was facing east, and the moon was already over the mountaintops. From my vantage point I saw the farmhouse, and I screamed for help as loudly as I could. Nothing happened so I took a deep breath and yelled the word every farmer fears, "Fire!"

The farmhouse door burst open, and two figures came running out.

"Help!" I cried. "Please help me."

The couple ran down the hill to the barn and looked up at me in wonderment.

"I'm locked in," I called. "Do you have a key?"

"No key," the man called back.

"Then please call the police. And tell them there's a dead man in here."

He turned his back to me and sprinted up the hill. Right past his house. I wondered why, until I remembered the Amish don't have phones. I hoped he didn't have far to go.

He returned in about ten minutes. "They're coming," he yelled. "You'uns okay in there?"

"I'm all right. Thanks."

By the time I'd maneuvered down the scary stairs and the even more scary ladder, I heard a siren. Trying not to look at Darious, I waited, and after a short while someone began to attack the barn door. The wood splintered as an ax broke through, and I saw a face peer through the opening. It might not have been the cavalry, and it certainly wasn't a knight in shining armor, but right then Luscious Miller looked better than anyone I could have imagined coming to rescue me.

He enlarged the hole he'd made and stepped through. "Wow," was all he said as he gazed in astonishment at the whirling carousel. A smile lit his face, and I knew he was experiencing the childlike wonder of it all. But the smile faded when he saw the body in the chariot.

"How do you stop it?" he asked.

"There's a switch inside the workroom, but it's locked."

Luscious picked up his ax and let me lead him to the workshop door. After a few minutes of being hacked, the door disintegrated. "Come on," he said. "Show me how to turn it off."

I pointed to the lever halfway up the wall. When he pulled down on it, the music stopped. I'd nearly forgotten how blissful silence could be, after listening to "In the Good Old Summertime" for more than an hour. I'd probably hear it in my dreams for years to come.

While I waited, Luscious examined Darious's body. I looked around for something to sit on and found several piles of cardboard boxes in one corner that looked fairly strong. I was resting on top of one of the piles when Luscious returned, looking shaken and pale. "I gotta call the coroner."

He pulled out his cell phone and made the call. Then he asked me to tell him why I was in an Amish barn on the edge of town with a dead body riding a carousel.

"Have a seat," I said, and waited until he sat on another pile of boxes. Then I told him everything that had happened from the time I arrived and discovered the body until I spotted the farmer and called for help. Luscious didn't interrupt, except to go *tsst, tsst* from time to time.

"But why did you come here in the first place, Tori? How well did you know this Darious guy?"

I had hoped I wouldn't have to explain why I was there. It would probably be relayed to Garnet before I got home that I'd had an assignation with a good-looking guy, who just happened to have his throat cut before I arrived.

More *tsst, tsst*s from Luscious accompanied my explanation of how I had first met Darious. He was hissing like a snake by the time I finished telling him I'd only come to the barn to tell Darious I wasn't interested in him.

"Seems kinda funny to me you had to come out here to tell him you wasn't gonna see him no more. Couldn't you have done it by phone?"

"He didn't have one." But I wouldn't have done it by phone, even if Darious had had one. Memories of when my ex-fiancé, Steve, called to tell me he was going to marry someone else still hurt. It was the coward's way to break someone's heart, and I couldn't turn around and do it to another person.

He took his policeman's hat off and smoothed his three strands of pale blond hair over his bald spot. "Still seems kinda peculiar."

To hide my irritation and embarrassment, I stood up and turned away from him. In doing so, I knocked over the box that topped off the pile I'd been using as a seat, and some newspaper-wrapped articles tumbled onto the wooden floor. A few items came unwrapped, and I stared aghast at them. Although I'd only seen the items once before, I recognized them immediately for their uniqueness. Then, they'd been in a glass display case in the Lickin Creek Public Library. Now, scattered about on the rough wooden floor were some of Gerald Manley's gutta-percha collectibles that had been stolen from the library last Sunday night.

Luscious recognized the collection almost as quickly as I did. "Holy cow," he said. "So that's where them things went to."

"The other boxes, Luscious. We'd better see what else is here."

We opened one box after another, and in one I found the hexagonal bracelet with seed pearls I'd last seen on Maggie's wrist at the library. And there were other things, too, that I didn't find very interesting but that were valuable Civil War collectibles, according to Luscious. Whether or not they had also been stolen, we didn't know. But when we opened the box of antique fire chief's trumpets that both of us knew had been stolen from the volunteer firemen's company museum, we knew for sure that Darious had been a thief.

"There are more boxes on the upper levels," I said. Without even looking into them, I was sure we'd find the antiques stolen from the Gettysburg collection. Anger surged through every inch of my body. Anger with Darious for deceiving me into thinking he was nothing more than a harmless carousel lover. And anger with myself for being so easily deceived. I knew carousels cost a small fortune. Darious had no visible means of support. I should have realized right away something wasn't right.

Henry Hoopengartner, the coroner, arrived and showed some mild interest in what we'd discovered. "Looks like we caught ourselves a rat," he remarked.

"We didn't catch anybody, Henry," I retorted. "The man is dead."

"I can see that," he said. "Question is how?"

"Why don't you examine the body and find out?" I snapped.

"Good idea. Wish I'd thought of that." He grinned and slowly moved toward the still carousel.

I stayed behind while he took his camera over to the carousel and snapped flash pictures from different angles. "Okay," he announced. "I'm ready to examine him. Luscious, can you give me a hand?"

I could sense Luscious's reluctance, but he knew his job and was up to it. Choosing not to observe the coroner at work, I concentrated on picking up the scattered gutta-percha jewelry and daguerreotype cases and rewrapping them in the crumpled newspaper pages, torn from the *Chronicle*. At least one of our subscribers had recycled!

Having finished my tidying up, I peeked out to see what was happening and wished I hadn't. I sat down on the high stool and surveyed the workroom. Darious and I had had one thing in common: We both survived on junk food. The worktable was covered with the remnants of former meals: two pizza boxes, a bakery box, half a dozen Chinese food carry-out containers, and many soda cans, as well as pieces of the carousel in various stages of repair. A horse's jeweled bridle lay waiting for Darious's hand to restore it to glory. Next to it was the picture of me from the *Chronicle* that Darious had framed, and I decided to take it with me. I wasn't really removing evidence, I told myself, because it didn't have anything to do with the crime. I slipped the cardboard back off the frame, and as it came out, so did a picture. Only it wasn't of me; it was a snapshot of Gloria Zimmerman, the animal control officer who lived with Moonbeam Nakamura. And it was signed LOVE ALWAYS, GLORIA. I folded it along with my picture and stuck both of them in my pocket. I had some questions to ask Gloria the next time I saw her.

Absentmindedly, I pushed aside the overflowing ashtray that offended my senses of sight and smell, and as I glanced at it, I realized where I'd seen similar cigarette butts recently. On the floor of Ethelind's parlor, where they had ignited a pile of my clothing that should not have been there. I hadn't thought much about it at the time of the fire, but now I recalled that Ethelind smoked only ugly brown cigarettes that resembled miniature cigars, not common American filter cigarettes like these.

I searched the workroom like a crazy woman, looking for flammable liquids, and of course I found many. I eliminated turpentine as being too smelly. Ditto lighter fluid, gasoline, and kerosene. The fire chief would have identified any of them immediately. Finally, I came upon a large drum containing seventy percent solution hydrogen peroxide, with a warning on the label saying it was an oxidizer, which would initiate combustion in other materials by causing fire through release of oxygen. I was afraid to open it, but as far as I knew, peroxide had no recognizable odor.

Darious was not only a common thief—there was also the strong possibility he had tried to murder me!

I frantically pulled open drawers, dumping contents of the desk and file cabinets on the floor. I found what I was looking for jammed into a box on a shelf, hidden behind a carved rooster head. A long blue skirt, blouse, white apron, and a white cornette, its angel-like wings crushed and sagging. Now I was sure Darious had not only set fire to my house, he'd also shoved me over the bannister at the college. Only by dumb luck had I survived either attempt to kill me.

But why? Why me? What had I ever done to him? The questions spun through my head, but the answers did not come.

CHAPTER 19

CASSIE HAD RUSHED OVER TO BE WITH ME AFTER I called her from the mansion. She intercepted the visitors who arrived in a constant stream bearing offerings of casseroles and cakes. In Lickin Creek, misery was a magnet, pulling people I'd never seen before to my back door.

"Let's put it on the dining room table," she suggested, surveying the quantities of food that covered the kitchen counter. "That way you can serve a buffet lunch."

"To whom?" I asked, following behind her with my arms laden down with Pyrex dishes. "Just who do you think is going to be here for lunch?"

"You never know," she said cryptically, making a small pile of paper plates near the edge of the table.

The first to arrive was Luscious Miller, accompanied by a stranger, a small man in an ill-fitting gray suit who reminded me of a mourning dove—no chin, poufy chest, and scrawny legs.

"Like you to meet John Strainge," Luscious said once they were inside.

"That's spelled S-T-R-A-I-N-G-E," the man said as he shook my hand.

"Strange spelling," I said. He didn't smile. I guess he'd heard that one before.

Before Luscious could tell me why the strange Strainge man was there, the door swung open and Henry Hoopengartner entered.

"Please come in," I said.

"I already am in," Henry said, not getting it. Cassie wiped the smile from her lips and removed a dish of baked lasagna from the oven.

"Everything's ready," she announced.

"Would you like to have lunch?" I asked the three men.

Of course they would. In fact, they followed Cassie like the children of Hamelin following the Pied Piper.

As the men loaded their plates with food, I heard knocking at the back door. "That would be Chief Yoder," Luscious explained. "I asked him to drop by."

The fire chief was already inside by the time I reached the kitchen. And, "Yes, I would like a bite to eat, thank you."

The six of us sat down in Ethelind's large front parlor, the one that had been recently refurbished due to fire. Henry and Mr. Strainge sat on the modern couch that Ethelind had unwillingly bought to replace the charred Empire sofa. It was much nicer to lie on but not nearly as elegant-looking. Cassie and I sat side by side on the piano bench, while Luscious and the fire chief took the carved rosewood chairs that I knew from experience were even more uncomfortable than they looked.

I picked at my food and waited for the men to tell me why they were there. Surely they hadn't just dropped in for lunch! They appeared to be in no hurry as they all went back for second helpings.

After a long, quiet interval, where the only sounds to

be heard were the sounds of chewing, lip smacking, and an occasional dainty belch, Cassie asked if anyone would like to have dessert.

"What do ya got?" Chief Yoder asked.

"Pumpkin, apple, shoofly and Montgomery pie, molasses cake, cornstarch cake, cracker pudding, cherry fritters, and sticky buns. Shall I continue?"

"No sticky buns for me," Henry Hoopengartner said with a shudder. "That's what that poor bastard was eating when his throat was cut."

Luscious shook his head solemnly. "Just imagine, you're sitting there, quietly minding your own business, when zap . . ."

"Looks like he tried to grab the guy behind him. All he managed to do was yank out a big hunk of his own hair. It was right there in his hand." Henry smiled at me as if talking about a man's death throes was normal at mealtime.

"Please!" I screamed. "I don't want to hear this."

"Sorry," the two men said in unison.

"Why don't you tell me who Mr. Strainge is, and what he's doing here today," I said.

Luscious nodded. "Okay. But first, let me explain how he got here."

"Whenever you're ready," I said.

"After I got back to the office, I got to thinking that a working merry-go-round was a real peculiar thing to find in a barn. And because all them things in the boxes was stolen, I thought maybe the merry-go-round was stolen, too. So I called my nephew Sam and asked him to check the Internet and see if he could find something out."

"And did he?" I asked.

"Sure did. Didn't take him long, either, so his

mother made him go back to middle school for the afternoon."

"So what did this sixth- or seventh-grade genius determine?" I'd get the story out of him even if I had to pull it out word by word.

"This." Luscious handed me a black-and-white laser printout. "$10,000 REWARD," I read, "for information leading to the return of this carousel." Below the message was a photo of Darious's carousel, only it had been taken many years ago, for it was out-of-doors, under a pavilion. Happy-looking children straddled most of the animals.

"It looked like the same merry-go-round to me," Luscious said.

"It is, I'm sure of it. I recognize my favorite animal, the hippocampus."

"So I called the number. Turned out to be this gentleman, Mr. Strainge."

Mr. Strainge took up the narrative. "When I got Chief Miller's call, I told the wife I was going straight up to Lickin Creek to check it out for myself. It's my carousel. No doubt about it."

"You're sure of that?" I wanted to doubt him, but in my heart I knew he was right.

"It was made by the Dentzel factory in 1920 for my pap-pap's amusement park down in Boiling Springs. It ran there until my father closed the park in 1950. He had the carousel took apart and stored it in the barn on his farm in Dillsburg. It's my farm now, since he passed."

"So how do you think it got to Lickin Creek?" Cassie asked.

"I'm getting to that," Mr. Strainge said, frowning slightly. "Three summers ago a young guy came by, driving an old pickup truck, and offered to do farm work for nothing if we'd give him a place to stay. I told him he could sleep in the barn if he liked, and he said that would suit him just fine. He'd been injured during Desert Storm, he said, and all that Agent Orange Juice he drank there gave him Gulf War syndrome. Said the docs at the veterans' hospital told him fresh air was the only cure."

Cassie threw an amused look my way. I pretended I didn't notice.

"Me and the wife both got jobs down in Harrisburg because farming don't pay enough to leave us stay home, so we was glad to have the help. Especially when it didn't cost us nothing except for his meals. Round about the end of that September, he just up and disappeared one day. I didn't mind too much because most of the hard work was done.

"In fact, I never gave him another thought till a few months later. That's when a couple of men showed up at the door with a magazine—I think it was called *American Carousel*—something like that. They showed me an article about collecting carousel horses, and I'll be darned if there wasn't a picture of my pap-pap's carousel right there in the magazine.

"I told them it was stored in my barn, and they got all excited and said they'd be willing to pay me a million dollars if the animals was in restorable condition. A million dollars! The wife near burst with excitement. We went right down to the barn, and guess what . . ."

"The carousel was gone," I said.

"Yep. Every last bit of it. All I could think of was that young guy spent all summer hauling it away while me and the wife was at work. He must have seen the article about it, too, and tracked it down just like the collectors, only he got to me before they did. The buyers was real disappointed, and they suggested I offer a reward. I thought ten thou was too much, but they reminded me I'd get a million from them when I got it back. They took care of putting ads in the carousel magazine and on the computer. It's been so long without any word that I darn near forgot about it. That is, till Chief Miller called this morning."

"The young man you think took it—do you remember his name?"

"Oh yeah, it was Darren Detweiler. I thought he was related to the Detweilers over in Littlestown. He never said he weren't. Good-looking man the wife said often enough. If you like that type."

Yes, I wanted to say, *I liked that type.*

"I got a picture of him." He pulled an envelope out of the inside pocket of his suit jacket and handed it to me. "I was snapping a picture of the wife with my new John Deere, and it turned out he was in the background painting the house."

I had to force myself to look at the photo. Behind the large yellow tractor and the dumpy little woman was a golden-haired, bare-chested man, so busy with his paintbrush that he never knew his picture was being taken. Darious hadn't changed at all in three years. My eyes misted over, and I passed it over to Luscious.

"So I guess the reward's yours, little lady. I'll see you get a check as soon as I get my million bucks."

"I don't want it," I told him. "Why don't you give it to Luscious's nephew Sam? He's really the one who did all the work in finding you?"

Luscious beamed with pride. "That'll take care of Sam's college."

One semester of college is more like it, I thought, but I didn't disillusion Luscious.

Mr. Strainge shook hands all around and left. Now we were five, Cassie, Luscious, Chief Yoder, Henry

Hoopengartner, and me. I wished they'd all go and leave me alone to process what had happened, but they all seemed firmly ensconced in their places.

"Now that he's gone, I've got some bad news for you," Chief Yoder said with a cheerful smile that seemed out of place. "I had the contents of your teapot analyzed, and it was loaded with Ambien, a prescription sleeping medicine."

"I knew there was something in it," I said.

"Worse news," Luscious added. "We found a half-empty prescription bottle among Darious's personal effects."

"I'm not surprised. I'd already decided he was the one who tried to kill me. I just don't know why . . . I thought he liked me."

Cassie patted my hand reassuringly. She seemed to sense something had gone on between Darious and me. "I'm sure he did, Tori. But when he discovered you were a reporter, he probably thought you were tracking down the antiques he'd stolen. Remember I told you P. J. has received several threats to her life. It comes with the job, Tori."

"I wonder if he's also the one who shot Professor Nakamura . . . while aiming at me?"

Luscious and Chief Yoder exchanged glances. Luscious cleared his throat and said, "We found some guns in the barn. I've sent them out for a ballistics check, to compare them to the bullet that was in Nakamura's chest. I have a feeling we'll find out Darious was the guy what shot at you. There's something else you should know, Tori. I hate to tell you this because I know you and he was kinda . . . friends."

"Not friends. Acquaintances. Tell me."

"There's a good chance one of them guns killed Dr. Washabaugh. We'll know for sure in a day or two."

"But why would he have done that?"

"Probably looking for drugs." Luscious opened his eyes wide trying to look wise, but the result was merely that he looked pop-eyed.

"The kind of man who'd steal from a fire department would do anything." Chief Yoder was full of righteous indignation.

"One more thing," Luscious began.

"What else?" I groaned.

"His name wasn't Darious DeShong or even Darren Detweiler. Fingerprints identify him as Douglas Digby from Pittsburgh, a felon with a record as long as my arm: DUIs, armed robbery, assault with a deadly weapon . . ."

"Please don't tell me." I couldn't bear to listen to any more evidence against Darious. Evidence that proved to me all too well that my atrocious taste in men was still alive and well. With the exception of Garnet, all my life I'd been attracted to the wrong kind of men, ones who were good-looking and charming on the outside, but inside were rotten to the core. Did it have something to do with my father being that kind of man? Maybe the time had come for me to join a therapy group and look into this major character defect.

"Why don't you two stop telling me bad things about Darious and tell me who you think killed him?"

They looked at each as if nothing like that had ever crossed their minds. Finally, Luscious spoke up, "He was involved in lots of shady deals. I figure one went bad. Double-cross, maybe."

Henry and the fire chief nodded their agreement. To me, it looked as if they didn't care. The borough was rid of one of its more unsavory residents, and that was all that mattered.

After the three men left, Cassie and I busied our-selves with cleaning up, carrying the half-full casserole dishes back to the kitchen, throwing out the paper plates, putting the silverware in the dishwasher. While I was refilling the cats' dishes with Tasty Tabby Treats, the phone rang.

"I'll get it." Cassie picked up the receiver and said, "Hello, Miracle residence."

I liked the sound of that.

"Who's calling? . . . Just a minute please." She covered the mouthpiece and whispered, "Someone wants to talk to you . . . a woman . . . she won't give me her name. Sounds upset."

"Probably someone who wants me to rush over and take a five-generation photo before great-great-grandma dies." I took the phone from Cassie and glanced at the caller ID unit, then said into the receiver, "Hello, Lillie."

The woman's voice on the other end was faint. I couldn't tell if it was because of a bad connection or because she wasn't talking into the mouthpiece. She gasped and asked, "How did you know it was me?"

"It's a journalistic secret. What can I do for you?"

"Do you remember me? Lillie White? You done come and talked to me at the Brick Shed House."

"Yes, Lillie. I remember. How can I help you?"

"There's something you said . . . I want to know . . . can you . . . like, you know . . ."

Impatiently, I said, "Lillie, would this be easier face-to-face? Do you want to meet me at my office?"

"I don't have a sitter. Can you come here? To my place?"

She gave me the name of a building, and I said I'd be right over. After I hung up, I asked Cassie if she knew where the Overholtzer Arms was.

"It's on Main Street, about a block and a half south of the *Chronicle* building, on the west side of the street."

"Now if I had my handy-dandy Girl Scout compass with me, I'd know exactly where that was, wouldn't I?"

"Turn left, cross the next intersection, the Overholtzer is on the right side of Main Street, before you cross the next street. It would really help if you would learn directions, Tori. Can't you remember Main Street runs east and west?"

"Sure. I just don't know which way is east and which is west."

After a little trouble getting the car to start, I drove to the Overholtzer Arms, which was a Late Victorian brick building overlooking a bend in the Lickin Creek. Its balconies, large windows overlooking the waterfront, and stone gargoyles peering down from the roof were reminders of Lickin Creek's glory days. I imagined this building, at one time, had been a prestigious place to live.

Sagging floorboards creaked as I crossed the front porch and pushed open the door. The hallway inside was dim and smelled of mildew. After my eyes adjusted to the darkness, I spotted a row of doorbells set in the wall to my right. I peered at them until I found one that said L. WHITE and pushed it. Somewhere upstairs a door opened and a woman called out, "Who is it?"

"Tori Miracle."

"Come on up. Be careful of that railing. It wobbles."

Not only did the railing wobble, the whole staircase swayed as I groped my way up in pitch-blackness to the third and top floor.

Lillie was waiting for me at the top of the stairs. Without her thick stage makeup and with her hair pulled back into an unadorned ponytail, she looked about twelve years old. She held open the door to her apartment and urged me to enter.

The living room was tiny, even by my New York standards. The furnishings were a green sofa, a reclining chair upholstered in mauve velour, two white plastic end tables, a wicker coffee table with the white paint peeling off, a floor lamp, and a large TV. That was it. There was no place more depressing than my Hell's Kitchen apartment, but this was definitely a runner-up in the not-fit-for-man-nor-beast category.

A little girl sat on the bare wood floor in front of the TV, watching cartoons with her thumb in her mouth. Her free hand clutched a faux Beanie Baby. She didn't acknowledge my presence.

"She don't hear so good," Lillie explained. "Want a soda?"

I shook my head, sat down on the edge of the sofa, and watched her refill two glasses from a half-empty Coke bottle on the coffee table. She handed one to the child and took a long drink from the other before sitting on the recliner.

"Looks like we're in for a weather change," she said. "Turned kind of cool after that windstorm."

"Mmmm," I agreed. Local custom called for starting every conversation with a discussion about weather conditions.

"Good thing. I don't like hot weather."

"Mmmm,"

"Maybe if I had an air conditioner."

"Always heard you don't need air-conditioning in Pennsylvania."

"That's true. Fresh air's always the best. The first killing frost always hits near Halloween."

That was enough weather-channel chatter for me. "Lillie, what was it you wanted to talk to me about?"

She took another long swig of her Coke. "It's something you done said to me on Sunday. I wanted to ask you if . . . like . . . you know . . ." Her voice trailed away, and she began to shred a Kleenex into little bits of confetti.

"Please, Lillie. Just ask me. I don't have all day."

"It's what you said about Kayla's dad."

Who's Kayla? "I'm sorry, Lillie, but could you give me a little hint? I don't know what you're talking about."

"Kayla," she said, nodding at the little girl on the floor. "You said I could track her dad down with dee and ay. Can you tell me how to go about it?"

"Sure. It's a DNA test, just the letters DNA. A lab can compare people's blood samples to prove paternity." She looked blank, so I added, "Prove who the dad is. I believe they can even do it with swabs from the inside of the mouth. Do you want to find Kayla's dad?"

Lillie's ponytail bounced as she vehemently shook her head. "If he don't want to be her dad, then I don't want him nowhere near us. We're getting along just fine without him."

"Then why did you want to know about DNA testing?"

"When you was talking to me the other day, it got me thinking. Do you know if they can test a guy's DNA after he's dead?"

"Of course," I said. "If they can get a tissue sample. Why do you ask?"

She patted her skinny midsection. "Because Mack promised me that this kid would have everything it deserved, and I want to make damn sure it gets it."

"You're pregnant! By Mack Macmillan?"

She smiled and nodded. "Mack never had no kids

with his other wives. He was real excited about the baby. Wanted us to be a real family."

"Did he tell you he had cancer?"

Her eyes opened wide with surprise. "Mack didn't have cancer. He would of told me."

"He knew, Lillie."

"If he'd known, he would of made a will and put me and the baby in it. He said he'd take care of us, no matter what."

I must have been exhausted because suddenly a vision flashed through my brain of me sitting in an attorney's office preparing for my own death. *And to my neighbor Murray Rosenbaum. I leave my aspidistra.* I shook the crazy idea away; I don't even know what an aspidistra is. I just like the sound of the word.

"You probably should call your lawyer," I suggested.

"Yeah, right. People like me don't have lawyers."

I tore a page from my notebook, wrote down Buchanan McCleary's name. Not only was he the borough solicitor, but he had his own private practice and loved to champion the underdog. They'd be a match made in heaven, of that I was sure.

As I crossed the room I reached down and gently touched Kayla on the shoulder. The child looked up and smiled at me. I gave her a thumbs-up sign that caused her to giggle. "Have you sought out any help for her?" I asked Lillie as she held the door open for me.

"Like what? I don't have no money for fancy doctoring."

I sighed. This was what happened when children had children. "Try Easter Seal," I suggested.

"Mack's wife volunteers there, teaching sign language, and I sure don't want to bump into her."

When I was back on the street, the cold wind rushing down from the mountains felt good to me after the cloying atmosphere of the small apartment. I buttoned my sweater and wondered if this was the start of that "killing frost" Lillie had mentioned.

At least now I understood why Lillie had told me Mack Macmillan was going to marry her. Quite possibly, she was right. As I got into my car, it occurred to me to wonder why a man would commit suicide when he was excitedly expecting his first child. Sure, he'd been told he only had about ten years left, but from my thirty-something viewpoint, ten years was a long time, especially for a man who was already in his seventies. He'd told Lillie he'd take care of her and the child—did that mean he'd changed his will in their favor? I decided the person to ask was Buchanan McCleary.

I drove the couple of blocks to his office in the old Pizza Hut building the borough council had bought to use as a town hall annex. Buchanan had told me it was a real bargain because it shared a parking lot and snow removal costs with the Church of God. That church, located in what used to be a service station, had a new sign up: NO JESUS, NO PEACE. KNOW JESUS, KNOW PEACE. How easy life must be for the faithful, I thought. There certainly wasn't much peace in my life these days.

Perhaps it was my overactive imagination, but I was positive I smelled garlic as I entered through the glass door that faced the parking lot. Buchanan, six foot eight if you counted his seventies Afro, came around the desk to give me a hug and a peck on the cheek.

"Ugh!" he said, straightening up and rubbing his back. "Wish you'd grow about eight inches."

"I will if you'll agree to shrink by the same amount."

A grin crossed his dark, handsome face. "How about a cup of Darjeeling?" He'd once told me tea drinking was a habit he'd picked up when he was a Rhodes scholar in England.

"I'd love some."

While he busied himself at the hot plate in the corner, I wondered how his relationship with Garnet's sister, Greta, was going. They were both aging hippie activists who espoused many causes, such as the rain forests, the whales, dolphins, the Bay, and recycling. If I'd met two people who were destined to be soul mates, they were Buchanan and Greta.

Buchanan was reputed to be the best lawyer in the tri-state area, and his private practice was quite lucrative. I often wondered why he worked for the borough council as a part-time attorney, but then I realized, that Buchanan, with his penchant for good deeds, probably thought of the work he did for the borough as his charitable contribution to Lickin Creek. He came back carrying two blue-and-white Spode mugs full of fragrant hot tea. He'd remembered I like mine with milk and sugar.

"What do you hear from Garnet?" he asked, taking his seat behind the giant library table that served as his desk.

"He called Wednesday."

"Will he be coming home before he leaves for Costa Rica?"

I had no idea. "Of course," I said.

"Damn shame about that young man getting himself killed. Luscious told me it looks like he was responsible for the recent rash of button-and-bullet robberies. Sounds like someone he double-crossed got revenge. No honor among thieves."

"What do you mean by 'buttons and bullets'?"

"That's what we call most of the Civil War collections around here. Most contain a lot of objects, but none are particularly valuable."

"But there were some really important artifacts

stolen from the Gettysburg museum, weren't there? Did everything turn up in the barn?"

Buchanan shook his head. "Not everything. The two rangers who were at the barn all morning stopped by the police station an hour ago to tell Luscious the rarest items are still missing."

"Anything in particular?"

"General Meade's sword, for one, and some battle flags. They left some photos to help Luscious identify them if they should turn up. Luscious came by to use my scanner to make some copies." He pulled three pieces of paper out of his in-box and handed them to me. "This is the clearest. You can easily read the letters and numbers on the banners."

I studied the photos. Two showed the banners. The third was of the sword, and something about it bothered me, but I didn't know why.

Putting the pictures to one side, Buchanan leaned back, cocked his head, and looked quizzically at me. "May I ask why you have honored me with this visit?"

"I want to know about Mack Macmillan's will. Has it been filed for probate?"

Buchanan nodded. "It has. Shouldn't take long at all to take care of the few bequests he made and wind it up."

"Were there any unusual or unexpected bequests?"

"Not unless you count the ten grand he left to the animal shelter. I guess his conscience got the better of him."

"So you know about the puppy mills?"

"Sure. Everybody does. And thanks to Mack, it's still not illegal to run one."

"Can you tell me how long ago the will was written?"

"Of course. He came to see me at my office, the real

one, not this place, about a month ago. Asked me to tear up the trust he'd written immediately after he and Charlotte were married. He replaced it with a simple will, the kind that costs about fifty bucks, leaving the bulk of his estate to Charlotte. When I pointed out to him that his estate was large and complicated and better served by the trust, he told me to mind my own business. That he knew what he was doing."

"I wonder why he did that," I said, thinking of Lillie White and the baby she was expecting. Had Macmillan lied to her about taking care of her and the child? For all that it was worth, I didn't even know if she'd told me the truth about his being the father. Maybe she saw his death as an opportunity to grab some of his money for herself.

"What if there was a child?" I asked.

"But he and Charlotte never had . . . Wait just a minute. Are you telling me there *is* a child?"

"There might be. It hasn't been born yet."

"But Charlotte . . . uh . . . isn't she a little old for . . ."

"Not Charlotte, Buchanan. Another woman."

"That explains why he didn't let me scratch that line out of the will."

"What line?"

"The one that's in most standard wills—leaving half the deceased's assets to be divided up among his children."

"If what you're saying is true and there is a child, it could change things. Give me the woman's name."

"I'll have her call you," I said. For once, I decided, I would not be caught in the middle of another Lickin Creek scandal.

CHAPTER 20

Halloween Morning

FRIDAY WAS MUCH BUSIER THAN USUAL AT THE *Chronicle*. We had to toss out the entire front page to make room for articles about Mack Macmillan's suicide and Darious DeShong's murder. Cassie also reminded me that the mayor wanted something in the paper about Woody and Moonbeam rescuing me from sure death. Now that he had been cleared by the D.A. and was not waiting to go to trial, the mayor had decided to honor him at a ceremony at The Accident Theatre next weekend.

President Godlove called to ask me if I'd suffered any ill effects from tumbling over the balcony. Was it my imagination, or did he sound very cool? Maybe he would have preferred to let Woody take the blame. It probably would have looked better for the college if the chairman of the board of trustees had been the victim of a stupid accident rather than a suicide.

We proofed, we pasted, we moved, we inserted, and we deleted. And finally, in the late afternoon, the *Chronicle* was ready to go to the printer. Due to Cassie's valiant efforts on the telephone, we were down only a handful of subscribers, and with any luck, in a week or two even they would forget what they'd been angry about and resubscribe.

When I arrived home, I was ready to collapse from exhaustion. After feeding the cats, changing their litter boxes, and eating half of a can of chili I found in the refrigerator, I checked the doors and windows to make sure all were locked and climbed the stairs to my bedroom on the second floor.

There, I ripped off my clothes, tossed them in the direction of the chair, and pulled on my Tin Woodman nightshirt that said IF I ONLY HAD A HEART. My jeans missed the chair and landed on my dresser, jiggling the little carousel-horse music box Darious had given me, which began to play "In the Good Old Summertime." I practically flew across the room to turn it off. I'd never be able to listen to it again. In fact, it was going to the Salvation Army thrift shop next week. I covered it with my sweater so I wouldn't have to look at it, and went to bed with my cats.

I slept sporadically. The events of the past few days danced through my head as if I were viewing them through a kaleidoscope. A vision of Darious sitting in his golden chariot with a horrendous gash in his neck that nearly separated his head from his body kept floating through the dreams. Sometimes the pieces almost formed a picture that made sense, then they would break apart into a meaningless jumble. As I dozed off at sunrise, I was thinking there was something about Darious I needed to remember. Something he'd done? Something I'd seen at his barn? What was it? Fred's paw stroking my cheek woke me, and I jerked to a sitting position, groped for the clock, and nearly had a panic attack as my foggy brain tried to deal with how late it was and what I should wear to this afternoon's wedding.

Much to my chagrin, yesterday I'd learned that Woody had not called me Monday evening to ask me out on a date. The real reason for that call, which I never gave him time to get to, was to invite me to his and Moonbeam's wedding, to take place this very afternoon on the Gettysburg battlefield. When Moonbeam had called yesterday afternoon to make sure I was coming, she'd been very surprised that I knew nothing about it. As if she needed to convince me to come, she read off the names of about two dozen guests she thought I knew who had already accepted. I assured her I wouldn't miss it for the world.

The occasion deserved my good black silk suit with the sequined collar and cuffs. I'd bought it in a nearly-new shop two years ago, and despite the designer label's having been cut out of it, I knew what it was. I thought it made me look a little thinner than I really was, and in New York it often went to the theater with me. It hadn't yet had an outing in Lickin Creek.

I found my black heels in a box in the storeroom, and when I put them on I was surprised at how uncomfortable they were after many months of wearing nothing but sandals and sneakers. Oh well, I'd soon grow accustomed to wearing them again. I tottered down the stairs, hanging on to the railing for dear life and hoped that would happen soon.

There were cats to feed and water and mail to gather from the hall rug where it lay after having been dropped through the slot in the front door by our stubborn mailman, who refused to come to the back door. "I've always delivered it here, and I'm not going to change now" was his answer when I pointed out the perils of the front porch roof. Lickin Creek natives had two phrases I heard over and over. The first was "It's the way we've always done it," and its evil twin was "We've never done it that way."

In the kitchen, I heated a cup of yesterday's coffee in the microwave and tried to make some sense of the thoughts and dreams that had come to me during the night. By the time I'd finished drinking the coffee, I came to the conclusion that I knew who killed Darious DeShong. But I didn't know why. I called Luscious to ask him a couple of questions about the crime scene that would prove me right. The nitwit on the end of the line told me she thought Luscious was out.

"You *think* he's out? You're only five feet away from his desk. Can't you look?"

In a minute she was back. "I was right. He's out. You want I should take a message?"

I told her what I wanted to know and waited while she looked for a pencil to write it down. "Tell him to call me later this afternoon, after four at . . ." I had to think for a minute. "At General Pickett's Restaurant in Gettysburg."

"Okeydokey. What did you say your name was?"

"Tori Miracle!" I slammed the phone down.

If I was right, I would confront a killer this afternoon. If I was wrong . . . well, I'd been wrong before. It's embarrassing but not the end of the world.

I tossed the advertising circulars into the trash, put the bills on the kitchen table, and thought about quickly fixing something to eat. Not enough time. Instead I grabbed a Snickers bar from the refrigerator to eat on the go.

"Come on baby, turn over," I muttered furiously at my car, and after a few grunts of protest, it started.

While Halloween might seem like a strange choice for a wedding day, Moonbeam and Woody had truly beautiful weather for their special occasion. The

weather was crisp, the sky clear, and if sunshine was a
good portent, then the bridal couple was destined for
happiness.

I got around the traffic circle with no trouble, and
then consulted the little map Cassie had drawn for me.
At the Lutheran Theological Seminary, I turned down
Confederate Avenue and drove along Seminary Ridge,
which became a one-way street on the battlefield. I
drove past several beautiful monuments and nearly
missed seeing the tiny brown-and-white sign on my
right that said AMPHITHEATER. I left my car next to a
statue of General Longstreet, which looked strange
standing on the bare ground instead of being raised on
a pedestal as the other statues were. Someone, I noticed,
had tucked a miniature Confederate flag into a space
under the general's arm. The area smelled of mold and
decay, and the ground beneath my feet was oddly
spongy. I walked past a row of green SaniPots and
down the hill to where benches built of landscaping
timbers faced an odd-looking A-frame building with a
small stage in front.

By the time I reached the wedding party, I was hobbling and wished I hadn't worn high heels. I also
wished I hadn't worn the black suit. No matter how
sophisticated and stylish an outfit is, there are right
places and there are wrong places for everything. And
this was definitely the wrong place for black silk and
sequins. Nobody had told me I'd be sitting in the sun,
or that most of the guests would be wearing Civil War
costumes. Once again, Tori Miracle was dressed wrong
for the occasion.

Among the hundred or more guests seated on the
benches, I recognized many. It pleased me that several
nodded and waved when they saw me.

Gloria Zimmerman, who was the maid of honor in a

gray silk hoopskirted gown, stepped onto the stage. I guessed this meant something was going to happen soon. At least I hoped so. I was anxious to ask her about her relationship with Darious, but I figured I could do that at the reception. While the overhanging roof of the A-frame provided Gloria some shade, the rest of the guests were not so lucky; they were busy fanning themselves with little pieces of paper. Those of us who arrived late, and there were many, had to stand in the sun, which seemed to grow bigger and hotter with every passing minute.

Charlotte Macmillan stood alone on the edge of the crowd, dressed in what my friend Murray Rosenbaum always called "mother-of-the-groom beige." I was surprised, at first, to see her there but then I realized that Moonbeam must have invited everybody in town. I tried to edge closer to her. But I was sidetracked by a reenactor who saw by my suit I was an outsider and was determined to tell me everything there was to know about staging a Civil War–era wedding.

Janet Margolies and Lizzie Borden had taken shelter under a tree, far off to the right. They waved at me. I tried to squeeze through the crowd to get to them, but it was an impossible task. The two women standing next to me took it upon themselves to tell me who the other wedding guests were. Their own names were Maybell and Grace. They looked identical except Maybell had purple hair while Grace's was snow-white. Grace was grumpy; rather than assume she was always that way, I blamed it on the heat.

"Can't imagine why anybody would want to get married in a place where so many men died," she grumbled.

"Whatever floats their boat," Maybell said with a wicked grin.

Grace sniffed and pointed out the tall, handsome middle-aged Asian gentleman pushing Ken Nakamura's wheelchair. "That's the bride's ex-husband. Probably here to celebrate the end of his alimony payments." She snickered.

President Godlove was also present, surrounded by a half-dozen professors from the college, including Helga Van Brackle. "They're not really friends of Moonbeam's," Maybell, of the lavender hair, told me. "They're just here because of Professor Nakamura."

More people were arriving every minute, most of the men in uniforms while the women wore hoopskirts, feathered hats, and crocheted gloves. If the pace kept up, soon there would be more people in the amphitheater than had fought at the Battle of Gettysburg. Vesta Pennsinger, in a long gingham gown, glanced my way but pretended she hadn't seen me. At least she had the good sense to look embarrassed.

"They're coming," someone called, and the crowd surged forward. Maybell put a restraining hand on my forearm and held me back.

"You'll be able to see from here," she informed me.

Sure enough, the crowd separated into two parts, and a covered wagon drawn by a team of beautiful horses rode into the center of the parking lot. Woody, wearing a blue dress uniform, sat tall on the bench beside a young man in a black suit and flat straw hat who reined in the horses. When they came to a halt, Woody jumped to the ground with unexpected agility for a man of his size. He straightened his sword, adjusted the tilt of his hat, tightened the gold sash around his waist, then walked around to the back of the wagon and lifted the canvas revealing . . .

The guests gasped. And so did I, for Moonbeam Nakamura was not only the most beautiful bride I'd ever seen, she was also the most unusually dressed. For her grand occasion she'd chosen a cloth-of-gold sari and had twisted ropes of gold in the single blond braid that hung down her back. Instead of a veil, she wore a gold tiara with a red jewel in the center. A delicate nose ring and a small green stone glued between her eyebrows completed the bride's ensemble. Tiny bells on her anklets tinkled as Woody lifted her from the wagon and set her on the ground.

If Captain Woodruff of the Federal Army of the Potomac found anything strange in his bride's clothing, it did not show in his face. He looked at her with such love and admiration that my cheeks burned with discomfort at witnessing the private moment.

They slowly walked down the aisle to the shelter and stepped onto the platform, he in polished boots, she with bare feet. There they were joined by their attendants, several young women in long cotton gowns and three men in blue wool uniforms.

The minister wore a normal-looking white cassock, and the ceremony was traditional and not at all what I had expected when I first saw Moonbeam's wedding outfit. But Moonbeam didn't disappoint me. After the minister stepped aside, Tamsin Nakamura, radiant in a flowing white robe, walked toward the stage, gently pounding a tambourine. From somewhere in the crowd, a woman's voice began to chant, and soon others joined in. The ceremony that followed was an interesting and quite original blend of Zen, Tao, goddess worship, Native American shamanism, Hinduism, and Tibetan spiritualism. And it climaxed with a performance of didgeridoo music played by an Australian aborigine. "He's from Baltimore," Grace shouted in my ear.

A woman turned around, looked at me, and said, "Shhh."

When the female shaman used a turkey feather to fan sacred smoke in their faces, the couple kissed, officially ending the ceremony.

The audience had been stunned into silence throughout the unusual ceremony, and now a few nervous giggles signified relief that it was over. Woody ignored them, stepped to the edge of the platform, and held his arms high over his head until he had everyone's attention.

"Moonbeam and me want to thank you'uns for being here and sharing our happiness. Now we want all of you'uns to make up a car parade and follow our wagon to General Pickett's All-U-Can-Eat Buffet Restaurant."

A roar of approval rose from the assemblage. Grace whispered in my ear, " 'All you can eat' is the magic phrase here in south-central Pennsylvania."

"So I've noticed," I said. "I think I've gained five pounds since I've been here, just from breathing the air."

Two lines of Union soldiers formed a tunnel of sword blades for the newlyweds to walk through, while the ecologically correct guests tossed breadcrumbs, instead of rice, at them. The last soldier in line swatted Moonbeam on the rear end with the flat side of his sword, and she giggled. Gloria followed closely behind the couple, and I pushed forward and tried to catch her attention. She noticed me and waved.

"Gloria, I need to talk to you," I yelled.

"Later, Tori. I've got to get out of these seven layers of clothing before I melt," and she was gone.

Maybell and Grace were swept away in the rush to the cars, while I walked in a dignified manner, very slowly, on blistered feet. Every guest but me had worn sensible flat shoes. But then they had probably known in advance it was going to be an outdoor wedding with limited seating. As soon as I got home, I vowed, the high heels were going in the garbage—not even the Salvation Army bag. I didn't want to be responsible for any other woman suffering similar agony.

By the time I'd managed to stagger to my car, the parking lot was nearly deserted. I dug vainly in my purse trying to find my car key, then spotted it where I'd left it—in the ignition switch, in the on position. I turned the key and said my usual little prayer, but this time the Automobile Goddess wasn't listening. P. J.'s car had come to the end of the road.

CHAPTER 21

"CAN I GIVE YOU A RIDE TO THE RESTAURANT?"
Charlotte Macmillan leaned in the window
on the passenger side and smiled at me.
"Sounds like your battery is dead."

"It's my own fault," I said. "I left the key in the
ignition, and it must have drained the battery." I got
out and kicked a front tire in frustration. The only
thing that accomplished was to hurt my already sore
toes.

"Ride with me, then," Charlotte said.

"I'd better stay with the car. Will you please call
Triple A from the restaurant?"

"I insist. You don't want to miss the bridal procession."

"My car . . ."

"Hardly anyone comes here in the off-season," she
said. "It will be perfectly safe."

Reluctantly, I followed her to her Mercedes SUV.
She tossed me the keys. "I'm very tired. Will you drive,
please?"

"I don't know how," I said, staring helplessly at the
Mercedes's complex dashboard.

"Nonsense. It's automatic transmission. Just turn the key. Take a right as you leave the parking lot."

I pulled slowly onto the road, hoping to catch a glimpse of the tail end of the bridal procession. But it was nowhere to be seen. We drove for a long time on the deserted road.

"Turn right just up ahead."

I did as she ordered, and drove past the park service visitor center and the Cyclorama building. "Turn right again, then make a left." Charlotte's voice was flat, as though she were very tired.

I turned into a long driveway lined with red, white, and blue banners. The sign said GETTYSBURG NATIONAL TOWER.

"The park service has been trying to get this torn down for years," Charlotte said. "People say it ruins the skyline. Park over there." She pointed to a weathered wood building.

"This doesn't look like General Pickett's Restaurant," I said.

She pulled the keys from the ignition and dropped them into her purse before I had a chance to react in any way. "Let's go," she said. I stared at her and saw her eyes, looking at me from behind her mask, were bloodshot. I felt distinctly uneasy.

Charlotte took my arm as if we were old friends, and we walked up to the brown building with a sign over the door that said SUTLER'S STORE in yellow letters. Inside, standing behind a central desk, was a young man who smiled at us as we walked in.

"Two tickets, please, Joey."

"I'm real sorry, Mrs. Macmillan," the man behind the window said, "but we're closed for repairs."

"Oh, come on, Joey. We'll just be a few minutes. I

want to show my friend the view of Gettysburg, and she won't be here tomorrow."

He looked like he was about to change his mind.

"That's okay," I said. "I really don't like heights anyway."

The man laughed. "That's what they all say. Okay, Mrs. M., just because it's you, I'll let you go up—but don't tell my boss." He handed her a couple of tokens.

Charlotte laughed girlishly. "Don't worry, Joey. No one will ever know. Come on, Tori."

"I don't want—" Something jabbed me just above my waist.

Charlotte leaned close and whispered, "This isn't one of those toy guns they try to sell to women. This one can blow your head right off your shoulders." For the benefit of the young man, she said loudly, "Let's take in the view, Tori."

As the elevator rose three hundred feet through the metal struts of the tower, I closed my eyes, not sure whether I was more frightened of Charlotte's gun or the dizzying ride. I've always thought if I were trapped in a high building by a fire, I'd be one of those people who'd die before climbing down a fireman's ladder.

A bump told me we had reached the top. "Out," Charlotte ordered.

I opened one eye to a narrow slit, saw through a glass window how high we were, and clung to the grab bar inside the elevator. My knees were jelly, and I was close to collapsing. "Can't," I whimpered.

"Big baby." Charlotte pushed me in the back, propelling me onto the glassed-in observation platform. "Open your eyes, Tori. Both of them. If you're too chicken to look down, just look at me."

When I opened my eyes, I saw the cannon-size gun she was pointed at me. I focused then on her masked face, and it seemed as though her eyes had grown larger and blacker.

Keep your eyes on her, Tori. Don't look over the edge. I fought back the panic that threatened to engulf me. I wanted to get her talking—to postpone the inevitable for as long as I could. Without looking away from her face, I asked, "Why are you doing this? I don't understand."

Charlotte laughed. "Mack's cousin's daughter, Reba, answers the phone at Hoopengartner's Garage and police station. Nothing very exciting happens there, so when you called and asked her to relay some questions to Luscious having to do with Darious DeShong's death, she couldn't wait to tell someone. So she called me. Now what I want to know is, what gave me away?"

If I hadn't been sure before, I was now. "The sticky buns you brought him as an excuse for being there. Everyone around here bakes sticky buns but the ones in Darious's workshop were from the bakery in Gettysburg you always shop at. I saw the box and it was dated that day." The date was one of the things I had wanted to ask Luscious about. "And the hank of hair Darious pulled from your head as he was dying. Tests have already proven it was yours." The other question I had for Luscious—was the blond hair Darious clutched in his hand his own or someone else's?

Unconsciously, she raised one hand and touched the side of her mask. "There's no proof I even knew him."

"But there is. I've seen two copies of a photograph of your husband in a Civil War general's uniform. And, having just seen a picture of General Meade's sword, I realized that the sword Mack wore in the picture was the missing sword from the Gettysburg collection. His ego couldn't resist the urge to be photographed with his stolen treasure, could it? Did he get a thrill out of having that picture on display in his office at the college and at home for everyone to see? Did he commission Darious to steal it, or did he simply pick and choose from whatever Darious brought him? How did a man like your husband get mixed up with a common thief like Darious in the first place?"

"Questions, questions, questions. My grandma used to say to me, 'Charlotte, you'll go to your death with a question on your lips.'"

I hoped I wouldn't. But there didn't seem to be any way for me to escape. The pounding in my chest had slowed down a little while I was talking, but it had started up again. My heart felt as if it was about to burst from my chest.

"I don't mind answering your questions now," Charlotte said. "It won't matter." My knees threatened to buckle when she said that, and I had to concentrate on her mask to keep myself from fainting from fright.

"You asked how Mack met Darious. I introduced them, Tori. Months before my accident, I was riding on the battlefield and came across Darious, hunting for artifacts with a metal detector. When he realized I wasn't going to report him, we started talking about collecting, and I told him of Mack's constant search for good-quality Civil War collectibles. He said he had some items Mack might be interested in. Mack was delighted to buy them with no questions asked. One thing led to another, and before long Darious was 'picking over' various collections for certain pieces Mack wanted. I suppose he planned to sell the other things to other 'collectors.'"

"And after Mack's suicide, you killed Darious to keep him from talking about the sales and to protect your late husband's reputation?"

"Good guess, Tori. But wrong motive."

"What then?" I asked. "You might as well tell me why. I'm obviously not going to tell anyone."

"I eliminated Darious because he was a blundering idiot. He couldn't do anything right."

"Like what?"

"Like killing you, for one thing."

"It *was* Darious who shot at me."

"Shot and missed. He couldn't even set your house on fire properly. When you survived being pushed off the staircase at the college, I decided I'd had enough."

"But Darious liked me. I know he did. I don't understand why he would want to kill me."

"That carousel was all he cared about. When I learned you'd visited him, I told him you were conducting an undercover investigation about carousel robberies for a story. When you showed up the second time, he believed me. I invited you to come riding, let Darious know by cell phone when we left so he had time to hide in Devil's Den, then led you to where you'd be right in his sights."

"Why not do me in yourself?"

"I wanted to make sure I had an alibi when an attempt was made on your life." She sighed. "My grandma always said, 'If you want a job done well, do it yourself.' "

"But why me? What did I do to you?"

"When I suggested to President Godlove that he ask you to quietly look into my husband's death, I thought doing so would give me plausibility as the bereaved widow. I had no idea you'd take your assignment so seriously. You asked too many questions of too many people. I knew it would be only a matter of time before you figured everything out. You reminded me of a bulldog I had as a kid. Once he got hold of something, he wouldn't let go. You're the same way."

"I only did what I thought should be done."

"Exactly. But you were supposed to come to the conclusion that Woody Woodruff was a bumbler who accidentally put real bullets in the guns."

"But, Woody isn't the kind of . . ."

Charlotte sighed. "I know, Tori. I underestimated both of you. You got too close to the truth."

"What do you mean? The truth about what?"

She snickered. It wasn't a pleasant sound. "Oh, Mack committed suicide, all right. After I told him he would die painfully in less than a month. We agreed suicide made to look like an accident would be the ideal solution. He'd die quickly, I'd get the insurance money, and I'd split it with Lillie White to take care of her brat."

"How did you convince him he was going to die? The nurse at Dr. Washabaugh's office said he had . . . Oh my God. You killed Dr. Washabaugh, didn't you?"

"Technically no. Darious did it. To cover up destroying Mack's medical records. It was supposed to look like a robbery gone wrong."

"But Vesta was there; she told me how hard Mack took his diagnosis."

"She'd be dead, too, if she'd gone to work when she was supposed to. But Vesta has such a reputation for making up stories that nobody in their right mind is going to pay any attention to what she says. In this case, though, she was right about what she saw. She just didn't understand what was going on. You see, I interpreted for Mack using sign language, but what I told him was not what Dr. Washabaugh told me. Very simple. I'd interpreted everything for him for the last four years. He trusted me."

"And look what it got him. That's disgusting!"

Charlotte shrugged. "I did what I had to do. After we got home that day, while he was still in shock, I convinced him that staging an accidental death was the only way he could avoid dying slowly and painfully and still provide for Lillie and the baby. We planned his 'accidental' death down to the last detail. The plans were already under way for the mock execution, and it was easy for Mack to persuade Janet to let him play the convicted man. We even planned for me to be away for the weekend, so I couldn't be suspected of doing anything wrong. It was easy to change the ammunition; he simply substituted his key for the storeroom key while Janet Margolies was in the bathroom, then went back later that night to reload the guns."

"And his plan would have worked, if he'd switched the keys back again."

"He was supposed to bring the key and the ammo home and put them in the safe. After all the fuss died down, I'd be able to dispose of them. But when I opened the safe to get them, they weren't there. I guessed, wrongly, that he'd managed to get rid of them on Friday night. I never realized he'd done something as stupid as putting the evidence in his desk at the college."

"What was the purpose of his leaving a suicide note, then, if you wanted it to appear to be an accident?"

"That was a CYA letter. You know, cover-your-ass. If somehow the authorities came to suspect what happened and that I'd had something to do with his death, I was to bring it out. We never thought it would get to that point—not with that idiot Luscious Miller running the police department. If you hadn't come by with your prattle about Wonder Wads and suicide, that letter would still be in the safe, and I'd have enough money to make a new life for myself."

"And so would Lillie White," I pointed out.

"Like I'd share it with that tramp. Wasn't it enough she stole my husband's love from me? The only reason he turned to her was because he couldn't stand to look at me after I was burned." The hand holding the gun dropped as if she'd forgotten it was there. "He told me he was going to leave me . . . was going to marry her . . . I loved him too much to let that happen."

"Was Darious involved in the plot to kill your husband?"

"Hell no, Mack was his goose who laid golden eggs. But I knew Darious was so crazy to get money to refinish that carousel, he didn't care where it came from, so I offered him part of the insurance money to kill Dr. Washabaugh and make it look like a robbery gone bad. He was a man with no morals, Tori. He tried to blackmail me!"

Like she had scruples! "So you killed him."

"I had to, to keep him from talking. Just like I have to kill you, Tori."

"That was a bluff, Charlotte. If he'd gone to the police, he would have implicated himself. You didn't have to kill him. You didn't have to kill your husband either. I'm sure he would have provided for you."

"There was no money left. Mack was the worst businessman in the world. Even the farm had a double mortgage. There was no way he could have supported two families. But it wasn't really about money," she said. "I could never give him children, and that's the one thing he always wanted. With the baby coming and me so ugly, he said he never wanted to see me again. I couldn't let that whore have him. I'd devoted myself to taking care of him and all he cared about was having a baby. He didn't love me. He probably never did."

Charlotte's empty left hand rose. "Look!" Before I realized what she was doing, she pulled the mask up over her head. Her sleek blond hair tumbled loose, covering her face, and she swept it back. "Look," she cried again. "Look at me."

I stared at her in silent shock. I don't know what I had expected to see, but this was definitely not it.

"Have you ever seen anything so hideous?"

"Charlotte . . . you're . . . you're beautiful!" The face she had uncovered was unblemished, so far as I could see.

"No," she wailed. "I'm ugly. There're scars beneath my skin—maybe you can't see them, but Mack could. He couldn't bear to look at me after the fire. Or touch me. He said nobody would ever want me again. Then he said he was going to leave me. Leave me alone. Alone and hideous. And poor. You understand why I couldn't let that happen, don't you, Tori?"

No, I did not! Charlotte been responsible for three deaths: her own husband, Dr. Washabaugh, and Darious. And she'd nearly killed Professor Nakamura and me. I could not feel any sympathy for her.

I also knew the only reason she'd told me all this was because she had no fear I would tell anyone. And the only way she could be sure of that would be to kill me. This was the end. Tori Miracle would be another casualty on the battlefield of Gettysburg, only there would be no beautiful monument erected in my memory. I'd be lucky if my father sprang for a tombstone.

"We're going up to the top," Charlotte announced. She pointed to a flight of metal steps while keeping the gun trained on me.

"Please, don't make me go up there," I whispered.

"Climb, or I'll shoot you right now."

Even another minute of life was precious at that moment, so I climbed with Charlotte close behind me. We emerged onto an open-air platform near the top of the tower, with only a waist-high metal railing between us and the blue sky beyond. Stacks of metal gratings lay on the floor, waiting to be placed around the edge so that no one could fall or jump off.

"Walk over to the railing," Charlotte ordered. "And don't try any funny stuff."

I minced my way to the edge, where I grabbed hold of the railing and hung tight. The world spun around me, and I already felt the terror of my death plunge. She wasn't going to shoot me, I realized. She was going to force me over the railing. Make it look as though I'd fallen by accident. But I wouldn't climb over it. She'd have to shoot me first.

"Don't turn around," she said. She wasn't going to shoot me. A blow on the head would knock me senseless, then she could simply shove me over. The mark the gun made on my skull would never be noticed amid the trauma caused by the fall.

"I'm not a bad person," Charlotte said. "Circumstances forced me to do what I did."

"How many more people would you have been forced to kill, Charlotte?"

"Only one more. Lillie White was next."

I steeled myself for the blow that would surely follow what I was going to say next.

"You're not as smart as you think, Charlotte. Your husband outwitted you."

"What are you talking about?"

"Mack was no dummy, Charlotte. He must have known you wouldn't share the insurance money with Lillie. That's why he left the Wonder Wads and the keys in his desk instead of bringing them home. He knew someone would find them there and figure out his death was a suicide. Then you'd have to produce the suicide note to save yourself from being charged as an accessory to insurance fraud. The letter might save your skin, but it also meant you wouldn't get the insurance money."

"That's ridiculous. Besides, there's other money—the collection is probably worth a million dollars."

"Your husband wrote a new will, Charlotte."

Her gasp of surprise told me I was right. Macmillan had double-crossed her.

"He left half his estate to his unborn child, Lillie's baby. While half a million dollars might seem like a lot of money to some people, it wouldn't support your lifestyle for long."

Behind me, there was absolute silence. I'd apparently shocked her into silence. I braced myself for the blow. Please let it be over with quickly, I prayed.

"Didn't you hear me, Charlotte? Your husband outsmarted you. He made sure his child would be cared for and that you would be out of the picture." I looked over my shoulder at her, but I didn't see her. I spun around, still gripping the rail. She was gone. She must have slipped down the stairs while I was talking. For some reason, she had decided to spare me.

I slid down the stairs, two at a time, to the observation room. The elevator door stood open. There hadn't been time for her to ride it down. She had to still be up here with me, somewhere. I leaped inside the elevator and pressed the down button. After a long, frustrating wait, the door slid shut and the elevator lurched downward.

I stood an inch away from the door, ready to spring from the elevator as soon as it came to a stop. When at last it opened, I ran screaming for help toward a small group of people standing in a semicircle. Why did they pay no attention to me? I stopped. Something was horribly wrong. They were staring at a crumpled object on the ground. As if I were walking underwater, I slowly moved toward them and saw that the object was beige and streaked with red. And as the realization of what it was hit me, my wobbly knees gave way, and I collapsed in a heap on the sidewalk.

CHAPTER 22

SOMEONE HELPED ME UP AND LED ME TO A BENCH near the small pond at the foot of the tower. Another brought me a cup of ice water, and I dipped my fingers in it and rubbed some on my cheeks and forehead. I'm not sure when Luscious Miller arrived, but he was suddenly there.

"How did you know to come here?"

"I heard on the scanner that a woman had fallen from the tower. I knew you was in Gettysburg for the wedding, and I kind of thought I'd find you in the middle of things." He turned bright red. "I was afraid it was you what fell, Tori. I prayed for you all the way over the mountain."

I took his hand and squeezed it, loving him for his unabashed concern. Suddenly, we were nearly overrun with white police cars. The only differences I could see was that the park rangers' vehicles had green stripes on the sides, the Gettysburg police cars had blue stripes, and the state police cars had black stripes. Close behind the white fleet came an ambulance and the Adams County coroner.

With little confusion, the allied forces herded the witnesses, three tourists, Joey from the Sutlery, and a groundskeeper into one area, then turned to me for an explanation. My heart sank when I recognized one of the rangers who had interrogated me at the visitor center. His grin told me he recognized me as well.

I turned my back on the grisly scene and spent about fifteen minutes explaining what had happened. Then another fifteen minutes explaining why it had happened and why I was involved. Luscious, bless his heart, stood by my side with an avuncular arm around my shoulders. Fortunately, one of the park rangers had been to Darious's barn to identify the stolen items from the park's collection and was able to verify parts of my story. Both rangers were ecstatic when they learned they were going to get General Meade's sword and other treasures back. After ordering me to go home and stay there until they could come and question me some more, the police and the park rangers went back to measuring, photographing, and taking affidavits from the witnesses who were huddled together near the revolving entrance to the tower area.

While Luscious and I walked to the Lickin Creek police car, slowly on account of my sore feet, we saw three cars hurtling down the driveway toward us. The first screeched to a stop and was nearly rear-ended by the car behind, which in turn was gently bumped by the car behind it. When the dust and noise settled, I realized Woody, Moonbeam, and Tamsin were in the backseat of the front car. Professor Nakamura sat in the front seat beside the driver, his son.

Moonbeam climbed out, bells atingling, and embraced me. "We just heard someone from the wedding had fallen from the tower. You and Charlotte were the only guests missing. I was so afraid it was you, Tori." She burst into tears.

I patted her back. "I'm not always the victim of foul

play; it just seems like it's been happening that way, lately."

Gloria Zimmerman emerged from the second car. She'd changed from her gray silk gown to a slinky silver mini dress that wouldn't have gone around one of my thighs. Helga Van Brackle and Dr. Godlove got out of the third car and assessed the damage done to their bumper. Gloria was the first to see the body, now covered with a white cloth. "What happened?" Her voice was barely more than a whisper.

I was too exhausted to talk, so Luscious filled them in with what he knew.

"Charlotte was a murderess . . . I can hardly believe it. She did so much for everybody in the community. Good people like her don't kill other people." Moonbeam shook her head, nearly dislodging her gold tiara, and Woody put a protective arm around her.

"Look," I said, "I really want to get home. Can we talk later?"

They moved their cars so Luscious could get out. As we went around the traffic circle, I realized they were following us. I groaned. "When I said later, I meant later as in next week, not later as in twenty minutes from now."

Luscious patted my hand. "I'm sure they just want to show you how much they care."

"For me, or for Charlotte?" That wasn't a very nice thing to say, and Luscious sensibly chose not to answer it.

When we were assembled in my large front parlor, I confronted Moonbeam and Woody. "Shouldn't you two be at your reception?"

Moonbeam smiled. "They won't miss us. Right now you're what's important. Besides, we brought some champagne. We can celebrate right here."

Nods and smiles all around confirmed what she said. Even Helga didn't look as disagreeable as usual.

With Tamsin's assistance, I set the dining room table with the platters and bowls of food left over from my last two disasters. I hoped my neighbors had run out of patience with me and wouldn't be showing up on my doorstep with more goodies. We put everything out, except for the half-empty box of sticky buns Charlotte had brought, which I tossed in the trash. I didn't know if I'd ever be able to eat another.

"This is almost as nice as the General Pickett," Moonbeam said, surveying the table. "Let's have a toast. Where are your glasses?"

"In the sideboard, over there. I'll put on some coffee. Gloria, can you help me?" She looked surprised but followed me into the kitchen. I started the coffeemaker, then said to her, "I saw your picture—in a frame—in Darious DeShong's workshop."

She gasped. "You didn't think I had anything to do with his death, did you?"

While such a thought had crossed my mind, I didn't need to tell her that. "What was going on between you?" And a much younger man, I wanted to add.

"Nothing. Well, nothing anymore. We did have a thing going for a little while. I met him while I was investigating the puppy mill the Hostettlers ran at their farm. It was one of the worst I've seen; I gave them six weeks to clean it up or go to jail."

"They haven't," I said.

"I know. I should have gone back there, but I didn't want to run into Darious again. Tori, there was something wrong with that man. But he was gorgeous, don't you agree?"

I nodded, agreeing with both statements, Darious

was gorgeous, and there had been something wrong with him.

"I can't put my finger on it, but shortly after we . . . I mean . . . well . . . you know, I began to suspect he wasn't all he appeared to be. And that carousel . . . if you're rich enough to own one, you don't have to live in a barn. And you don't try to hide it. He'd disappear, sometimes for days at a time, and get furious with me when I asked him where he'd been. He hit me—once— that was enough. After that, he called . . . maybe half a dozen times. I hung up on him every time. Then that ended. I never saw him again."

"You were lucky to get away with only being hit," I said. "He tried to kill me. And he did kill Dr. Washabaugh."

"How do you know . . . ?"

"Charlotte confessed everything to me. She and Darious were truly a team made in hell. I don't know which of them was worse. Let's go into the parlor, so I can tell everybody at once what happened on the tower."

The eight people in the parlor had already helped themselves to food and had begun to eat. I sat down and waited for Gloria to fill a plate.

"How did you figure out Charlotte killed Darious?" Tamsin asked, too eager to wait. "Did you find a big clue?"

I smiled. "No big clues, Tamsin. I'm not really Nancy Drew." I drew a blank stare from her on that one. "The Hardy Boys? Sherlock Holmes?" Blank again. Kids these days. What do they read anyway?

"Champagne?" Moonbeam asked me.

"Just a little."

She filled a glass to overflowing and handed it to me. "Then how did you figure it out?" Moonbeam asked.

"I guess you could say there were a lot of little clues that didn't mean much until they were added up. As you know, my attention was focused on discovering how Mack Macmillan could have been shot. Everything pointed to an error on Woody's part, but somehow I couldn't believe that a professional like Woody could ever make such a tragic mistake."

Moonbeam smiled at Woody, who beamed back at her.

"But nobody else had access to the room where the guns were, except Janet Margolies, and although I learned she resented Macmillan because he decided to put a road through her family's business, I couldn't really picture her, at nine months pregnant, doing such a thing.

"So that meant someone else had to have access to the key, and according to Janet the only person who could have gotten hold of it was Mack himself. I knew he had the opportunity to load the guns, but I also had to look for a reason. What would make a man stand in front of a firing squad when he knew it would be firing real bullets at him?

"The answer came when Vesta Pennsinger, Dr. Washabaugh's assistant, told me Mack had been devastated when he heard his cancer diagnosis. That was what suggested suicide to me. I thought perhaps Charlotte had helped him plan his death, but when I confronted her with my suspicions, she produced a suicide note, in Mack's handwriting, absolving her completely. Case closed, I thought."

"Wait a minute, Tori," Moonbeam interrupted. "More champagne anybody?" She poured drinks all around while Woody opened another bottle.

When they'd settled down, I continued. "Case closed—until the next day when I learned that Lillie

White, Mack's mistress, was expecting a baby, and he'd told her very recently that the child would always be provided for. Buchanan McCleary told me that Mack tore up his trust recently and had written a simple will, which had the clause in it that stated half his estate was to go to his children. I think, Luscious, if you read Mack's will, you'll find that that provision will cover Lillie's baby."

"Providing her baby is Mack's child," Helga sniffed.

"There's always DNA testing," Moonbeam said, refilling her glass.

"I still didn't have any reason to suspect that Charlotte killed her husband, though. After all, she was at Penn National racetrack that weekend. Not until last night . . . when I couldn't sleep and was mulling everything over—I remembered she always interpreted for him, converting everything said to him into sign language. And Vesta had told me how upset he was when he learned about the cancer. Naturally, he would be upset, for using sign language that Vesta and the doctor didn't understand, she told her husband he was going to die slowly and painfully, and very soon."

"But she loved him dearly," President Godlove said. "That was obvious. At faculty parties she never left his side. Seemed to adore him." He wiped his mouth with his paper napkin. "Now you're saying Charlotte convinced her husband he was dying and coerced him into planning his own death so she could get his insurance money? That sounds rather improbable."

"But I can understand how she did it," Helga said. "She made him so dependent on her, interpreting for him even when he was in Congress, that he trusted her completely. He was enchanted by her, as if she were a witch casting a spell. She stole him right out from under me."

"What was he doing under you?" Moonbeam giggled. Too much wedding champagne, I thought.

"Pas devant les enfants," Woody said, looking at Tamsin and surprising me.

"I'm old enough to know what's going on, and I'm in second-year French," Tamsin huffed.

"What made you suspect her?" Gloria asked.

I answered President Godlove's question, which had almost been lost in the champagne-induced gaiety. "Her heart was broken when he told her about Lillie and the baby and asked for a divorce. Her passionate love for him turned to passionate hate, almost overnight. She'd rather see him dead than with another woman. She knew she could persuade him to commit suicide, but she was a practical person. If he was killed in an accident, she'd get the insurance money. She convinced him she'd share it with Lillie. That was all the assurance he needed. He still trusted her."

"This is awful," Ken Nakamura's son spoke for the first time. "I really don't think Tamsin should be listening to this."

"Leave her be," Moonbeam snapped. "She's almost grown up. As you'd know if you ever spent any time with her."

The ex-husband's jaw clamped shut and his face reddened. Moonbeam and Tamsin exchanged knowing smiles.

"There's a thin line between love and hate," Moonbeam said with a hiccup. I couldn't tell if she was talking about Charlotte and Mack or herself and her ex-husband.

"How did you figure out she killed Darious?" Tamsin asked eagerly.

"More little clues. When we found the stolen antiques in his barn, we discovered that much of what was there had been stolen from Gettysburg, but the most valuable article of all, General Meade's sword, was gone. Later I remembered seeing it in a photograph—of Mack—hanging in his office for everyone to see."

"What?" President Godlove looked as if he were about to have a fit. "That picture . . . the one in his office . . . in the general's uniform? What nerve!"

I waited for him to stop sputtering and continued. "So that proved there was a connection between Darious and the Macmillans. In his barn, enough evidence was found to convince me that it was Darious who had tried to kill me three times."

Like little birds, words fluttered through the air: *Oh my! Can't believe it! Poor Tori! What a shock! Tsk-tsk.*

"The night Darious was killed, I found a picture in his workroom that led me to suspect the wrong person." Gloria shifted nervously in her seat.

"I'm not going to say who that person was . . . there was no connection with the crime. But at the same time I saw the photo, I also noticed a box of sticky buns, from the new Gettysburg bakery Charlotte liked to use. In fact, she'd dropped a box off here after my first near-death experience. The bakery dates its product, and the box had that day's date on it. I assumed that Charlotte dropped by, carrying a box of treats as an excuse for being there, then killed him as he sat on the carousel eating."

"Oooh, neat-o!"

"Don't be juvenile, Tamsin." Moonbeam was curled up in a ball on the sofa, with her head in Woody's lap.

"I just could not figure out why she did it. I thought it probably had something to do with the stolen goods we found there."

"Why did she come after you at the wedding? She

couldn't have known you'd figured all this out." Doctor Nakamura asked.

"I'd already ruined her chance of getting her husband's insurance money. And she was faced with losing half of whatever was left to Lillie and her baby. She knew she was done for, especially after Reba called from the garage to tell her I was asking questions that would eventually point to her." I glared at Luscious. "You need to tell Henry to hire more trustworthy people."

"Like you can get anything better for minimum wage," he muttered, and drained his glass.

"Was she going to kill you?" Tamsin asked.

"I think she planned to. But she realized it would be futile; even if I died, someone else would look at all the clues and figure it out sooner or later. She knew that the lock of her hair in Darious's hand would identify her eventually. And so, she jumped instead." I didn't mention that my taunts about her husband had most likely been the final straw that led her to jump; I didn't feel very good about that.

The silence that fell upon the group was broken first by Moonbeam's gentle snores, and then by the front doorbell.

"Who could that be?" I wondered.

"Trick-or-treaters," Luscious said. "It's already past seven."

I opened the front door and peered into the darkness. There was a large moving van in the circular driveway.

"You Tori Miracle?" a male voice called out.

"Yes. Who are you?" I strained to see who was there.

"Got a delivery for you."

"Can you bring it around to the back? I don't trust this porch roof."

"Sorry lady. Truck's too big to go back there." A burly man in a Grateful Dead T-shirt materialized from the darkness. "Here's the message that goes with it."

I opened the envelope.

> *Dear Ms. Miracle, After we bought the carousel firm Mr. Strainge, he told us you refused the reward he offered. We will honor your request to give the money to young Sam Miller, but we also want you to have something as an expression of our gratitude for finding the carousel. We understand the hippocampus is your favorite animal. Sincerely, Rick Langley and Bill Moorehead.*

"Oh no!" I exclaimed. "It can't be."

"Where do you want it, lady?" The man stood on the porch, holding the aqua-blue hippocampus in his arms.

"I don't want it. Please take it back."

"No can do. Do you want me to leave it here on the porch, or can I come in and set it up for you like I'm supposed to?"

I stepped aside. "Better bring it inside."

The people from my parlor, with the exception of Moonbeam, gathered around to watch as the beautiful steed was set on a wooden base in the front hall.

I tried to tip the man, but he refused, another sign that I was a million light-years away from New York City.

My guests, no, my friends, left shortly after, Woody carrying Moonbeam over his shoulder as if she were a golden-wrapped package of elderdown. Tamsin kissed me good-bye and left with her father and grandfather. Gloria walked out with them. Luscious swigged down the dregs of the last bottle of champagne and thanked me. I urged him to stay for coffee, but he wouldn't hear of it. "We'll drive him home," President Godlove said, and he and Helga led the bewildered young officer to their car.

"Trick or treat, give us something good to eat." The four children standing on the back steps held king-size pillowcases open to make it easy for me to add to the loot. I pretended to be scared, which they seemed to find discomfitting, then sprinkled a few miniature Snickers bars in each bag. They scampered away, and I noticed a parent holding a flashlight standing in the shadows beneath a huge tree. He waved at me and followed them at a close distance.

As I popped a Snickers bar into my mouth, I noticed one of the children had dropped a mask. I picked it up and started to call out to them, but they were already out of sight.

Back in my kitchen, my very quiet kitchen, I laid the mask on the table. It was the kind that always scared me. Clear, colorless plastic. You could see through a mask like this, but the face beneath would look strange, almost alien. The mask would allow no expression to show through.

I poured a glassful of fresh cider for myself, then, noticing the cats were wild-eyed and panic-stricken at having gone at least an hour since their last meal, I poured Tasty Tabby Treats into their bowl before sitting down with my cider and a ginger cookie from the Farmers' Market.

The mask stared up at me, and it occurred to me that all the people I'd been involved with recently had worn masks. At first I thought I'd seen them as they really were, but beneath the transparent masks there was something else. Perhaps everybody wore a mask, I thought. Maybe even I had been wearing one for years, letting people see me but not really know me.

Charlotte, of course, was the most obvious because she had worn a real mask. The face she hid beneath the elastic was beautiful by anyone's standards, but she had seen herself as hideous. She was loved by her students at the college, volunteered hours of her time working with hearing-impaired students, and acted as an interpreter for the library. No matter what the Charlotte who wore the mask had done, the Charlotte known to the people of Lickin Creek and Gettysburg would be missed.

Her husband, Mack Macmillan, had worn a mask for years. "Mack Macmillan—a man like you." He'd been elected over and over to represent the good old boys of his district, and he wore the mask of a humble man whenever he was out in public. But at home, he lived in luxury hardly ever seen in Caven County, allowed lobbyists to buy his votes, collected stolen treasures, owned a strip joint, and kept a mistress. Not exactly the image he'd tried to portray all those years.

Who else? Woody Woodruff's mask had come off to reveal a much nicer person than I'd expected to find. He wasn't really a letch or a leech, but a kind person who worked hard and truly seemed to be in love with Moonbeam. I hadn't seen past the mask there.

Then there was Darious. I winced at the thought of him. Beautiful Darious, Apollo in his golden chariot, the artist who sacrificed his morals and finally his life to bring a carousel back to life. How could anyone who appreciated beauty as much as he did have turned out to be so rotten?

Lillie White wore a tough, slutty-looking mask, and while she wasn't exactly the "prostitute with a heart of

gold" beloved by so many writers, since she'd know-
ingly had an affair with a married man, she was a child
struggling as best she knew how to support a child,
now two. Life might be a little easier for her now, I
thought, for the DNA tests would surely prove Mack
Macmillan had fathered her baby. Her baby would in-
herit all that was left of Mack's estate.

Helga Van Brackle had covered her passion for
Mack with a prim, schoolmarm mask. Ken Nakamura
had hidden his family's tragedy beneath a smiling face.
Vesta Pennsinger pretended to be a caring professional,
but her gossipy persona was the real Vesta. Thank
goodness for that, I thought, or I'd never have realized
how Charlotte had fooled her husband.

Moonbeam Nakamura was one of the few people I
could think of who was just what she appeared to be. A
good-natured kook without a mean bone in her body. I
wasn't sure about her daughter, the sullen teenager
who'd announced before she left that she finally had
found a purpose in life. Unfortunately it was go-cart
racing. Woody had cringed when he heard it, but I was
sure Moonbeam, when she came to, would be grateful
that her daughter was showing an interest in something.

Another person who was just what she appeared to
be was Cassie. Good old dependable Cassie, who'd
kept the paper going despite me. Thank goodness some
people are just what they seem.

I'd left Garnet for last. Did I really know him? I
wasn't sure. I thought I did, but then when he'd
abruptly left me, it occurred to me that maybe I didn't. I
was willing to spend more time finding out, though. As
soon as he got settled in Costa Rica, and I could take
some time off from the paper and finishing my book, I
might head down to Central America for a long visit.

Even Lickin Creek wore a mask; on the surface it was a charming, old-fashioned town, but under its placid surface rumors and gossip moved as quickly and as surely as sewage sludge flowed beneath the streets.

My thoughts were interrupted by someone pounding on the back door. I shoved Fred from my lap, grabbed the sack of Snickers bars, threw open the door, and screamed.

Instead of the children I had expected to see, there stood a nun wearing a blue habit and a fluttering cornette. The nun's face was hidden by a dime-store skull mask.

Her hand came up to pull off the mask, revealing my friend Maggie Roy, the librarian.

"I didn't mean to scare you," she said. "I thought it would be funny—me dressing up like the ghost of the Lickin Creek College for Women."

I breathed deeply three times to slow my pounding heart then said, "It is funny, Maggie. It's just that I've had a bad day. If you've got time, why don't you come in and hear about it?"

"I was hoping you'd ask," Maggie said. She bent over and picked up a large box, which I hoped didn't contain sticky buns. "I brought a pizza—just in case—and a video. You told me once you love old sci-fi movies, so I got *The Day the Earth Stood Still*. Have you ever seen it?"

I smiled and stepped aside so she could enter. "Of course I have, dozens of times. It's my favorite. *Gort, Klaatu barada nikto.*"

She was taken aback for a moment by my quote from the movie, then responded with, "You're welcome. What language is that, anyway?"

Sticky Buns

Dough ingredients:
3½ to 4 cups all-purpose flour
⅓ cup granulated sugar
1 teaspoon salt
2 packages active dry yeast
1 cup warm milk (scalded then cooled to about 120 degrees)
⅓ cup butter, softened
1 egg

Syrup ingredients:
1 cup packed brown sugar
½ cup butter
¼ cup dark corn syrup
¾ cup pecan halves, chopped if desired

Filling ingredients:
2 tablespoons butter, softened
½ cup chopped pecans
2 tablespoons granulated sugar
2 tablespoons packed brown sugar
1 teaspoon ground cinnamon

Mix together 2 cups of flour, ⅓ cup granulated sugar, the salt, and the yeast in a large bowl. Add milk, ⅓ cup butter, and the egg. Beat on low speed 1 minute, scraping bowl often. Beat on medium speed 1 minute, scraping bowl often. Stir in enough remaining flour, 1 cup at a time, to make dough easy to handle.

Turn dough onto lightly floured surface; knead

about 5 minutes, until smooth and elastic. Place in greased bowl, turn greased side up. Cover and let rise in warm place about 1½ hours or until it has doubled in size.

Grease rectangular pan, 13×9×2 inches.

Heat 1 cup brown sugar and ½ cup butter to boiling, stirring constantly. Remove from heat. Stir in corn syrup. Cool 5 minutes. Pour into pan. Sprinkle with the pecan halves.

Punch down dough. Roll out into a rectangle, 15×10 inches, on a lightly floured surface. Spread with 2 tablespoons butter. Mix chopped pecans, 2 tablespoons granulated sugar, 2 tablespoons brown sugar, and the cinnamon. Sprinkle evenly over the dough rectangle. Roll up tightly, beginning at the 15-inch side. Pinch edge of dough into the roll to seal it. Stretch it and shape the roll to make it look even.

Cut roll into fifteen 1-inch slices. Place slightly apart in pan.***

Let rise in warm place about 30 minutes or until doubled in size. Bake as directed.

Heat oven to 350 degrees. Bake 30 to 35 minutes or until golden brown. Invert immediately onto heat-proof serving plate or tray. Let pan remain in place for a minute so the caramel can drizzle over the rolls.

*** If desired, at this point you can cover the pan with aluminum foil and refrigerate it for at least 12 hours. Then follow the baking directions. This is nice, if you want to surprise your family or guests with hot, fresh sticky buns for breakfast.

Janet Margolies's Easy Sticky Buns

Dough ingredients:
1 package Pillsbury Hot Roll Mix
1 cup hot water
1 egg
2 tablespoons butter

Syrup ingredients:
1/2 cup melted butter
1 cup light brown sugar
2 tablespoons water
1 teaspoon vanilla
3/4 cup pecan halves
3–4 tablespoons light or dark Karo syrup

Filling ingredients:
1/4 cup melted butter
1 cup brown sugar
handful of raisins
1/2 cup chopped pecans
cinnamon to taste

Heat oven to 375 degrees.

Stir hot roll mix in a large bowl and prepare according to package directions by stirring in 1 cup hot water, butter, and egg until dough pulls away from the sides of the bowl. Turn dough out onto a lightly floured surface. With greased or floured hands, shape dough into a ball. Knead dough for 5 minutes. Cover dough with a large bowl and let rest 5 minutes.

While dough is rising, put all the syrup ingredients (except nuts and corn syrup) into an 11" by 18" baking pan and stir gently over low heat. Dribble corn syrup over all to prevent sugaring. Lay pecan halves on top of the syrup.

Roll out on floured surface into rectangular shape, about ⅛ inch thick. Spread with ¼ cup melted butter, sprinkle with 1 cup brown sugar, shake cinnamon over sugar, and sprinkle with raisins and chopped nuts. Roll as for jelly roll, stretching it out to about 36 inches. Slice into 40 equal slices and place facedown in the prepared pan—5 across and 8 down.

Cover this pan with a towel and let rise about 30 minutes.

Bake at 375 degrees for 25 minutes. Remove from pan immediately by flipping it over onto a tray covered with tin foil so the chewy goo is on top of each bun.

Can be frozen and reheated.

ABOUT THE AUTHOR

VALERIE S. MALMONT is also author of *Death Pays the Rose Rent* and *Death, Lies, and Apple Pies,* the first two novels in the Tori Miracle mystery series. She lives in Chambersburg, Pennsylvania.